CHOOSING ROSE

OTHER WORLD SERIES BOOK SIX

RAMONA GRAY

EK PUBLISHING INC.

Cover Art by
The Final Wrap

Edited by
L. Nunn Editing

CHOOSING ROSE

OTHER WORLD SERIES BOOK SIX

Rose Morris likes order and routine and science. What she doesn't like is being sucked into the glowing orb she and her team have been studying. Unfortunately, the big blue alien named Vida who appeared out of the last orb doesn't care. He's forced Rose and the rest of her team through the latest orb with him, and now she's on another world where chaos rules and science might as well be witchcraft.

Vida is determined to return to his home world, even if that means jumping through every orb he comes across. If he must drag a tiny human and her companions through the orb with him, so be it. The new world - an island surrounded by a vast ocean - may be perfect for his needs but it isn't home. He'll do what he's always done, survive in the new world and wait for another orb to appear.

When Rose is separated from the rest of her team, dangerous animals, killer vegetation and angry locals force her to rely on Vida for protection. As he teaches her how to survive in the new world, their mutual attraction is difficult to resist. Rose knows Vida wants to return to his world, so why does she keep hoping he'll choose her instead?

Note: This is Book Six in the Other World Series. It is a stand-alone book in the series and you DO NOT have to read Books One to Five before reading this one.

CHAPTER 1

"Crap, crap, crap...CRAP!" Rose banged her hands on the steering wheel of her useless car before climbing out. She slammed the door shut and locked it. A pointless gesture considering the damn thing wouldn't even start. She hurried across the parking garage toward the elevator.

She ran through the lobby of her apartment building and out to the street. It was pouring rain and she stared up at the dark sky as lightning flashed. She covered her head with her arm and stood at the edge of the sidewalk. A taxi was careening down the street and she waved frantically at it as the rain soaked her long, blonde hair.

The taxi screeched to a halt in front of her and she climbed into the back seat. The front seat was separated from the back with a thick layer of plexiglass and the driver's disembodied voice floated out of the speakers hanging haphazardly from the ceiling.

"Where to, lady?"

"The Franklin Center, please."

The driver pulled out into the street and Rose rapped on the plexiglass. "By air, please."

"It'll cost ya extra."

"I know, that's fine. I'm in a hurry," Rose said with an impatient sigh.

She clutched at the door handle when the driver flipped a switch and there was a loud grinding noise below her feet. The car shivered wildly and lurched sideways as Rose quickly buckled her seat belt.

"Can this thing even handle air?" She wondered out loud.

"Don't you worry, lady. Baby might be showin' her age but she's still got all the tricks," the driver replied.

There was another painfully loud grinding sound and Rose made a breathless shriek when the car lurched upward. Her stomach dropped to her feet and the driver grinned cheerfully at her through the rearview mirror. "Can you handle air, lady?"

"Yes," Rose flapped her hand at him, "I'm fine."

"There are bags in the seat pocket in front of you. Use 'em if yer gonna puke."

"I'm not going to puke," Rose said. "Just get moving, would you? I'm really late and I - "

She shrieked again as the cab rose another hundred feet then took off in a burst of speed. The driver honked his horn and cursed at the car hovering next to them. "Get the hell out of my way, ya miscreant!"

Rose peeked out the window and immediately wished she hadn't. The people standing on the street below them were the size of ants and her stomach made an unpleasant heave. God, she hated travelling by air in well-maintained cars. Doing so in one that looked like it might drop from the sky at any moment made her want to vomit. She didn't have much of a choice though. She started work in exactly seventeen minutes and with the morning rush hour, she'd never make it by ground. She jumped when a loud crack of thunder made the car shake and a jagged streak of lightning lit up the sky. She closed her eyes and clung to the door handle as the cab made another unpleasant sway.

"I KNOW, I KNOW. I'M LATE." ROSE SCURRIED INTO THE LAB. She hung her coat on the hook and grabbed her lab coat, slipping into it as she tucked her purse under one of the tables.

"Relax, the orb isn't due to appear for another three hours and Solomon isn't even here yet." Brody was studying something under one of the microscopes and didn't notice when Rose frowned.

"He's not here yet?"

"Nope." He adjusted the dial on the microscope before typing a note on the tablet sitting next to it.

"But he left the apartment early this morning," Rose said. "He said he was going to the lab."

Brody shrugged. "Don't know what to tell you, Rosie-girl. He's not here."

Rose checked her phone. There were no messages from Solomon and she sent him a quick text before slipping it into the pocket of her lab coat. "What are you looking at?"

"Another skin sample from Subject Blue Balls."

"Don't call him that," Rose replied.

Brody glanced at her. "What else should I call him? Subject 10387? If the big guy won't tell us his name, I gotta call him something."

"Is there any change?"

"No. He's getting drier by the day. If he keeps this up, he'll be completely dried out within the next couple of days. His internal organs are starting to show signs of shutting down."

"Crap," Rose said. "I can't believe he's been with us for a month and we still can't figure out how to rehydrate him."

Brody gave her an odd look. "We do know."

"We know what?"

"How to rehydrate him. Figured it out the second day. Didn't Solomon tell you?"

"No, he – I had no idea," Rose said.

Brody gave her a thoughtful look. "Weren't you on holidays when the big guy came in?"

Rose nodded and he smiled cheerfully at her. "That's why you didn't know."

"But I specifically talked to Solomon about rehydrating him and he said they were still working on it."

"That's weird," Brody said. "We rehydrated him a few times the first week."

"How?"

"Just plain old water. Dunk the big guy in some water and his body starts to rehydrate. Makes sense considering the gills behind his ears. Did I tell you that Solomon had me put a piece of the big guy's flesh in the haloden liquid? I don't know why. He's crazy if he thinks we could grow another one just from the flesh. I mean, I know haloden liquid can regenerate human limbs, but this guy isn't human. The haloden didn't do anything at all. Rose? What's wrong?"

Rose squeezed the edge of the lab table. "I asked Solomon if he tried water and he said yes. He said it didn't do anything. He lied to me, Brody."

Brody gave her an uncomfortable look. "Rose, listen – I know Solomon is your fiancé but he's also the boss. I'm sure there's lots of stuff he doesn't tell a couple of lab monkeys like us."

"He lied to me," Rose repeated.

Her head snapped up and she stared at Brody. "If he's so

close to dying, why aren't we rehydrating him?"

Brody cleared his throat. "I don't know."

"Don't start lying to me as well, Brody."

The short, redheaded man sighed. "Solomon wants to see how long he can go without being rehydrated."

"Are you kidding me? He does know he's dying, right?" Rose said.

"I gave him the report yesterday. He looked it over and told me to leave things the way they are."

"Son of a…"

"Rosie, where are you going?"

Rose stormed out of the lab. Using her keycard, she accessed the elevators that led to the lower level. She tapped her foot impatiently as the elevator took her down fourteen floors. When the doors opened, she hurried down the hall and used her keycard to open the last door on the left.

Subject 10387 was lying motionless in the bed. Both of his arms were strapped down as were his legs. He stared up at the ceiling as she approached the bed. She studied him silently. His skin was a dusty blue colour and it was so dry and cracked that she could see blood seeping through the hospital gown that covered his massive chest. She studied the small black horns growing from his temples. His thick black hair had lost its sheen and clung listlessly to his scalp. His eyes were the colour of warm amber. When his gaze shifted to her, she felt a weird almost painful cramp of pleasure deep in her belly.

His lips were a slightly darker shade of blue, as were his nails. She touched his arm, wincing when flakes of skin shed away. There was a cup with a damp sponge sitting on the table next to the bed and she swiped the sponge across his dry lips. His mouth opened a little, enough for her to see the tips of his fangs, and his tongue flickered out to lick at the sponge. She set the sponge down and poured water into a glass before holding it to his mouth. He drank eagerly, and she gave him a second glass of water before returning it to the table.

She cleared her throat as he continued to stare at her with those unnerving amber-coloured eyes. When her hand tightened on his arm he winced, and pain flashed across his face. She crossed the room to the sink that was in the corner, filled a jug with water and marched back to the bed. She hesitated only briefly before pouring the water over his left arm. His skin sucked up the moisture and she poured more, watching with disbelief as the skin began to heal.

"Holy moly," she breathed before emptying the jug over his entire forearm. She traced the now smooth skin with the tips of her fingers. "It works."

She gave the silent, blue man a look of regret. "I'm sorry. I didn't know."

He didn't reply. In the month he had been here, locked up like an animal, he hadn't spoken a single word. She didn't know if he spoke English or if he could even understand a word she said to him. Despite that, she talked to him almost every time she came into the room.

She spent more time in here than was probably necessary, but she was fascinated by the giant blue man who had appeared from the orb. The woman that was with him was human and a real pain in the butt. She had told them all about her version of Earth. It sounded remarkably like their world. Solomon kept her for only two weeks and did minimal testing on her before turning her over to the Eternity Corporation. Rose wished she had thought to ask the woman if she knew the blue guy's name before Solomon tossed her out of the lab. She certainly had no problems with talking. In fact, she never shut up.

She got more water and sponged his face, paying careful attention to the cracked and bleeding skin around the horns. The relief on his face as she sponged him with water was palpable and another surge of guilt went through her.

"I really am very sorry," she said. "Solomon lied to me, said he didn't know how to help you. If I had known I wouldn't have let it get this far. I'm so sorry."

She sponged water over his throat and the top of his chest. "I'll talk to Solomon and we'll - I don't know - get you into a bath or something, okay?"

She brushed her hand over his cheekbone. "Is that a little better at least?"

He nodded, and her eyes widened. "You understand me."

His eyes shifted to the sponge she held in her hand and she quickly swiped it across his throat again before sliding it under his hospital gown. She squeezed the sponge, letting water drip over his chest and he made a soft hissing sound.

"I'm sorry. I know that hurts." She used her other hand to rub his arm. "Gosh, I feel so awful about this."

She brushed his hair back from his forehead and dipped the sponge into the water before squeezing it across his chest again. "Can you speak English? Will you tell me your name?"

He remained silent and she sighed before dipping the sponge into the jug. When she turned back to him, he was staring directly at her.

Her mouth dropped open when he said in a low, hoarse voice, "Vida. My name is Vida."

She closed her mouth with a snap. "It's nice to meet you, Vida. My name is Rose. Like the flower. Do you have roses where you come from?"

He shook his head.

"Do you have flowers?"

A nod this time. She sponged more water onto his chest. "Why didn't you tell us before that you could speak English?"

He gave her a look that clearly suggested she was an idiot. She kind of was. They had basically been torturing him since he came out of the portal. Why would he talk to them?

"Where am I?" He asked.

"You're in a lab in a city called New Eston. Where are you from?"

"How long have I been here?"

"Almost a month. Can you tell me how old you are or where you're from?"

"Where is the woman that was with me?"

"Vida, I get that you don't want to tell us anything, but giving us something means getting something in return. If you cooperate, they'll be more...generous with you. You would be rehydrated, maybe even allowed outside to get some fresh air."

She shouldn't be making these types of promises. Truthfully, she had no idea what they would do for Vida if he started cooperating. She'd only been working at the lab for six months now, and this was the first time something had come through an orb since she started.

She knew there had been other creatures to come through orbs, but they were no longer at the lab. The Eternity Corporation gave Solomon three months to do testing before they swooped in and took the subjects to who knew where.

"Where is the woman?" Vida repeated.

"She's, um, not at the lab anymore." She checked her watch. "I'm going to find Solomon and talk to him about rehydrating you, okay? In the meantime, think about what I said. It's in your best interest to cooperate with us."

CHAPTER 2

The woman's low laugh stopped Rose from barging into Solomon's office. She slowed and then peeked in through the open door. Marissa, the newest lab tech, was standing next to Solomon. Solomon's office overlooked the portal room and they were both staring out the window at the lab technicians preparing for the portal's opening. She supposed Marissa was standing a little closer than necessary to Solomon. She decided she should feel more jealousy than she did.

She leaned against the doorway. Solomon was a good looking guy and lots of the women in the lab flirted with him. Besides, she wasn't the jealous type – never had been.

"So, explain to me again how the portals work, Dr. Markel." Marissa's voice always sounded like she was on the verge of an orgasm.

"I've told you, it's okay to call me Solomon inside the lab too." There was a warmth to her fiancé's voice that she hadn't heard in a long time. "I don't know how the portals work. It's not my department, is it?"

"No, I guess not," Marissa replied. "Thanks so much for letting me watch the portal opening. I'm really excited."

"Of course." Solomon held a tablet in his hand and he swiped across the screen. "After the portal closes, you can come with me while we analyze the data."

"What if something comes through?"

"It won't. This portal is one that sucks in people, not spits them out." He grinned at her. "Maybe next time."

"Is the blue guy dead yet?" Marissa asked.

Rose shook her head at the woman's callousness.

"Not yet," Solomon said as he scanned his tablet.

"Can I see him?" Marissa asked.

Solomon shook his head. "Only certain personnel are allowed in."

"You let Rose see him." Marissa's voice was thick with jealousy.

Solomon glanced up at her and grinned. "No need to be jealous, Marissa. You know you're special."

"I wanted to see him before the Corporation picked him up," Marissa said as she placed one hand on Solomon's back and rubbed. "Please, Solomon?"

"Maybe. He's not much to look at right now. The thing's drying out like a fish. We're going to do a few more days without hydration and then we'll rehydrate. Maybe I'll try and sneak you in -"

"He won't last a few more days."

Both Marissa and Solomon turned. Solomon gave her an oddly guilty look before hurrying forward and pecking her on the cheek. "Rose, I didn't hear you come in. You know Marissa, of course."

"I do. Hello, Marissa."

"Hello, Rose." Marissa gave her a cool look before turning and staring out the portal window again.

"Marissa is just, uh, helping me with some data before the portal opens. She's going to be watching today."

"I heard. Solomon, we need to talk about Subject 10387."

Solomon frowned. "Is there something wrong?"

"In private." Rose stared at Marissa.

"Marissa, could you give us a moment, please?" Solomon said.

Marissa turned and stared at him. "Seriously? You said I could watch the portal opening."

"It's not going to happen for another few hours," Solomon said. "Plenty of time. Don't worry, you won't miss it."

"Fine." Marissa gave him a huffy look and walked past them before slamming his office door shut.

Rose frowned at Solomon. "Is she always this disrespectful to her boss?"

"Marissa is just very passionate," Solomon said. "Now, what did you need to speak to me about?"

"You lied to me about Subject 10387. You figured out how to rehydrate him on the second day."

Solomon shrugged as he studied his tablet. "You're a lab monkey, Rose. I'm not required to tell you everything."

His dismissal of her job stung but she ignored it. "There's a difference between lying and holding back the truth, Solomon."

He sighed and glanced quickly at her. "When I offered you this job at the lab, you said you wouldn't let our personal relationship interfere with it. Do you remember that, Rose? Yet, here you are questioning me about my -"

"I would ask the same questions even if we weren't engaged. You're letting Subject 10387 suffer needlessly." She couldn't bring herself to tell Solomon his name or that he

11

spoke English. It felt like a violation of trust to Vida. "He needs to be rehydrated now."

"He's fine," Solomon said dismissively. He scrolled across the screen on his tablet and she felt a burst of uncharacteristic anger toward him.

"He is not fine. He's dying, Solomon."

"Hardly."

"His internal organs are shutting down."

"He can survive it for another day or two."

There was a knock on the door and Peter, another lab tech, stuck his head into the room. "Solomon? There's a problem with Subject 10387."

"What kind or problem?"

"He's, uh, been partially rehydrated."

"What? Who the fuck…"

Solomon turned and stared at Rose. She gave him a defiant look and he squeezed the bridge of his nose. "Leave us, Peter."

"Should I go ahead with the tests today or…"

"No point now," Solomon said. "Leave."

Peter closed the door and Solomon glared at her. "What the hell did you do, Rose?"

"He was dying."

"He wasn't!" Solomon shouted. "For fuck's sake, Rose, do you have any idea how many days of testing you've just fucked up?"

"You were torturing him, Solomon! Maybe he's not a human, but that doesn't give you the right to-to torture him. If the Eternity Corporation found out that you were -"

"Oh my God, Rose. Even you can't be that fucking naïve." Solomon rolled his eyes. "The Eternity Corporation does a lot worse to these things that come out of the portal than I ever will. I have a limited time with these creatures and thanks to you, I have to start all the fucking tests over again."

"Solomon, you can't let him dry out like that. It hurts him, okay? You can't possibly be okay with that. You're a good guy, you're not -"

"I'm paid to do a job, Rose, and I do it. You should be fucking fired for what you've done. Do you get that? I can fire you and send you out on your ass for this little stunt. I am so sick and tired of your fucking bullshit!"

She recoiled from his red, throbbing face and the spittle that was flying from his mouth. She had never seen Solomon act like this and a trickle of fear went down her spine. "Solomon, you're scaring me."

He glared at her before stepping back and raking one hand through his dark hair. "Fuck, I should never have hired you."

"Are you firing me?"

"I don't fucking know. Honestly, I don't have time for this bullshit. I've got a portal opening in less than three hours and a meeting with the Corporation in half an hour, where I need to come up with an explanation for why my tests on Subject 10387 are now fucking useless. Just… get out of here, Rose. Go back to your fucking cubicle and enter data in your fucking computer while I figure out how to fix this mess you've gotten us into."

"Solomon, torturing and -"

"Get out!" He roared at her.

She stumbled to the door and yanked it open. Marissa nearly fell into the room with a startled squawk and Rose stared at her in disbelief. "Were you eavesdropping on us?"

Marissa straightened her lab coat, her pale cheeks flushed, before glancing at Solomon. "Is there something I can do to help you fix the problem, Solomon?"

13

"Like what?" Rose said. "You're just a lab tech, like me, and -"

"Go, Rose!" Solomon glared at her. "And stay away from Subject 10387. Do you hear me? Don't go anywhere near him."

Feeling like a toddler who'd been reprimanded, she walked out of his office. The door closed firmly behind her and with her cheeks burning, she returned to her cubicle.

ROSE, DON'T DO THIS. PLEASE, YOU'RE GOING TO GET US FIRED or something worse.

She ignored her inner voice and checked her watch as she stopped in front of Vida's room. Fifteen minutes until the portal opened. She had spent the last three hours in the lab, staring blankly at the latest tests on Vida. Knowing he was being deliberately tortured ate at her belly like acid. How could she be so stupid? Did she really think that the lab even gave one shit about whatever came out of the portal? She should never have taken the job here, but she had, and she'd be damned if she sat back and let her employer torture an innocent person.

Rose tried to look nonchalant as she pressed her card against the lock. For a moment, nothing happened and her stomach curdled. Had Solomon already changed her security clearance? The light clicked to green and she took a deep breath and walked into Vida's room. Daryl, one of the techs, was studying the computer screen above Vida's bed. He glanced at her before shaking his head. "Boy, you fucked up, Rose."

She bristled. "I wouldn't call refusing to let someone die a slow and painful death, fucking up, Daryl."

"Oh yeah? I don't think Solomon agrees. The water you poured on this blue moron has fucked up his research. He has to start all over again and I hear he's pretty pissed with you."

"He's not a moron," Rose snapped.

Daryl glanced at Vida and shrugged. "He looks like a moron. Guy can't even speak English."

"He's from another world, you idiot."

Daryl just rolled his eyes. "Whatever. Why are you here?"

She took a deep breath to calm her nerves. "Solomon wants to see you in the lab."

"Why?" Daryl gave her a suspicious look. "The portal opens in less than ten minutes. Why would he want to see me now?"

"He didn't say, and I didn't ask," Rose said. "Maybe he's finally going to let you watch a portal opening."

Daryl's eyes lit up and he gave Rose a spiteful grin. "Aw, did Solomon's wittle girlfwiend get kicked out of the wab?"

Rose didn't reply, and Daryl laughed before heading toward the door. "About time Solomon let someone else watch. You don't even have a goddamn degree."

"Screw you, Daryl."

He grabbed his crotch and pumped his hips at her. "Is Solomon gonna withhold sex to punish you? Anytime you need that itch scratched, you come see me, sweetheart. I'll scratch it for you."

She made a noise of disgust and Daryl laughed and strolled out of the room. She hurried over and shut the door before glancing at the security camera mounted just below the ceiling. Fuck, she'd forgotten all about the cameras. Her resolve wavered before she marched forward resolutely. If she couldn't erase the video before they watched it, then she'd just have to accept that she'd be fired.

Fired? What if they do more than fire you, Rosie? What if they throw you in jail?

She ignored her frantic inner clamoring. Solomon was her fiancé for God's sake. He would undoubtedly be pissed if he discovered it was Rose who freed Vida, but he wasn't going to throw her in prison.

He was so cruel to you earlier, Rosie!

Yeah, he was, but he always got weird and kind of mean before a portal opened. It was just his way of dealing with the stress.

This is such a bad idea, her inner voice moaned.

No, what was a bad idea was watching a man die when she could save him.

She set the plastic bag on the floor and gave Vida a nervous smile. "It's time to leave."

His amber eyes studied her silently as she grabbed the covers and threw them back. "Can you – oh my gosh! Oh, Vida."

She stared in horror at his legs. They were heavily muscled, but the skin was split open in multiple spots. His hospital gown fell to mid-thigh and dried blood coated his legs from the edge of the gown to his ankles. His feet were just as bad, the soles cracked wide. She could only imagine the pain he was in.

"Can you walk?" She asked.

He hesitated before shaking his head. She scurried to the sink and filled the jug with water. She unstrapped his legs and poured the water over his legs and feet before returning to the sink. It took eight jugs of water before his skin was somewhat healed. She was pouring the ninth jug over his feet when he moved his legs experimentally.

She glanced at his face and he said, "I can walk."

His voice sent a weird little shiver down her spine.

"Good." She dropped the jug and unstrapped his arms. "Sit up slowly."

He sat up and she helped him swing his legs over the side of the bed. He swayed and she steadied him with a hand on his chest. He was so big they were the same height even with him sitting and her standing. She studied his face as he closed his eyes and sucked in a few deep breaths.

"Vida, do you feel faint?" His blue skin maybe looked a little less blue...she couldn't tell for sure.

"A little."

"I'm sorry, but we have to hurry," she said with a nervous glance at the door. She didn't think the security team monitored the cameras in these rooms twenty-four hours a day, but she didn't know for certain.

She opened the bag and pulled out a pair of hospital pajamas. "These were the biggest ones I could find."

She knelt and slid the pants over his feet and up his legs. "Can you try standing?"

He pushed up off the bed and when he swayed again she said, "Use me to balance."

He rested one heavy hand on her shoulder as she pulled his pants up underneath the hospital gown. The pants were way too short, but they fit well enough around his waist and hips.

She stared up at him. This was the first time she'd seen him standing and while she knew he was big, she was unprepared for just how big. The top of her head only came up to the middle of his chest and even after being trapped in a bed for a month, he was still heavily muscled and powerful looking.

She leaned around him and untied the gown before peeling it off his upper body. Despite the water she'd given him earlier, his skin was cracked and bleeding again and she

17

winced. His upper body was hairless, and she stared at his abs for a moment. Holy moly, he looked like he was carved from granite. Lust was making an unexpected appearance in her belly and, without thinking about it, she traced her fingers over his abdominal muscles.

His hand tightened on her shoulder and she raised her gaze. There was an inscrutable look on his face and she blushed furiously. "Uh, I'm sorry. I shouldn't have done that."

He didn't reply, and she said, "I have a boyfriend. Dr. Solomon is my fiancé, actually."

More silence and feeling incredibly stupid she reached for the shirt. She shook it out as he let go of her shoulder and sat on the bed again. She helped him into the shirt. It was much too small and clung like a second skin across his chest and shoulders.

"I'm sorry," she said again. "It's the biggest size we have."

He just shrugged, blood was already beginning to seep through the shirt, and she bent and pulled hospital slippers out of the bag. She put them on his feet. They were ridiculously small, but she crammed them on anyway.

"This will work until I get you out of here," she said as she straightened. "We have to move quickly. Can you?"

"Where are we going?" He asked.

"We're leaving the lab."

"To go where?"

"I – well, to my apartment I guess, and then I'll figure something out."

She hadn't thought this through, but she supposed that's what happened when you came up with a rescue plan on the fly.

He was giving her a skeptical look and she sighed impatiently before tugging on his arm. "Stand up, please. I know it's not a great plan, but this is our best chance at getting you out of here, okay? Solomon and most of the other techs are preoccupied with the orb right now. We have about ten minutes to get out of the lab before someone notices you're missing."

"Is it one that takes or gives?" He asked as he took a few unsteady steps forward. Pain flashed across his face, but he kept moving toward the door.

"What?" She glanced at the security camera again. Already she was thinking about how she could sneak into the security room and erase the videos later.

"Does the orb take or give?" He asked.

"Uh, takes," she said distractedly as she reached for the door.

Before she could touch the handle, the door opened, and she stared wide-eyed at the two security guards standing in the hallway.

"What are you doing, Ms. Morris?" The taller one asked.

Crap. She rubbed her suddenly sweaty hands across her pants. "I'm taking him for some further testing. Move, please, we're running behind."

The guards stared at each other before the big one sighed and entered the room. Rose backed up a step when he pulled the long, black wand from his belt. The wand emitted an electric shock and she swallowed thickly as he pushed a button and electricity crackled between the two metal prongs at the end of it.

"Ms. Morris, we've been watching and listening to you from the security room," the guard said as he glanced at the security camera. "This thing can't leave the lab and you know that."

"He's not a thing," she said. "He doesn't deserve to be locked up and – and tortured."

The smaller guard shook his head and took out his own wand. "Ma'am, step away from the creature and let us do our jobs."

"No!" Stupidly, she stood in front of Vida and glared at the two men. "You're not zapping him with those things. It could kill him."

"Then tell him to get back in the bed," the guard said.

He raised the wand and Rose wanted to be brave, but she automatically took a step back. She ran up against the solid body of Vida and squeaked in surprise when his big arm slid around her waist.

"Hey! Take your hands off of her," the guard said as he took another step forward.

"It's fine." Rose held up her hands. "Just calm down. It's fine and - "

"Hands off of her now, asshole," the guard repeated.

Rose clutched at Vida's arm when he lifted her up. He turned and set her to the side before giving her a gentle push in the back. "Move, little flower."

He gave her another push that sent her stumbling forward before he turned to face the guards. "Step aside, humans."

The first guard grinned at his companion. "Light him up."

Rose screamed when the guards lunged forward. Vida grabbed the biggest guard's arm, stopping him from sticking him with the wand. The guard's eyes went big and he screamed hoarsely when Vida yanked his arm to the right. There was a loud crack and the guard screamed again as the wand fell from his hand.

"You broke my arm!" He wailed.

Vida grabbed him by the back of the skull and shoved him head-first into the wall. He slithered to the ground, his eyes rolling up in his head as the second guard jabbed Vida in the side with his wand. There was a crackling sound and Vida's big body froze for a second or two before he turned to stare at the man.

"Oh fuck," the guard whispered. He zapped Vida again. Vida made a growling noise and grabbed the wand from the man's hand.

"No, please," the security guard whispered as he held up his hands. "Don't kill me. Please don't...ungh!"

Vida pressed the wand against his stomach and the man jerked and twitched as urine darkened the front of his pants. Vida zapped him a second time and he fell to the floor. Her heart pounding in her chest and her legs shaking, Rose stepped over the guard with the broken arm.

"Are you all right, small flower?" Vida asked.

"I – yes," Rose whispered.

"Good. Let's go."

"Are you okay?" She stared at the burnt mark on his shirt.

"Yes, we must leave before more humans arrive."

"Right," she said shakily.

She followed Vida out into the hallway. Vida looked down at her. "Which way to the orb?"

"What?"

"The orb," he said. "Take me to it."

"No," she said. "I can't take you to the portal. That's where everyone is. We'll be caught. We need to get out of the lab."

"You will take me to the orb," Vida said. "I will leave this place through it."

She stared at him before shaking her head. "Vida, the orb won't take you home. We don't know exactly how the portal works, but we know there are many different worlds. The orb will probably take you to another world. Do you understand?"

"The orb," Vida said with maddening patience. "Take me to it."

"I won't," she said.

Vida sighed, and she moaned in panic when he took her arm in one hard hand and pulled her close. He traced the end of the wand against her stomach. "I have no wish to use this on you, little human. But if you do not tell me where the orb is, I will."

Her stomach muscles clenched in and she glared at him even though she was terrified of being zapped. "You asshole! I'm trying to help you!"

"I know," Vida replied. "That is why you're going to take me to the orb."

"I can't," she whispered. "They'll kill you."

He smiled at her, revealing his razor-sharp fangs. "I don't think so. Take me to the orb, little flower. I will not ask again."

She hesitated and then said, "Left. We go left."

———

OKAY, SO THIS WAS BAD. VERY, VERY BAD. SHE HAD BEEN certain that she and Vida would be stopped before they made it to the portal room, but in the five minutes it took to get to it, they hadn't seen a single person in the hallways. Where the hell was the rest of the security team?

Vida pulled her to a stop. They were just outside of the room and she took a shuddering breath when Vida reached for the door.

"Vida, don't do this," she whispered. "They'll kill you."

He ignored her and pulled on the door. It didn't open, and

he stared at the card key clipped around her wrist. She sighed and handed it to him. He pressed it against the sensor and the door unlocked with a quiet click. He opened it, pulling her into the room behind him. They were in the observation room. It was a large room with six rows of tables, loaded down with computers and other equipment, all facing toward the second door and the giant glass window that lined the far wall. Above the window on the wall, a giant digital clock counted down the time to the portal opening. It was currently at three minutes and thirteen seconds.

The room was full of people, most of them Solomon's colleagues, although she could see a few admin and IT people. There wasn't one security person, and she bit back her groan of dismay as Vida prodded her in the back with the electric wand. "Where is the orb opening, human?"

"There." She pointed to the far door and Vida prodded her again.

"Move, little human."

She walked toward the door, Vida's hand on her shoulder and the wand in her back. The room gradually quieted as more and more people caught sight of them. By the time they reached the door, you could have heard a pin drop.

She glanced behind her. Everyone was standing completely motionless and staring at them with identical looks of shock and panic. She couldn't blame them. If she'd seen a giant blue man with horns come walking into the observation room, she probably would have been frozen stiff too.

"Call security," she said to the frozen observers as Vida used her card key to open the door. He herded her into the portal room, following closely behind her. The door swung shut and she stared at the group of people standing in the room. Solomon was there, as were Brody and Marissa. Four other lab techs were studying the tablets they held in their hands, and Daryl was standing in front of Solomon. The room was completely void of equipment or furniture.

Solomon gave Daryl an impatient glare. "Look, Daryl, I don't know why Rose told you to come over here, but I didn't…"

"Rose? What's going on?" Brody gave her a cautious look. "What's he doing in here?"

"Holy fuck." A lab tech named Randy looked up from his tablet. "It's Subject 10387. Jesus, he's even bigger than I thought."

"Why's he in here?" Leslie, her long dark hair pulled into a ponytail, glanced at another of the lab techs. "John, why's he here?"

"I - I don't know."

"Guys, we need to get out of the room." A third lab tech, Rose thought his name was Peter, picked at his acne-pocked face before glancing at his watch. "The portal is opening in less than two minutes."

"Rose, what are you doing with him?" Solomon asked as Marissa grabbed his arm.

"Solomon, I'm sorry," Rose said.

"I am leaving in the orb and you will not stop me," Vida said.

Solomon's mouth dropped open. "He speaks English."

"Guys, seriously, we need to go," Peter said again.

"Call security," Solomon said. "Call them right now."

"They're already here," Brody replied.

Vida released her, and Rose turned to see five men carrying guns come bursting into the observation room.

"Move, little flower." Vida brushed past her and her eyes widened when he ripped off the cover to the door sensor.

"Vida, no, don't! We'll be trapped if you -"

He pressed the electric wand against the sensor and pushed the button. Electricity sizzled into the sensor, there were sparks and the smell of burnt wires drifted into the air. She could hear the security team pounding on the door and she stared at the pale faces of her coworkers as they crowded up to the glass and stared at them.

"What have you done?" She whispered. The air was starting to crackle with electricity and Marissa made a frightened scream when a gust of wind ripped the tablet from her hand.

"Where is it coming from? Where is the wind coming from?" She babbled as she followed Solomon and the others toward Rose and Vida.

"Shit." Brody yanked on the door handle before pounding on the glass window. "We need to get out of here right fucking now."

"Impossible." Randy, his face oddly serene, took off his glasses and tucked them into the breast pocket of his lab coat. "That glass is bullet proof and they'll never get the door fixed in time."

"What the fuck are you saying?" Daryl grabbed him by the collar and shook him as the wind picked up and began to howl.

Randy tore away from him and straightened his lab coat. "What I'm saying, you idiot, is we're about to go through the portal."

"No! No, this cannot be fucking happening." Solomon shoved Brody out of the way and grabbed the handle to the door, twisting and turning it. "Get me the fuck out of here! Get me out of here right fucking now!"

"Brody!" Rose grabbed the redhead's hand and he held it tightly. His face was pale, and he gave her a sick look of fear.

"Rose, I think we're fucked and not in a good way."

"Maybe it won't happen, maybe it won't…"

There was a pulse of bright light. Rose threw her hand up to shield her face as Marissa shrieked in fear. The wind grew even stronger as the orb appeared. Leslie and John were closest and the first to be sucked in. As they disappeared, Marissa screamed again and bolted for the window. She pounded on it, sobbing and screaming for help.

Rose could feel the power from the orb, could feel it's relentless pull as first Daryl and then Peter were sucked into the orb. As Randy was lifted off his feet, he gave them a dry smile. "See you on the other side."

He was gone before she could blink. Vida stepped past them and walked directly into the orb's light. It flashed bright and the big man vanished. The light pulsed brighter, she squinted and held tight to Brody's hand as they were lifted into the air. Behind her, she could hear Marissa and Solomon screaming, and she cried out when she was ripped away from Brody and sucked into the light. There was a brief and intense flash of pain and then…darkness.

CHAPTER 3

"Rose, wake up."

A hand was patting her cheek. Her head was pounding, and she wanted to ignore the hand and drift back to the darkness.

"C'mon, Rose, look at me."

She blinked and then squinted at the face above her until it came into focus. A light rain bathed her face in moisture and she could hear the distant rumbling of thunder. "Brody? Wh-what happened?"

"We went through the orb. Can you stand up?"

"Yeah, I – I think so."

Brody helped her to her feet. A wave of nausea went through her and she swayed. He steadied her, and she squinted up at him again. "Where are we?"

He barked harsh laughter. "Your guess is as good as mine."

"Solomon! Where's Solomon?"

"There." Brody pointed to his left. Solomon was sitting on the ground. He had a stunned look on his face and, weirdly, Marissa had her arm around him and was resting her head on his shoulder.

"Is he okay?"

Brody shrugged. "I think so."

"Why does my head hurt?"

"Looks like you knocked it against something." He tugged her head down and pressed on the top of her head. She hissed out a breath. "Sorry. You've got one hell of a goose egg starting."

A flash of blue in the dim light caught her attention. Vida was standing apart from the others. He had taken off the too-small hospital shirt and his skin glistened with rainwater. He studied her silently for a moment before turning and staring up at the trees.

"How long was I out?"

"Just a few minutes. When we first got here it was storming like crazy, but it's already starting to slow down."

"We're in a jungle." Rose stared at the lush vegetation that surrounded them. The air was humid and warm. Now that the rain had almost completely stopped, she could hear a low roaring noise behind her.

She turned, wincing a little when it made her head ache and her vision blur. "Holy shit. Is that a cliff?"

"Yeah. If the portal had opened twenty feet behind us, we'd be dead right now."

Randy joined them, cleaning his glasses on his wet shirt before poking them back on his face. "We could have survived. There's water – an ocean from the looks of it. The drop wouldn't have been enough to kill us."

"I can't swim," Brody said.

"Solomon and I can't swim either," Rose said.

"Well, then I guess the three of you would have died." Randy's voice was matter-of-fact.

"Thanks, Randy." Brody scowled at him.

"I'll be right back." Rose walked over to Solomon and crouched in front of him. A wave of dizziness passed over her and she bowed her head, taking a few deep breaths until it passed. When she raised her head, Solomon was staring blankly at her.

"Solomon?" She touched his face. "Solomon, say something."

"He's in shock. Leave him alone." Marissa hugged him a little tighter.

"We're all in shock." Now was probably not the time to be a bitch, but something about Marissa bugged the crap out of her.

She touched Solomon's face again. "Hey, snap out of it."

He blinked at her. "Rose?"

"Yeah. Can you stand?"

"We went through the orb."

"Yeah, we did. Stand up for me, okay?"

She stood and hooked her hand around his arm. She tried to ignore her irritation when Marissa took Solomon's other arm and helped him stand.

"Are you hurt?"

Solomon shook his head. "No, I don't think so. We went through the orb."

"Yes," she said patiently. "We need to get moving."

"Where?"

She shook off her frustration with him. "We need to find shelter. It'll be dark soon and I don't think we should stay in the jungle at night."

Solomon looked around blankly. His gaze landed on Vida and animation seeped into his slack face. "He did this." His voice rose higher. It was full of anger and darkness. "He did this to us."

29

"Solomon, keep it down." Brody looked around. "We don't know what the fuck is in this jungle with us."

"Do you have any idea what you've done, you asshole?" Solomon glared at Vida as he staggered forward a couple of steps. "Do you?"

"Shh," Rose said. "Solomon, now isn't the time to -"

"Now isn't the time? Now isn't the fucking time, Rose? We are in the middle of a fucking jungle on a completely different fucking world because of that giant blue piece of worthless shit! I think now is the fucking time!"

She took a step back as Solomon's hands clenched into fists. "I'm going to fucking kill you. I'm going to bash your fucking blue brains in with a goddamn rock."

"Enough," Brody said. "Solomon, he'll kick your ass. Just relax."

Rose watched in horror as Solomon bent and pried a rock out of the dark earth. The others stared at each other uneasily as Solomon started toward Vida.

"Solomon!" Rose grabbed his arm. Solomon snarled at her and shoved her back. She stumbled, tripped over a root and fell on her ass.

"Rose, are you okay?" Brody helped her to her feet.

"Yeah."

"Solomon's lost his mind." Brody watched as her fiancé stopped a few feet away from Vida.

Vida had moved until he was standing at the edge of the cliff. He stared silently at Solomon before turning his head to stare at the water below. With a low grunt, Solomon threw the rock at Vida.

"Watch out!" Rose's cry echoed through the forest.

The rock hit Vida squarely in the chest. Solomon's triumphant grin faded when Vida didn't even flinch. He stared at the rock at his feet before turning and diving off the cliff.

"Vida!" Rose stumbled forward. Brody and Randy were right behind her and they stared down into the crashing, tumbling waves. There was no sign of Vida and they watched the water for almost two minutes.

"He's dead," Randy announced. "Must have hit his head on a rock or something."

"He has gills." Brody gave him an exasperated look. "He can breathe under water, you idiot."

"What I want to know," Daryl had joined them at the edge of the cliff, "is how old Subject Blue Balls got free and took Rose as a hostage. He was locked up tight when I left."

He stared at Rose who took a nervous step back.

"How did he get free, Rose?" Brody asked her.

"I…"

"She was with him when I left. In fact, she lied to me. She told me that Solomon was going to let me watch the portal opening, but when I got to the lab, he didn't know what the hell I was talking about. Isn't that right, Solomon?"

Solomon nodded as Marissa clung to his arm. "Yeah, that's right."

"You got something you want to tell us, Rose?" Daryl asked.

She glanced at Solomon, but he was studying the trees around them. She took a deep breath. "I didn't know he was going to -"

"Guys? Who the fuck is that?" Randy's voice had grown weirdly high-pitched.

Rose swung around. Her eyes widened as she stared at the man that had emerged from the jungle. He was very tall, close to seven feet was her guess, and his skin was a pale pink.

Long, blonde hair fell past his waist and his eyes were a vivid blue.

When he grinned at them, Brody made a noise of disgust. The man's abnormally large teeth were a mottled green and they ended in sharp points. His tongue flicked out, long, dark red, and forked at the end.

"What the hell?" Brody grabbed her arm. "Is his... what the fuck is happening with his jaw?"

"It's getting bigger," Randy said.

"That's impossible," Brody replied.

He took a step toward the man and Rose tugged him back. "Brody, wait."

John was standing a few feet from the pink man. As the man opened his mouth and his teeth protruded outwards, John made a terrified squawk and stumbled back.

Rose gasped when the pink man darted forward and snatched John into his embrace like he weighed nothing more than a feather.

"John!" Brody started forward, his steps faltering when the pink man made a howl of undeniable delight. The skin around his mouth was peeling back and his teeth and gums were jutting out even further.

With another low howl, the man clawed John's head back by his hair and buried his mouth in the lab tech's exposed neck. John shrieked as the others watched in horror. Blood sprayed out in a glistening arc and John beat frantically at the creature's arms. It hugged him tighter, sucking and tearing at his skin.

John's screams became muted gurgles and his madly-swinging arms slowed until they hung limply at his sides. The creature dropped him indifferently to the ground and Rose's gorge rose when she saw the blood and tatters of flesh hanging from the creature's mouth. As she watched, his tongue flicked out and grabbed a piece of dangling skin, dark with John's stubble, that hung from its lower teeth. It slurped it into its mouth with a smacking sound.

"We need to go. Right now." Rose's voice was so shaky and filled with fear, she hardly recognized it.

The others had backed away until they were standing in a loose cluster near the edge of the cliff. The creature cocked its head and gave them an undeniably hungry look before taking a step toward them.

"Fuck, yes," Brody said.

"Solomon?" Rose reached for his hand but before she could grab it, Leslie made a low moan of fear.

"Uh oh." Randy's throat worked convulsively. "There's more, guys."

"What do you mean – more?" Solomon asked.

"More!" Leslie's voice was shrill. "More of those fucking things!"

She pointed to her left. Two more of the pink creatures had emerged from the trees.

"We go right," Brody said. He grabbed Rose's hand. "C'mon."

He took two steps toward the thick curtain of vegetation sprouting to their right, before stumbling to a stop.

"Brody?"

"Oh fuck."

Rose peered around the redhead's body. Another two pink creatures were emerging from the trees. "Fuck. Now what do we do?"

Brody glanced around wildly as the five creatures moved toward them. "Shit, I don't know."

"Think of something!" Daryl snarled. "Before we end up as their goddamn meal!"

Brody picked up a thick branch that was near his feet. "We fight."

"We fight?" Daryl said. "You're fucking kidding me, right?"

"Do you have any better ideas?" Brody said.

"No," he shouted. "But we don't stand a fucking chance against those things. They're gonna -"

"We gotta jump." Randy was staring over the cliff at the water below.

"We'll be killed if we jump," Solomon said.

"No. The height won't kill us. It's our only chance." Randy glanced at the advancing creatures. "We have to jump."

"He's right." Peter joined Randy at the edge of the cliff. "We can survive it. We jump and swim to shore."

"Or get smashed into the rocks by the tide," Marissa said.

"Better than getting our fucking face sucked off," Daryl said. "Let's go."

"Wait," Rose grabbed Brody's hand again. "There are three of us who can't swim."

"And that's our fucking problem, how?" Daryl asked.

"Fuck you, Daryl," Brody said.

"Fuck you, you goddamn faggot!" Daryl shouted. "You think -"

"Enough! We have to jump now," Randy said.

The creatures were drawing closer. One of them flicked its tongue out and another sniffed the air like a dog, but they didn't increase their almost leisurely pace toward them.

"Brody, take my hand and we'll jump together," Randy said. "When we hit the water, I'll help you to shore. Okay?"

"What about Rose and Solomon?" Brody asked.

"Peter and Daryl can help Solomon and Rose," Randy said.

Peter grabbed Solomon's hand and dragged him toward the edge of the cliff. Rose tried not to grimace when Daryl took her hand. "I don't think I can do this."

"You have no choice," Randy said. "C'mon, let's go."

He tugged Brody to the edge of the cliff and Rose watched in fear as the two men jumped. They were followed by Leslie. Peter jumped, taking Solomon with him before Rose could even say goodbye. Daryl pushed Marissa closer to the edge, and Rose glanced over her shoulder.

The five pink men had gathered together, and they were staring curiously at them. The one on the far right turned to stare at the creature next to it as they slowed to a stop.

"Marissa, jump!"

"I can't," she moaned.

"You have to!" Daryl tried to push her off the cliff and Marissa shrieked and clung to his arm.

"No, I can't!"

The pink creatures suddenly bolted toward them and Rose screamed. "They're coming!"

Daryl glanced over his shoulder and bellowed a curse before running for the edge of the cliff. He dragged Rose and Marissa with him. As he leaped off the cliff, Rose felt the fingers of one of the creatures skate across her back before she was falling with horrible and stomach-dropping speed to the water below.

They hit the water with a hard splash and panic immediately flooded through her. The water was crystal clear and she could see the feet of the others, kicking hard as they pushed toward the surface.

She held Daryl's hand in a death grip as he kicked for the surface. She took a huge, gasping breath of air when her head broke the water. "Daryl!"

"I've got you. Just relax, Rose." His arm slipped around

35

her chest and held her tight as a wave surged toward them. "Hold your breath!"

She held her breath as the wave crashed over them. She could see the others under water, their faces pale and wavering, and then they were popping back up to the surface.

"Let's go. Brody, relax your upper body and kick your legs for me." Randy, holding Brody around the upper chest, swam toward the shore.

Rose clung to Daryl's arm around her chest, watching as Peter pulled Solomon toward shore. Solomon's face was pale and more frightened than she'd ever seen him. She tried to smile reassuringly at him, but Marissa had joined them, and Solomon's gaze hovered on her face as she swam next to them.

"What was that?" Leslie's face was pale and frightened as she treaded water.

"What are you talking about?" Daryl said.

"Something just brushed my leg."

"It's just seaweed." Daryl started to swim after Randy and Brody.

"It isn't. It was rough and -"

Daryl cursed in surprise when Leslie was jerked under the water.

"Leslie!" Rose cried. Daryl's arm tightened painfully around her ribs. "Leslie!"

Another wave crashed over them, dunking them under the surface of the cold water again. Rose's eyes widened in horror. Leslie, her long dark hair floating around her face, was in the mouth of a massive sea creature. It was at least thirty feet long with the scaly skin of an alligator and four flippers to propel it through the water. Its mouth was filled with three rows of razor sharp teeth and dark blood clouded the water as it sunk those teeth into Leslie's midsection.

Rose had one last glance of Leslie's frightened face before the creature bit her in half. Leslie's upper body sunk down, her intestines curving and dipping in the water like delicate sea snakes, as the creature crunched up her lower body and swallowed it. It dove for the remainder of Leslie's body as Daryl kicked his way to the surface, dragging Rose with him.

"What the fuck was that?" Daryl screamed.

Rose grabbed Daryl's neck in a death grip as he let go of her. "Don't leave me!"

The others were already halfway to the shore and Rose screamed when Daryl tore her hands away from his neck. "Daryl!"

"I'm sorry!" He pushed her away and she thrashed frantically. "You'll slow me down – I can't die like this!"

"No!" She watched in horror as he swam away from her. She tried to swim after him, paddling her hands in the water, but the weight of her clothes combined with inability to swim had her sinking below the surface within seconds.

The creature was back, swimming up from below her and she screamed, bubbles spewing from her mouth, when she saw the long strands of Leslie's dark hair wrapped around a few of the creature's teeth. Bits of scalp still clung to the hair and Rose screamed again when a pale hand, its nails painted a bright red, drifted out of the creature's open mouth.

It swam straight for her and she immediately began to inhale water. She wanted to be dead before the creature tore her apart. As her lungs filled with water, blackness edged into her vision. The creature was almost on her and she wanted to close her eyes, but she couldn't look away from its widening mouth. Dimly, she was aware of something big, blue and moving impossibly fast heading toward her, but the darkness was all around her now. She dove into it with a feeling of relief as her body was jerked forward.

———

SHE FLOATED IN THE DARKNESS. THE PAIN FROM HER HEAD was gone, and the panic washed away by the soothing black. She wanted to stay here forever, but a deep voice was calling for her. She tried to ignore it, but it was insistent. Demanding.

Her mouth was pried open, warm hard lips covered them and there was painful pressure on her lungs as warm air was forced into them. It fought with the water for the right to live in her lungs, and she had the overwhelming urge to cough. More air pushed in and she was rolled roughly to her side as she coughed wretchedly. Ocean water spewed from her mouth and she sucked in a harsh gasp of air and coughed again. More water erupted from her lungs and a warm hand rubbed her back until the coughing stopped.

She was eased onto her back and she stared at the man leaning over her.

"Vida?" Her voice was hoarse and faint.

"Hello, little flower."

"I – what happened?" Her head was still aching, and she touched the goose bump gingerly as Vida watched.

"You were about to be eaten by the creature in the sea. I saved you." Vida's voice was matter-of-fact, like he saved a drowning woman from a massive and terrifying alligator shark hybrid every week.

"Why?" She whispered.

"As repayment for saving my life."

Rose studied the sky above her. The rainclouds had dissipated, and the sky was the same blue colour as home. "Is this your world?"

Vida shook his head. "It is not."

She tried to sit up and Vida placed one heavy hand on her abdomen. "Stay still."

He was stretched out next to her and she stared at his face. His blue skin was smooth and vibrant looking. The cracks around his horns were gone and his lips were no longer chapped and dry.

"You look better," she said.

He grinned at her. "I feel better."

His hand was still resting against her stomach. Her shirt had ridden up and she could feel the warmth from his hand seeping into her skin. It made a funny little shiver go down her back, and she studied the contrast of his blue skin against her white.

"Can I sit up now?"

"Slowly." He moved his hand and sat up before sliding one hand under her neck. He helped her ease into a sitting position. She turned her neck carefully and moved all of her limbs. She was already a bit stiff, but nothing seemed broken or permanently damaged.

"Thank you for saving me, Vida."

"Why do you not know how to swim?"

"I don't know. I just never learned."

"You should learn."

"Yeah. Do you know where my friends are?"

He stood and then lifted her easily to her feet. She swayed and didn't object when he put his arm around her waist to steady her. "The ones who abandoned you are down there."

He pointed to her left. The others were about a hundred feet away and she lifted her arm in acknowledgment when Brody waved at her. "They didn't abandon me."

"I watched the weak one push you away and deliberately choose to save his own life."

Before she could reply, Vida released her and stepped back. "Goodbye, small flower."

"What? Wait, where are you going? You can't just leave."

Vida was already heading toward the edge of the jungle and she took a couple steps after him. "Vida! Wait! You have to stay with us."

He turned. "Why? So you can keep me prisoner again?"

"No, it's not like that now. There were these creatures in the jungle and they killed John. It's best if we stick together for safety. You'll need our help to survive."

Only a small, white lie. Personally, she was pretty sure that out of all of them, Vida had the best chance of survival. They needed him.

"I do not need your help," Vida said. "Goodbye, flower."

He jogged into the jungle and disappeared.

"Rose!"

Brody yanked her into his embrace and hugged her. She returned his hug and smiled up at him when he kissed her forehead.

"You okay, Brody?"

Brody nodded. "I'm fine. Are you?"

"Yeah," she said. "Thanks to Vida. He saved me."

She stared at Daryl who flushed and looked away. She stepped away from Brody and reached for Solomon. Marissa had her arms wrapped around his waist and Rose gave her a pointed look. "Think I could hug my fiancé now?"

Marissa turned bright red and let go of Solomon. As she stepped away, Solomon frowned at Rose. "There's no need to be rude, Rose. She's just scared."

She stared up at him in disbelief. "I almost died five minutes ago, Solomon. We're all scared."

He made no move to touch her or hug her, and she

wrapped her arms around her own torso. "What is going on with you?"

"What is going on with me? We're on another fucking world, in case you've forgotten." Solomon said.

"I haven't forgotten, I -"

"Where did he go?" Randy suddenly said.

"Who?"

"The blue guy." He stared in the direction of the jungle that Vida had disappeared into.

Rose shrugged. "I don't know. He just left."

"Why wouldn't he stay with us?" Peter asked.

"Maybe because we tortured him for a month," Rose replied.

"We weren't torturing him. We were doing research." Solomon's tone was defensive.

"We were torturing him," Rose said flatly.

"Rose, you don't -"

"I hate to break up your little love spat, but we've got more trouble." Daryl pointed to the thick jungle behind them.

Three men – God, Rose hoped they were men – emerged from the jungle. All of them were wearing military fatigues, and while one carried what looked like a homemade spear, the other two carried handguns.

"Solomon, what do we do?" Marissa whimpered.

He didn't reply. His usual brash and take-charge personality had completely disappeared. Rose tried not to judge him. They were on a different world and it was a lot to take in.

The men were only a few feet in front of them now. The biggest one, he was dark haired with dark eyes and tattoos covering both of his arms, raised his gun. "Hands up."

Rose and the others raised their hands obediently. The second man with the gun studied them before nudging the leader. "They look human."

"Doesn't mean they are," the leader grunted.

Rose stepped forward, wincing at the wet squishiness of her socks and tennis shoes. The leader's gun raised a fraction of an inch, but he didn't aim it directly at her.

"We're human," Rose said.

"You're from Earth?" The second gunman couldn't hide his excitement.

"Yes," Rose said.

"Holy shit," the second man said.

"We don't know that it's our Earth," the leader said.

"You got cars on your Earth?" The second man asked.

Rose nodded, and the man gave the leader another excited look. "Shit, they're from our world. You got planes and shit like that?"

"We do. We have air cars too."

"Air cars?" The leader asked.

"Cars that fly," Brody said. "You don't have them?"

"Fuck." The second man spat in the sand before sighing. "Not the same Earth."

"Maybe they developed the technology in the last couple of years," the third man said.

"Maybe." The second man gave Brody a hopeful look. "How long have the flying cars been around?"

"Since before I was born," Brody said.

"Double fuck."

"How did you survive?" The leader asked. "The pinkies have been eating everything that comes through the orb lately."

"Pink creatures with teeth?" Rose asked.

The leader glanced at the others with him before nodding.

"They-they did eat one of us. His name was John. They surrounded us, and we-we jumped off the cliff," Rose said.

"Motherfucking pinkies." The second man lowered his

gun. "I can't believe one of the fucking sharkgators didn't get you in the water. It's their spawning season and they're all over this side of the island."

"I – something did come out of the water. It – it killed Leslie. It ate her." Rose blinked back the tears. She hadn't been particularly close to Leslie back on their world, but both she and John were dead because of Rose.

"Big alligator-shark looking thing?" The man asked. "Rows and rows of fucking goddamn teeth? Scales and flippers?"

"Yes."

"Yeah, that's a sharkgator. You're goddamn lucky, you know that?"

"Not that lucky." Brody pushed a trembling hand through his red hair. "Two of our people are dead and we haven't even been on this fucking world for half an hour."

The second man grinned at him before shoving his gun into the holster at his hip. "Welcome to hell, Red."

CHAPTER 4

"What is this place?" Daryl asked as they emerged from the trees into a natural clearing. Sturdy looking wooden huts with thatched roofs were in a neat circle around the perimeter of the clearing. A makeshift clothesline was strung between two trees and clothes hung limply from it. She studied the yellow bushes that were planted in front of every door of the huts. More of them were tied to the doors and there were yellow bushes planted every few feet around the clearing. Tucked back in the trees was a small wooden structure. It had more of the yellow bushes planted around it and draped across the door.

There was a crude table to their left. Its legs were made from round, fat logs and its top was a thick slab of smooth rock. A wooden bucket sat on the table, next to clay mugs, bowls and neatly stacked plates. A large firepit was in the center of the circle. A fire was burning and a man wearing military fatigues was cooking the body of an animal on a spit over the flames. He turned the spit slowly and didn't look up when their group stood near the fire.

"Where are the others?" The leader asked.

"Patrick's in his hut with Talla. Doc is in his hut and Duncan's on watch."

Rose followed the leader's gaze upward. She blinked at the man sitting in the tree above them. Unlike the other men, he wore a plain t-shirt and beige coloured pants.

"Where's Arden?" The leader said.

"I have no idea where that fucking fairy is, and I don't care," the man grunted.

Brody stiffened beside her, and Rose took his hand and squeezed it.

There were a couple of fallen logs set up around the fire and the second man pointed to them. "Have a seat. It's not fancy or comfortable, but it's better than the fucking ground."

"What is this place?" Daryl repeated.

"This is home, boy," the man said with a laugh.

"Don't call me boy," Daryl snarled at him.

The man arched his eyebrow before glancing at the leader. The leader shook his head slightly before turning to face them. "Have a seat. We'll get you some food and water."

Rose stepped toward him and tried to smile. "Thank you. We-we appreciate your help. I'm Rose, by the way." She held out her hand and the man stared at it for a moment before shaking it.

"I'm Teagan." He pointed to the second man with the gun. "This is Wallace, the guy cooking is Davis and that's Brian." Brian nodded to them and set his spear on the ground. He grabbed a mug and dipped it into a bucket. He drank the water in three large swallows before wiping the mug with a rag and setting it next to the bucket. He dipped more mugs into the bucket and handed them out as Rose and the others sat down on the logs. Rose took Solomon's hand and he gave her a distracted smile. Marissa was sitting on the other side of him, and he didn't object when she took his other hand.

"Are any of you hurt?" Teagan asked.

"Rose banged her head when we came through the portal," Brody said. "She's bleeding."

"It's fine now." Rose took the mug of water from Brian. "Thank you." She took a cautious sip of the water. It was cold despite the hot mugginess of the air. She drank it down eagerly as Solomon sniffed suspiciously at his.

"Should this be boiled first?"

"Doesn't need to be." Wallace sat down on the log next to Peter. "Trust me, we've been drinking the water without boiling it for months."

Teagan had crossed the clearing to disappear into one of the huts. He was gone only a few minutes before he reappeared with another man. This man was smaller, although Rose supposed that most men looked small compared to Teagan. Teagan wasn't as big as Vida, but he had to be at least 6'4", maybe taller.

"Hey, Doc. We got visitors and they're almost human." Wallace stretched his legs out and cracked his neck.

Brody was sitting on the other side of her and she heard his sharp inhale when the man named Doc moved closer. She didn't blame him. Doc was good looking with his shaggy blond hair and light blue eyes. His t-shirt hugged his muscular torso and Brody made another sharp inhale when he squatted in front of Rose.

"This is Rose. She hit her head coming through the orb," Teagan said.

"Hi, Rose. I'm Doc."

"It's nice to meet you." She shook his hand. "So, you're a doctor?"

"Mostly." He gave her an easy grin. "I'm what they call a SOCM."

"What does that mean?" Brody leaned forward and Doc

studied him silently for a moment. Brody flushed and held out his hand. "I'm Brody."

Doc shook his hand. The two men stared at each other. Rose wondered if she was the only one who felt the tension between them. Doc pulled his hand free and cleared his throat.

"Special Operations Combat Medic."

"So, you're in the military?" Peter said.

"Obviously," Daryl snorted.

"We're Navy SEALs," Wallace said.

"Oh, thank God," Peter breathed.

"You got the SEALs on your world?"

Peter nodded. "Yeah. Semper fi, right?"

"Careful now," Wallace said with another grin. "That's the Marine's motto."

"The what?" Peter asked.

"You don't have the Marine Corps in your world?"

"Never heard of them," Peter said.

"Huh, fucking bizarre." Wallace took the mug of water from Brian. "Thanks, dickhead."

"Fuck you," Brian said without malice. He sat next to Wallace and pulled his boots off. He poured the sand out of them and grimaced. "Fucking sand gets everywhere."

"It's in my crack right now." Wallace grinned at Peter. "You get used to it. I like to think of it as a natural exfoliator."

"Can you bend your head?" Doc said to her.

She bent her head and tried not to flinch when Doc pressed on the goose egg. He pressed around it before turning her head to the right and then the left. "Follow my finger with just your eyes, please."

She followed his finger as he stared at her. "Good. How do you feel? Any nausea or dizziness?"

"A little at first," Rose said. "Not now. I do have a headache though."

"Well, you might have a mild concussion, but I don't think it's anything too damaging. If you start to feel sick to your stomach and your headache gets worse, let me know. Okay?"

"Okay."

Doc stood and stared at the others. "Anyone else hurt?"

"My neck hurts," Brody said.

Doc hesitated before squatting in front of him. His voice was professional, but there was a tremor in his hand when he cupped Brody's neck. "Turn it to the right. Good. Now left. Where does it hurt the most?"

"Uh, right here." Brody touched just below his jaw. Doc pressed on it with his fingers and Brody made a low gasp.

"Sorry, did that hurt?"

"Uh, not too bad." Brody was staring at Doc's mouth and Rose watched as Doc leaned in a little closer. He probed at Brody's neck but now he was staring at Brody's mouth and she could see red creeping up both men's necks.

"How's this?" Doc rubbed his thumb over the spot just below Brody's jaw. "Painful?"

"No," Brody said in a low voice that only Rose and Doc could hear. "No, it feels good."

"Yeah?" Doc studied his mouth as he continued to rub slow circles with his thumb.

"Yes." Brody's voice was almost a moan. "Really good."

"Doc." Teagan's low voice spoke right behind Rose and she jumped a little.

Doc twitched all over and yanked his hand away before standing. He stared at Teagan who said, "Maybe you should help Davis with the cooking."

Doc nodded and walked away.

"The food will be ready soon," Teagan said.

"I'm not hungry." Marissa leaned her head against Solomon's shoulder.

"You need to eat," Teagan replied. "You need to keep your strength up."

Marissa ignored him, and Solomon squeezed her hand. "He's right, Marissa."

"Whatever," she said.

Teagan sat down next to Brody. "Tell me how you got sucked into the orb and then I'll tell you about this world."

"We're scientists," Brody said.

"No, I'm a scientist." Solomon gave him a look of disdain. "The rest of you are lab monkeys."

"Fuck you, Solomon," Brody said.

Solomon's mouth dropped open. "I'm your goddamn boss, and you'd better not forget that."

Brody barked harsh laughter. "My boss? We're not on our world anymore, you asshole. You fucking mean nothing to me."

"How dare you -"

"Enough." Teagan's voice was calm, but Solomon closed his mouth with a snap.

"Anyway," Brody said, "on our world, we know about the portals. The Eternity Corporation has facilities all across the world built just to contain them. They've been studying the portals, trying to understand how they work for the past five years."

"Have they figured it out?" Brian asked.

"No, not really. At least, they haven't told us if they have," Brody replied. "We work in the lab. We study whatever comes out of the orbs, do tests on them, find out about their world, that sort of thing."

"Then what happens to them?" Teagan asked.

Brody glanced at Solomon who shrugged. "I'm given three months to do testing and then the Eternity Corporation takes them."

"Takes them where?"

"I don't know. I've never asked," Solomon said. "When we know something's coming through the orb, we -"

"You know when it's one that spits something out instead of sucking you in?" Wallace sat up and leaned forward eagerly. "How do you know?"

"Well, I don't know personally," Solomon said. "The Eternity Corporation tells me."

"But how do they know?" Wallace persisted.

"I don't know."

"You're a fucking scientist," Wallace said. "You're telling me you've been studying these orbs for five fucking goddamn years, and you still don't know how they work?"

"I'm in charge of what comes out of it," Solomon said. "It's not my job to know if it's a give or take one, okay?"

"Well, fuck me sideways," Wallace spat.

"Wallace." Teagan gave him a warning look, and the man muttered another curse before sitting back.

"This could have been our chance, Teag," he said.

"Chance for what?" Daryl asked.

"To get off this fucking rock," Wallace replied. "If we knew that it's an orb that sucks, then we could leave."

"It won't take you back to your world," Solomon said.

"No shit, Sherlock." Wallace rolled his eyes before nudging Brian who had sat down beside him. "Can you believe this fucking douchebag?"

"Why don't you just go to the orb when it appears and see what happens?" Rose said. "Either it sucks you in like you want, or it doesn't."

"Told you, the pinkies have been waiting lately every

time an orb shows up. You think I want my fucking face sucked off?" Wallace said. "Besides, not everything that comes out of there is friendly. What if it's one that's just spitting something out and whatever it spits out isn't friendly?"

"You're in the military," Daryl said with a frown. "Aren't you supposed to be tough?"

Wallace gave him a withering look. "We are tough. You have no fucking idea. But you also have no fucking idea what it's like to live here. So keep your mouth shut."

"Enough, Wallace." Teagan glanced at the others. "He's right. It's too dangerous to approach the orb without knowing what it's going to do. Six months ago, it spit out this – this thing. It was the size of a dinosaur and it tore up half the island. It ate a bunch of the animals, and it killed and ate some of the locals before -"

"Locals?" Rose said.

"I'll explain in a minute," Teagan replied. "Anyway, this thing was running wild across the island until the pinkies took it down."

"Only fucking good thing those pink bastards have done," Wallace said.

"How many of the pinkies are there?" Peter suddenly asked.

"Only five but they are fucking dangerous," Wallace replied. "Teag wasn't kidding when he said that thing was the size of a dinosaur." He paused. "You guys have dinosaurs on your world?"

"Yeah, but they went extinct a long time ago," Peter said.

"Us too. Anyway, this fucking thing was huge and somehow the five pinkies took it down. They killed it and feasted on it for days. They didn't try to go after us for weeks after that. Too goddamn full to want human dinner. It was actually pretty fucking nice, now that I think about it."

"Keep going," Teagan said to Brody.

"There isn't much more to tell. We study whatever comes out of the orb until the Eternity Corporation takes it from us."

"How did all of you get sucked into the orb?" Teagan asked.

Brody grimaced. "A month ago, the portal spit out this big blue alien guy. We've been testing him for the last month and -"

"Torturing is more like it," Rose said.

Solomon frowned at her. "That blue guy wasn't human, Rose. He needed to be studied and -"

"His name is Vida and you were torturing him! You were letting him dry up like a damn fish for no reason. His organs were starting to shut down and you were putting him in incredible pain for what? Your damn research?" Rose could hear her voice rising and she tried to reign it in.

"Research that you destroyed when you poured water all over him!" Solomon glared at her. "I've made my decision by the way - you're fired."

"Have you lost your damn mind?" Rose said. "Do you think I care about my job? We are never going to see our world again, Solomon. Ever."

She stopped, dragging in ragged breaths of air as the others stared silently at them. After a long moment, Brody cleared his throat. "Vida escaped, took Rose as a hostage and made her take him to the orb. He wanted to try and get back to his world. It was getting ready to cycle up and he locked all of us in with it. We got sucked through."

"Where is this Vida now?" Teagan asked.

"He jumped off the cliff before the pink guys even showed up," Brody said. "He looks like a human, mostly. He's gotta be close to seven feet and he has blue skin and," he hooked his fingers by his temples, "small black horns and fangs. He breathes air like us humans, but he also has gills. He can breathe underwater and he needs water to live. He saved Rose from the alligator thing -"

"Sharkgator," Wallace said.

"I'm sorry?"

"It's a sharkgator. I named it. I'm excellent at naming shit around here."

"Uh, okay," Brody said. "Anyway, Vida saved Rose and then took off into the jungle."

"Why didn't he stay with you?" Teagan said.

"Because we tortured him!" Rose said heatedly. "He didn't want to be around the people who almost killed him."

"Well, he'll be dead soon anyway," Wallace said.

"What do you mean?" Marissa asked.

"Sweetheart, a human can't survive on this rock by themselves," Wallace drawled. "Forgetting about the pinkies, there are other animals that can kill you. Hell, even the plant life is dangerous in this place. Not to mention, the locals fucking hate us and try and murder us if they even catch a glimpse of us."

"Why?" Rose asked.

Wallace shrugged. "No idea. We think the ones who were here before us caused some bad blood."

"Before you?" Rose said.

"We didn't build any of this." Teagan leaned forward and rested his elbows on his knees. "Two years ago, our team was on a mission."

"What kind of mission?"

"Find and retrieve," Teagan said. "Before we could even get to our target, the orb opened up right in front of us and sucked all ten of us in."

"There are ten of you?"

"There was. Four of us have died since coming to the island."

"How did they…" Rose stopped. "I'm sorry. That's none of my business."

"Three of them were killed by the pinkies before we figured out how fucking dangerous they were," Teagan said. "The fourth, Garrett, died from an infection."

"What kind of infection?" Brody asked.

Teagan glanced at Doc. The man's face had paled, and he swallowed compulsively before nodding.

"Garrett had appendicitis," Teagan said. "It was really bad. Luckily Doc had his med pack when we were sucked in. He operated on him the best he could with what he had in his pack. He got the appendix out and sewed Garrett back up, but two days later infection set in. Without antibiotics, there wasn't anything we could do."

"I'm sorry," Rose said. "That's awful."

"No." Wallace's cheerful attitude had disappeared completely. "What was awful was listening to him scream when Doc cut into him without anesthetic or pain meds."

"Holy shit." Brody was staring at Doc. "How the hell did he even survive the surgery?"

"Garrett was a tough bastard. He was the head of our unit and the best man I knew," Wallace said.

"The best man *all* of us knew," Brian said.

There was silence for a few moments before Rose turned to Teagan. "So, now you're in charge?"

Teagan shook his head and glanced at one of the huts. "Patrick was second-in-command. He's in charge now. Anyway, we landed on this rock two years ago and we've been here ever since."

"How big is the island?" Rose asked.

"It would take about three days to walk from one side to

the other. But trust me, you want to stay away from the north side of the island."

"Why's that?" Brody asked.

"The pinkies live on the north side. We're on the south side and the locals are on the west end. It's better, safer, to stay on the south and east side of the island. Definitely don't go anywhere alone. We operate on the buddy system here." Teagan said.

"Were there any humans here when you first arrived?" Rose asked.

"No, just these huts and some tools and utensils, shit like that," Wallace replied.

"Why do the locals want to kill you?"

"No idea. We tried to make contact with them a few times, but each time there was aggression," Teagan said.

"A lot of aggression." Wallace rubbed at the scar visible on his neck. "They're damn quick with their spears and knives."

"Have you tried talking with them?" Solomon asked.

Wallace gave him such a look of disdain that Solomon flushed. "No, we tried interpretive dance. Ya think talking might be a better idea?"

When Solomon didn't say anything, Wallace snorted. "They don't speak English."

"So, it's just the six of you?" Peter asked.

"Nope. There's Talla, she got spit out about three months ago. Duncan up there," Wallace pointed to the man in the tree, "got spit out, eh, a couple weeks after us, maybe? And then there's Arden. I have no fucking idea how long that fucking fairy has been living on this rock."

Rose glanced at Doc. He had moved the animal to the stone slab table and was carefully cutting off chunks of meat from it. He had to have heard what Wallace said but he didn't seem upset by it.

She thought it was strange that the SEALs would throw around homophobic slurs when one of their own was gay. But, she mused, maybe they didn't know.

"Where is Arden anyway?" Brian asked.

"Who the fuck knows." Wallace cracked his neck again. "Probably off in the fucking jungle, petting his own damn willy again."

"I thought you said no one should go in the jungle alone," Rose said.

"Arden does what he wants," Teagan said. "He was living here in the huts when we stumbled onto them, and he seems to have an uncanny ability to avoid being eaten by the pinkies."

"I told you, it's because he's a fucking fairy." Wallace tapped his temple. "They got some kind of fucking radar that tells them when the pinkies are close. Remember when they attacked us at the falls? Arden fucking disappeared five minutes before the pinkies showed up."

He gave Brian a disgruntled look. "Fucking fairy could have warned us."

"Are they from your Earth?" Rose squinted into the trees at Duncan. He looked human from what she could tell.

"Nah. No idea where Arden is from, he's a closemouthed little fucker, and Talla is from a world that doesn't have any of the modern shit we do. Same with Duncan. His world is some kind of medieval place or some shit like that. He had never seen a gun, and he had a fucking sword when he came through the orb. An honest-to-god sword."

Wallace sat up straight and glanced at Duncan. "He's good with it too. You should have seen him take on the blowcat that went after us last month. Fucking thing had to weigh at least two hundred pounds and took us by surprise. We'd be dead if it hadn't been for Duncan and his fucking sword."

"Blowcat?" Brody said.

"Big fucking cat, kind of looks like a tiger only with blue stripes and this fucking hole in the top of its skull. It blows some kind of shit on you from that hole and it burns like a motherfucker. Normally, they avoid us, but this one was a mama and we got close to her den."

Wallace took the plate of meat that Davis handed him with a nod of thanks. "Duncan's stupid quick with that sword, but he's got a soft heart. He didn't kill the blowcat, just drove it off while the rest of us got the fuck out of there."

He shoved a piece of meat into his mouth and chewed. "Said he didn't want its babies to starve to death. Like we need more fucking blowcats on the island."

"So, you have no idea who built these huts?" Rose took the plate of meat from Doc. "Thank you."

He nodded and handed a plate to Brody. Their fingers brushed, and Brody's freckled skin took on a rosy hue. Doc studied Brody for a moment before moving on.

"No." Teagan was accepting his own plate of food from Davis. "Arden said they were empty when he found them."

"Maybe it was the locals who built them," Peter said.

"Nah, they got their community built behind the yellow bush. It's why they rarely get killed by the fucking pinkies."

Rose stared at Wallace. "What do you mean?"

Wallace pointed to the yellow flower bushes that were planted around the huts. "See those plants? They give off some kind of repellent that keeps the pinkies away."

"You're kidding me," Peter said. "Those things are afraid of plants?"

58

"I'm not. They hate those motherfucking plants. It's the only thing keeping them from attacking our camp."

"Why do they hate them?" Rose asked.

"No idea," Teagan said. "But Wallace is right. They hate them and avoid them like the damn plague."

"Why don't you have more of them?" Solomon asked. "If those plants keep them away, shouldn't you have them planted every few feet."

"They're not exactly easy to get," Teagan said. "They mostly grow on the west side of the island and the locals protect them."

"Can't blame them for that," Brody said under his breath.

"I got this," Wallace pointed to the scar on his neck, "trying to get more plants. One of them got me with a goddamn spear. Cut was deep too. If it hadn't been for Doc, I'd be fucking dead right now."

"It's fucking ridiculous," Brian suddenly grumbled. "They have more than enough of the plants. Even if we took a hundred of them, they'd be fine. They live behind a goddamn wall of them."

"Have you tried cutting some branches from the plants you do have and growing them?" Brody asked Teagan. "If you get a root system started, and the soil is good, you could grow as many as you want."

"Do we look like fucking gardeners?" Wallace grinned at him.

Before Brody could reply, a deep voice said, "When did our visitors arrive?"

Rose watched in amazement as all of the military men jumped up and stood ramrod stiff. She turned and stared at the man who had emerged from one of the huts. He was dark-haired and tall with a well-defined body. He was shirtless, and she stared at the tattoos that covered his upper chest before studying his face. A shiver went down her back. His eyes were cold and although there was a smile on his face, she could see no warmth in it. His gaze landed briefly on her and she had to suppress her immediate urge to stare at the ground. Cowering like a scared dog wasn't like her, but there was something about the man that made her feel uneasy and afraid.

"At ease, men." The man, he had to be their leader Patrick, waved a careless hand at Teagan and the others. They sat down and picked up their food again as the man moved toward the stone table. A woman came out of the hut. The military men didn't glance up from their food, but Peter and Daryl, even Solomon, stared openly at her.

Rose couldn't blame them. The woman was gorgeous with a body that the goddess Aphrodite would have coveted. She was close to six feet tall and she had long dark hair that fell nearly to her waist. She had full breasts and hips and she walked with a natural seductive sway that had Daryl practically drooling into his plate of mystery meat.

As the woman picked up the knife and cut chunks of meat from the still-steaming body, Teagan said, "They came out of the orb a couple of hours ago."

Patrick leaned against the table, watching as the woman added more meat to a plate. "And they survived the pinkies attack?"

"Not all of them. One was killed by the pinkies and one was killed by a sharkgator when they jumped off the cliff."

"They from Earth?"

"Not from our Earth." Teagan glanced at Rose.

"Is that right?" Patrick studied each of them for a moment. "You explain the rules?"

"Not yet."

Patrick took the plate of meat from the woman and ate a chunk with his fingers. "Explain them, Teagan."

Teagan sat his plate of meat on his thigh. "The rules are simple. You know the most important one – don't go into the jungle alone. Keep the noise level down. Help out around camp. That includes cooking, hauling water, and cleaning. Got it?"

Rose and the others nodded as Patrick ate another piece of meat. "Are any of you fighters?"

"They're scientists," Wallace said.

Patrick rolled his eyes before turning to Daryl who was openly staring at the woman's breasts. "Talla belongs to me and I don't share. Keep your eyes to yourself or I'll cut them out of your head. Understand?"

Daryl didn't reply. Rose grabbed Solomon's arm when Patrick dropped his plate on the table and moved across the clearing. He moved deceptively fast for a man his size and Daryl made a startled grunt when Patrick grabbed him by his lab coat and hauled him to his feet. His plate of food hit the ground, the meat sliding off to land in the dirt. Patrick shook him roughly before dragging the smaller man to his tiptoes and putting his face only inches from Daryl's.

"Do you understand me, maggot?" His voice was calm, but the back of his neck had turned a bright red. Rose crowded closer to Solomon, her heart thudding and her hands shaking so bad she could barely hold her plate of meat.

"Patrick -"

"Shut up, Teagan." Patrick didn't look away from Daryl's face. "Do you understand me, maggot?"

"Yes," Daryl whispered.

"Yes, what?"

"Yes, Sir, I understand."

"Good." Patrick released him. Daryl staggered back,

sitting on the fallen log with a harsh thud. His face was pale, and he stared at his plate on the ground without saying a word.

Patrick turned and studied the rest of them. "The rules are in place for a reason. This world is dangerous and without the rules, you won't survive. Without *us*, you won't survive. You need us. You do what I say, when I say it, and we'll get along just fine. Isn't that right, Wallace?"

"Yes, Sir," Wallace replied.

"Good." Patrick returned to Talla and she smiled at him before handing him the plate of food. "Now, let's eat our dinner like civilized folks and get to know each other."

CHAPTER 5

"Solomon, wake up." Rose pushed on Solomon's shoulder. He snorted and rolled away from her, burying his face in his folded up lab jacket that served as his pillow. She sighed and stared up at the ceiling of their hut. Early morning sunlight was shining through the cracks in the wood, but no light shone through the roof. Whoever had made the thatched roof had done a good job. Even with the middle-of-the-night rainstorm, no water had leaked through.

She sat up in the bed. It wasn't much of a bed, just a big pile of furs, but it was better than the ground, she supposed. Her body ached, and she rubbed at her back before gingerly touching the bump on her head. It was still tender, but the bump seemed a little smaller.

She put on her shoes before standing and heading toward the doorway. There was no door, just another fur hung across it. Unlike Solomon, she hadn't slept at all last night. She'd been too afraid, felt too guilty to sleep. It was her fault they were in this mess, and she wished to God she could go back and change it.

So, you would have let Vida die? You would have let

Solomon torture a living being in the name of science and research?

She pulled the fur back, blinking in the light before stepping out of the hut. She felt guilty about what had happened, but she didn't regret trying to rescue Vida. He hadn't deserved to die that way.

John and Leslie didn't deserve to die either.

She winced and rubbed at her forehead. No, they didn't, and she would carry the burden of their deaths for the rest of her life.

She walked quickly to the wooden structure behind the huts. It was an outhouse and, surprisingly, not that terrible to use. She peed and used one of the broad, smooth leaves piled next to her as toilet paper.

When she emerged from the outhouse, there was a man sitting by the fire. He was sharpening a long sword against a stone. He stood, placing the sword on the log beside him when she approached.

"Hi, I don't think we've met yet. I went to bed before you were, uh, finished your watch. I'm Rose."

"I'm Duncan." She didn't miss the way his gaze lingered on her small breasts and hips.

"It's nice to meet you."

"The pleasure is mine, Rose. Please, sit with me."

She sat down next to him. "Everyone else is still asleep?"

"Yes, other than Davis. He's on watch."

She glanced up into the tree. Davis was sitting in the tree and he nodded to her before studying the jungle around them.

"Were you on watch all night?" She asked.

"No. Only until about midnight. Brian took over for me for a few hours and now it's Davis."

"Oh."

"I've always been an early riser, even on little sleep."

Duncan stared into the fire and Rose took a closer look at him. Unlike the military men, his dark hair was long and pulled into a low ponytail at the back of his skull. He had surprisingly pretty green eyes with long dark lashes.

"I'm not usually," Rose said. "I just – I didn't sleep much last night."

"No, I imagine you did not."

"I don't want to be afraid, but I am. There isn't even a door on the hut, you know? What if those pink things attacked the camp at night, or another animal."

"We always have a guard at night. The yellow plants keep the pink creatures away and some of the more dangerous animals on the island have only wandered through the camp a few times. We killed them when they did." He studied her mouth. "If you wish, I would be more than happy to offer my services to keep you safe at night."

"Oh, um, that's kind of you, but I have a boyfriend. A fiancé actually – Solomon, the taller guy with the dark hair?"

Duncan's gaze slipped to her throat and he shifted away until there was more space between them. "My apologies, Rose. I did not know you were with someone. In my world, the women wear collars to show their attachment to a man."

"Are you serious? You make your women wear collars?"

"They wear it as a symbol of the man's love for them. When a man and a woman are sleeping together, he gifts her with his collar so that others will know she belongs to him."

"It sounds kind of barbaric and slavish to me. What if a woman doesn't want to wear one? Do you force her to?"

"Some men do, but that is uncommon. Most women gladly wear their man's collar. Although, the Lord Traven's beloved was one who did not wish to wear one."

"Lord Traven?" Rose asked.

Duncan smiled a little. "Traven was the lord of my home

65

and my best friend. He fell in love with one of his employees in his household when we returned from the war. She refused to wear his collar at first."

"She changed her mind?"

"Eventually, but it took some persuading on Traven's part."

He stared into the fire as sorrow flickered across his face. She patted his arm tentatively. "I'm sorry, Duncan. You must miss your friend."

"I do. I miss Traven and my world very much."

"Did you have a – a woman in your world?"

"I did not."

"Oh."

"Considering that I was sucked into a ball of light, it is probably for the best that I did not have a woman to miss me." Duncan gave her a wry smile. "Truthfully, I was very discontent with my life and yearned for a change. This, however, was perhaps a bit more than I wanted."

She smiled at him. "I bet it was."

"Tell me about your world, Rose. Was it a place much like the others' world? One filled with such magic like electricity and steel machines instead of horses?"

Her grin widened. The way Duncan said electricity was adorable. "It was. The steel machines are called cars."

"Cars, right. That's what Wallace called them. They go very fast and run on a liquid that burns."

"Gasoline. We used to use gasoline but most of our cars are electric now, even the air cars."

"Air cars?"

"They're cars that can fly like an airplane. Did the others tell you what an airplane is?"

Duncan nodded. "They tried to explain. I confess, I find it very difficult to imagine such things."

"I bet you -"

"Duncan, you bastard, you didn't fill up the water bucket yet."

Rose looked behind her to see Wallace standing at the stone table. He grinned cheerfully at her. "Morning."

"I'm on water duty this week." Teagan came out of his hut and took both water buckets when Wallace held them out to him.

"We need some more leaves too." Wallace scratched the stubble on his throat. "I'm about to take an epic shit, pretty sure I'm gonna clean out the leaves supply."

Teagan picked up a leather bag with a long strap and slung it over his shoulder. "Thanks for the warning."

"I got your back, brother." Wallace clapped Teagan on the back before ambling toward the outhouse.

"Now that we have more people, it may be prudent to build another outhouse," Duncan said.

"Probably. You seen Davis?"

"He's on watch. I will go with you to get the water." Duncan stood, and Rose watched as he picked up the sword and sheathed it in a leather scabbard around his waist.

"Can I come?" Rose stood, and Teagan studied her for a moment before nodding.

"Sure. Duncan, grab the flowers."

She watched as Duncan walked to one of the empty huts. He returned carrying some of the yellow flowers. They grew on long vines and the vines were twisted into circles. He placed one around her throat. He handed a circle of plants to Teagan who pushed it over his head and around his throat. Duncan put on his own necklace of yellow flowers before staring at the smaller circle in his hand. With a small grin, he plopped it on top of Rose's head like a crown.

"A little extra protection for you."

She gave him a shaky smile. The idea that the crown and necklace of yellow flowers would protect her from the horrifying pink men seemed absurd, but she had no reason to believe they would lie to her about it. She touched the soft petals of the flowers around her throat. They gave off a vaguely minty smell.

"Are these edible?"

"Don't know," Teagan said. "We haven't seen any of the animals eating them, so we assume no. Besides, we don't want to waste them by eating them."

"Right. Sorry, that was a stupid thing to ask."

Teagan shook his head. "It wasn't. But, yeah, don't eat anything until you ask one of us about it."

"I won't."

She followed Teagan and Duncan toward the edge of the trees. As they passed the clothesline, Teagan stopped abruptly. "What the hell?"

Duncan's hand dropped to the handle of his sword. "What is it?"

"Where the hell are my pants?"

"What?"

Teagan pointed to the clothesline. "My other pants were hanging here last night. They're gone."

"Are you certain?" Duncan studied the trees around them.

"Yes, I'm certain. When you only have two fucking pairs of pants, you keep track of them."

"Maybe Wallace or Brian took them by mistake last night in the dark."

Teagan scowled. "Maybe. C'mon, let's get the water."

———

"Holy crap."

"Yeah, it's pretty." Teagan was already kneeling at the edge of the water and filling up the first bucket.

Rose stared at the large waterfall as Teagan filled the second bucket before dipping his hand into the water and splashing some onto his face. She knelt next to him and dipped her fingers into the water. It was freezing cold and she cupped some water in both hands and drank.

"God, it's so cold," she said.

"The waterfall keeps it cold." Teagan had already moved away and was picking off the broad leaves from some bushes near the water. Duncan was staring into the jungle around them, his sword out and held loosely at his side. She hurried over and began to pick some of the leaves, stuffing them into the bag around Teagan's waist.

"How deep is the pool?"

Teagan shrugged. "Not sure. There's a drop off about ten feet from the shore, but no way to tell how deep it is."

"Are there any of the sharkgators in the pool?" She looked behind her shoulder at the water, shuddering a little.

"No. The pool isn't big enough for them and besides, I think they like the salt water. Most of the year they're living out in the ocean. They only come close to the island when they're looking to breed, from what we can tell."

He stopped picking leaves and pointed to the waterfall. "That right there is the closest thing we have to a shower. It's fucking freezing though so don't stand under it too long or you'll get hypothermia. Or you can bathe in the pool. It's just as cold though."

"Sounds great," Rose said.

A smile crossed Teagan's face. "There's a metal tub in one of the empty huts. You can use it if you want a warm bath, but you have to haul the water, heat it and empty the tub yourself. Most of us prefer the quick, cold shower method."

"Okay." She picked more leaves and handed them to Teagan who stuffed them into the bag.

"Soap is on limited supply though, so you're only given a certain amount per week." He eyed her long hair. "You might want to think about cutting your hair short so you don't use up your soap ration on it."

"What about Talla? She has really long hair."

"Talla gets extra soap."

"Why, because she's sleeping with Patrick?"

"Yes." Teagan's voice was unapologetic. "Sleeping with Patrick gives you certain perks."

"Is Patrick dangerous?"

Teagan stared silently at her and Rose picked another leaf before handing it to him. "I only ask because he seems... unstable."

"He has a quick temper. Do what he says, and there won't be a problem."

"So it's a dictatorship, not a democracy?"

Teagan sighed and turned to face her. "Patrick won't hurt you, but the smart thing to do is keep your head down and your mouth shut. Do you understand?"

"Yes."

"Good. We've got enough leaves, let's get back."

Teagan handed her the leather bag of leaves and she slung it over her shoulder. He carried the water buckets while Duncan led the way, his sword flashing in the light flickering down through the trees.

When they walked into the camp, Rose almost dropped the bag of leaves. She stared at the man sitting next to Wallace. He was short and stout with shaggy black hair and bright green eyes. He was naked from the waist up, his hairy belly protruding in front of him. He scratched at his belly-button then sniffed at his finger before casually flicking away the debris stuck under his nail. He was giving her a disgruntled look, but she barely noticed. Her gaze kept returning to the large blue gossamer-like wings that sprouted from his back. They quivered lightly, despite the lack of breeze.

"What's your problem, lady?"

The voice was deep and as rough as sand paper scraping across vocal cords. She stared in silent shock at the short man and he scowled angrily her.

"What's your problem?" He repeated. "You never seen a fucking fairy before?"

"I-I'm sorry," Rose said.

Wallace stood and took the bucket of water from Teagan. He set it on the table, dipped a mug into it, and pulled a toothbrush from the pocket of his pants. "Rose, meet Arden. Arden, this is Rose. Be nice."

"Yeah, yeah. Nice to meet you," Arden grunted.

Wallace dunked his toothbrush into the water and brushed his teeth vigorously. Rose sat down next to Duncan and tried not to stare at Arden's wings.

"Morning." Brody climbed over the log and sat next to her. He yawned and rubbed his eyes before resting his head on her shoulder. "How did you sleep?"

"Not well." Rose patted his leg. "You?"

"Not that great. Turns out that being sucked into an alternate reality plays hell on your sleeping pattern. Not to mention that jungle sounds aren't exactly the most soothing noise to fall asleep…"

Brody had caught a glimpse of Arden. The fairy curled his lip at him as Brody's mouth dropped open. "Is that a…"

"Fairy," Rose said.

"Holy shit," Brody breathed. "So, when they said fairy, they meant an actual…"

"Fairy," Rose repeated.

"You know I can hear you, right?" Arden glared at him.

"Sorry." Brody studied Arden's wings. "I've never met a fairy before."

"Yeah, well, I never met a redheaded moron before, but here we are."

Brody flushed as Wallace grinned around his toothbrush.

"Be nice, Arden." Teagan set the bucket of water next to the second one. "Who's on trap duty today?"

"Brian and me." Wallace finished brushing his teeth and stuck his toothbrush back in his pocket.

"Good. Don't forget to check the one by the falls."

"I won't."

"Holy shit. Does that guy have wings?"

Daryl's voice echoed across the clearing. Arden scowled and jumped up before stomping into a hut.

"Keep your voice down," Wallace snarled.

"Sorry, but seriously did that guy have wings?" Daryl stared at them and despite how tired and afraid she was, Rose started to giggle.

After a moment, Brody started to laugh too. Before long, Wallace and Duncan had joined in, and even Teagan had a smile on the face.

"You guys are assholes." Daryl turned and stalked back into his hut.

"He ain't wrong," Wallace said with a grin. He stood and clapped Brody on the back. "Come on, Red, I'll wake up Brian and we'll show you how to check the traps."

* * *

"TELL ME MORE ABOUT THIS VIDA CREATURE." PATRICK stared at Solomon.

It was late afternoon and everyone was sitting around the

fire. It hadn't escaped Rose's notice that Doc was sitting next to Brody. Their thighs were brushing, and Brody looked both pleased and nervous.

Solomon shrugged. "There isn't much more to tell. He's big, blue, strong and needs water to live."

"How strong?"

"Patrick, it doesn't matter." Teagan leaned forward. "You know he's dead by now."

"Maybe, maybe not." Patrick ran a lazy hand down Talla's thigh.

"Why are you so interested in him?" Marissa asked.

"Don't you worry your pretty little head about that." Patrick gave her a condescending look that set Rose's teeth on edge. "How did he escape again?"

"That's the million-dollar question, isn't it, Rose?" Daryl said. "You want to answer that?"

"What are you talking about?" Brody asked.

"I'm saying that Rose set that blue idiot free," Daryl said

"No, she didn't," Brody glanced at Rose, "she wouldn't do something like that. Would you?"

Rose gave him a nervous look. "I didn't know…"

"What the fuck did you do, Rose?" Solomon was sitting beside her, and he gave her a hard poke in the leg.

She flinched, and Duncan immediately stood with his hand on the handle of his sword. "You would be wise to keep your hands to yourself, Solomon."

Solomon gave him a wide-eyed look of fright and Patrick made a sit down gesture at Duncan. "Enough, Duncan."

Rose turned to Solomon. "You were torturing him. He would have died if I hadn't helped him. His organs were shutting down."

"So, what, you just decided to untie him and lead him straight to the orb?"

"No! No, I didn't know he would try and go back to the orb. I was going to get him out of the lab and then…"

"Then what?" Solomon asked. "What were you going to do with him? Do you really think you could have hidden a giant blue alien in our apartment? Christ, you are so fucking stupid! We're on this stupid fucking world because of you, Rose!"

He stood and stormed off to their hut. Rose started to stand, and Brody grabbed her arm. "I think he needs a minute."

She studied Brody. His face was pale, and he was giving her a sick look. "Brody, I'm sorry. I didn't mean for this to happen."

"I know."

"You're sorry?" Marissa stood up and glared at Rose. "You're sorry? All of this is your fault and all you can say is you're sorry? John and Leslie are dead because of you."

Rose winced. Her face was burning, her hands were ice cold despite the warm and humid air and she felt sick to her stomach. "I know, and I feel horrible about it. I didn't mean for any of this to happen. If I had known that Vida would lock all of us in with the orb, I would have…"

Daryl glared at her. "You would have what? Not tried to rescue the big blue fucking ape?"

"No," Rose replied. "I would have helped him escape, just not when the portal was opening up."

"You're such a bitch," Marissa spat. "I'm glad Daryl left you to die in the ocean. I just wish you had been torn apart like -"

"Marissa, shut up," Brody said.

"Fuck you, Brody," Marissa said. "And fuck you too, Rose. I hope you die a fucking horrible death on this stupid island."

She turned and stormed away to her own hut. Rose stared at the ground as Daryl stood. "She's right. You're a bitch and you're gonna get what's coming to you for trapping us all here."

He left, and Rose forced her gaze to Peter. He was staring at her and the disgust on his face made her want to vomit. "Peter, I'm sorry."

"Yeah." He stood and walked away.

Brody put his arm around her and she leaned into his embrace. He kissed the top of her head, avoiding the goose egg, and squeezed her hard. "It's okay, Rose. They'll get over it."

"They won't, and they shouldn't," she said. "Everything they said is true. This is my fault, and Leslie and John are dead because of me."

"It'll be okay," Brody repeated.

"Well," Patrick grinned at her and she swallowed down the trickle of fear she felt at the hard sheen in his eyes, "that was a fun show. Who's hungry?"

CHAPTER 6

R ose dunked the shirt in the water repeatedly until all of the soap was gone. Beside her, Wallace was dunking clothes as well and they worked silently. Wallace glanced around every few seconds, studying the trees and plant life that surrounded the waterfall.

"Where did he learn to do that?" Rose stared at Duncan. He was standing waist deep in the pool with a spear held high over his head. A mesh bag was slung across his chest and hung at his hip. He stared fixedly into the water, not moving a muscle.

Wallace shrugged. "Duncan knows a lot of stuff about surviving in the wilderness. Of course, he just calls it a goddamn regular old Tuesday. Truth be told, having Duncan around has saved our bacon more than a few times. Turns out, if you want to survive on a deserted island, you should have a guy from a medieval world with you. Duncan taught us how to build the traps, make spears, and skin the animals for their fur. Hell, he even showed us how to repair the roofs on the huts. He's a regular Mister Fix-It."

Rose smiled a little and Wallace winked at her. "Haven't

seen you smile in days, Rosie-girl."

She gave him a startled look. "Days? How long have we been here now?"

"Ten days," Wallace said.

"No, that can't be. Ten days already? Are you sure?"

Wallace wrung out the t-shirt and threw it into the basket weaved from dried grass. "Yep. Time has a funny way of getting away from you on this island. I noticed your friends still aren't talking to you."

She wrung the shirt dry and grabbed a pair of pants from the pile. She dunked them in water before smearing soap across them and rubbing them briskly. "No. Well, Brody is talking to me."

"Dick move from the others." Wallace sat back on his heels and watched Duncan.

"I don't blame them. It's my fault they're here."

"Sounds like it's that big blue guy's fault."

"That's nice of you to say, but it isn't true. Vida was only able to lock us in with the orb because I released him."

"You don't regret it though, do you?"

She scrubbed the pants against a large rock under the water. "Nope, I don't."

"Good for you."

She glanced at Wallace and he nodded. "I mean it. From the sounds of it, Vida was a prisoner and being tortured by your fiancé. Maybe your fiancé deserved what happened."

"John and Leslie were innocent."

He touched her shoulder and she stopped scrubbing the pants and looked at him.

"I know what you're going through, Rose. Believe me, I do. Innocent people have died because of my actions and while I'm not saying you ever forget that, it does get easier to live with."

"Does it?"

"Yes. Anytime you need to talk about it, I'm your man. Okay?"

"Thanks, Wallace. I appreciate it." She was a little surprised by his thoughtfulness. He had it completely hidden behind a thick armor of sarcasm and self-deprecation.

"Or, if you want to not think about it and just want to have hang-from-a-thatched-roof, hot and sweaty sex, I can be your man for that too."

Her mouth dropped open and Wallace laughed before scrubbing at another shirt. "Don't look so surprised, Rose. You're hot and smart and you have a great ass. And if you haven't noticed, there's a lack of women at our camp."

"I also have a fiancé," she reminded him.

"Do you, though?"

She stared at the pants in her hands. There were plenty of empty huts and Solomon had moved into one of them the night she had admitted to releasing Vida. Like the others, he was completely ignoring her. She knew how he was, and she had given him his space. Anytime they had a fight, he needed a few days to brood about it. Only, she hadn't realized how much time had passed. He'd never gone this long with giving her the silent treatment before.

Of course, she had gotten him transported to another world where it was very possible he would die a painful and horrifying death.

He lied to you, Rose. He told you that they didn't know how to rehydrate Vida, remember? He was putting Vida through agony and doesn't even seem to feel bad about it. Solomon isn't a good guy and it's time you admit it. Deep down you know he isn't. It's why you're not actually that upset about him ignoring you.

She was upset, dammit. She loved Solomon and she

79

needed him now more than ever. He wasn't perfect, but neither was she, and he still loved her.

Does he?

"Rose?" Wallace touched her arm and she gave him a faint smile.

"I think I do. I don't know. He's upset and when he's upset, he retreats and... never mind, none of this is your problem. Thank you for the, uh, offer of sex, but I'm going to pass."

"All right." Wallace gave her a cheerful grin. "But just remember, if you change your mind, it'll be hot *and* sweaty sex."

She laughed despite her anxiety and fear. "I'll keep that in mind."

She rinsed the pants and glanced at Duncan when the spear he carried dropped into the water with deadly accuracy. He lifted his arm and stared in satisfaction at the fish impaled on the spear, before pulling its body free and dropping it into the mesh bag around his hip. He resumed his position, the spear held above his head and his gaze searching the water around him.

ROSE STARED AT THE CEILING OF HER HUT. SHE SHIFTED IN the bed of furs before rolling to her side. The moon was very bright tonight and it shone through the cracks in the wall of the hut in thin stripes.

She sat up and wrapped a fur around her shoulders. It got surprisingly cold in the jungle at night, and she wished she had Solomon's body heat to snuggle up to. She was suddenly close to tears and she abruptly climbed out of the furs. It had been another two days since her conversation with Wallace at the falls, and Brody was still the only one who acted like she existed.

She deserved their anger, she knew she did, but their continued silence was starting to get to her. The tension and anger in the camp had put everyone on edge, and she knew it was only a matter of time before Patrick kicked her out.

He wouldn't, Rose. There's safety in numbers in this world.

Yeah, that was true. But she had a feeling that Patrick was growing impatient with the tension between her and the others, and that he didn't always think rationally. She wouldn't be at all surprised if he decided to fix it by just giving her the boot.

She paced back and forth in her hut. It wasn't that late, but everyone had retired to their huts almost an hour ago. She stuck her feet into her shoes and dropped the fur on the bed before heading to the doorway of the hut. A fur hung across it and she ducked past it and stepped into the clearing.

She glanced up at the tree that served as their watch tower. Daryl was on watch. He studied her for a moment and then flipped her the bird and looked away. She sighed and walked toward Brody's hut. It wasn't that late, maybe Brody was still up. If he was, she'd ask if she could stay with him tonight. The loneliness was crushing her tonight, and she couldn't stand being by herself in that hut for a moment longer.

She was walking by Patrick and Talla's hut now and her cheeks flushed when she heard the low sound of Talla's moans. She had tried to make friends with the dark-haired beauty over the past week or so, but Talla wasn't interested. She spent most of her time either sitting by the fire with Patrick, or in his hut with him.

Brody had told her that Marissa and Daryl had already

started making noise about the fact that Talla didn't do anything around the camp. She didn't help clean or cook or fetch water. Her sole purpose seemed to be – Rose grimaced a little – sleeping with Patrick.

She heard a low masculine grunt followed by Talla's breathless cry and she realized she had come to a complete stop outside of their hut. Her cheeks bright red, she hurried away. She knocked on the doorframe to Brody's hut and then ducked past the fur.

"Brody? Are you awake? Do you mind if I... oh!"

The moonlight filtering through the cracks in Brody's hut was just as bright as it was in hers. She had no problem seeing Brody and Doc lying naked on the bed of furs. They were kissing passionately, and she gave them a look of embarrassment when they broke apart and stared in surprise at her.

"Rose? What's wrong?"

"Nothing. I – nothing's wrong. I'm so sorry to interrupt." She backed up, reaching frantically for the fur that covered the doorway. "I shouldn't have just barged in like this. I'm so sorry."

Brody half sat up and Rose held out her hand. "No, no, don't, uh, stop. You and Doc stay right where you are. Have, um, fun."

Where the hell was the damn doorway?

"Rose..."

She gave them both another apologetic smile. "I'm very sorry." She turned, spotted the doorway and practically threw her body toward it. She stumbled past the fur and into the cool night air.

"Shit," she muttered as she hurried away. "You idiot, Rose."

She slowed down as she neared her own hut and stared at

Solomon's hut. After a moment, she took a deep breath and marched toward it. It was time to talk to Solomon. Twelve days was plenty of time to give him his own space. They needed to talk about what had happened and decide where they were going from here. Either they were still a couple, or they weren't, but she was tired of waiting for Solomon to decide. She had the right to know if he was going to hate her forever, for God's sake.

She lifted her hand to knock on the doorframe, her fist faltering to a stop. She cocked her head and leaned closer to the fur that covered the doorway. The unmistakable sound of Solomon moaning could be heard, and she smiled a little. If he was having a little sexy time with himself, this might be the perfect opportunity for her to reconnect with him. What man would turn down a warm and willing woman?

She stepped into his hut, her smile of seduction dying on her lips as she stared at his pile of furs. Solomon was on his knees, his pale body thrusting back and forth, and his head thrown back as he moaned with a stark sound of pleasure she'd never heard from him before. Marissa was on her hands and knees in front of him, her entire body jiggling wildly with every thrust of Solomon's cock. Her hair hung in her face and her hands were digging into the furs.

"Oh God," she moaned. "Fuck me with that big cock. Fuck me!"

"I'm fucking you, baby," Solomon panted. "I'm gonna fuck you so hard, you'll be walking bowlegged tomorrow. You like that? You like having my cock so far in your pussy that you... Rose?"

Solomon ground to a halt inside of Marissa. She squealed indignantly. "Don't call me that, you asshole!"

She lifted her head, tossing her hair back. "You think I

want to be compared to her tired old pussy or her – what the fuck? What are you doing in here, you stupid bitch?"

She glared at Rose with loathing as Solomon kneeled frozen behind her.

"Solomon, what are you doing?" Rose whispered.

Marissa brayed laughter. "What does it look like, idiot? He's fucking me."

Rose stared blankly at her before lifting her gaze to her fiancé. "Solomon? I know we're having trouble right now, but -"

"Right now?" Marissa laughed again as Solomon gave Rose a look of shame. "Are you that fucking stupid, bitch? You think we've just been screwing since we got to the island? Seriously?"

Rose's stomach churned, and she took a stumbling step backwards. "You-you're cheating on me with Marissa?"

"Rose, it isn't what you think," Solomon said.

"It's exactly what she thinks." Marissa laughed before making a little thrust back on Solomon's dick. She hissed in disappointment and glared at Rose. "Get out of here. Your ugly face is making him lose his erection."

"Solomon?" Rose whispered.

He didn't reply, and feeling sick to her stomach, Rose turned and ran out of his hut. Tears were streaming down her face and she ran blindly out of the clearing and into the jungle. She wanted to scream, she wanted to cry, she wanted to run back and punch Solomon in the face. Instead, she ran faster. She would go to the waterfall and sit for a while. Sit until the image of Solomon and Marissa having sex was no longer burned into her brain.

Her running turned into a slow jog and as the shock wore off and she started to pay attention to her surroundings, her hurt and her anger turned to fear. She should have been at the waterfall by now.

She stopped and stared at her surroundings. Nothing looked familiar, but it was dark, and she'd never gone to the waterfall at night before. No one went into the jungle alone and they definitely didn't go into the jungle at night.

Okay, don't panic. Just turn around and walk back the way you came. Easy peasy. You ran a straight line. Keep a straight line and you'll be back in the camp.

She turned around and started walking in the opposite direction. The sound of her heartbeat was very loud, and she tried to slow it down, tried to take deep breaths and ignore the panic that was eating away at her stomach.

Something made a squawking noise about three feet to her left. She walked faster, glancing behind her every few feet. After nearly twenty minutes of walking, she finally slowed to a stop.

She was lost.

She was lost at night in the jungle of a very dangerous world.

Shit.

OKAY, SO MAYBE STORMING OFF INTO THE JUNGLE IN THE dark wasn't her brightest idea. But, it happened, and now she was lost and probably about to die, and it was all because the man she loved had betrayed her in the worst possible way.

Do you love him though?

She stumbled to a stop before leaning back against the vine-covered trunk of a large tree. Of course she loved Solomon. He was her fiancé for God's sake. You didn't agree to marry someone you didn't love. Not that she was going to marry him now. Nothing ended an engagement faster than catching your fiancé banging away at another woman.

He sure seemed to enjoy it. You've never heard him make those noises when he was having sex with you. Did you see the look on his face? Pure ecstasy. Maybe he was fucking Marissa because you suck so bad in bed.

She swiped angrily at the tears running down her face. Okay, so maybe she wasn't the greatest at having sex, but Solomon was her first and any time she had tried to ask for advice or tips on what to do in bed, he had shut her down. Said it was fine and that she worried too much.

Besides, it's not like he was the world's greatest lover. Nine times out of ten she had to fake her orgasm. If she didn't, he just kept rutting on top of her, grunting and groaning and asking repeatedly if she was close. Solomon's penis was big, and the sex was always painful at first. Hell, it had gotten to the point where she was anxious and tense just thinking about sex with him.

Marissa didn't seem to be in pain. She looked like she was enjoying herself a lot. He was really giving it to her, wasn't he? Just going in deep and hard and not –

Shut up! Shut up! Shut up!

What the hell was she doing? She was lost, and the odds of her dying tonight were extremely high, and she was thinking about how awful sex was with her fiancé? She had bigger things to worry about right now. Like finding her way back before something came out of the dark and ate her for a midnight snack.

She needed to be with the others. Not that she wanted to be around her cheating fiancé and his lover, but on this world, you needed other people to survive. She pushed away from the tree, stepped forward and fell flat on her face.

"What the heck?" She sat up, rubbing at her stomach

where a root had jabbed into it and studied her ankles. Vines were wrapped around them and she reached down and tried to pull them off. Fear stabbed through her when they tightened.

"Oh shit." She yanked harder, trying to tear through the thick rope-like greenery with her nails. "Oh shit, oh shit, oh shit!"

The vines were creeping up her calves now and she shrieked and struggled to her feet. She reached out and grabbed the lower branch of the tree to her left and tried to pull herself free. The vines tightened again, and she screamed a second time when more vines came slithering out of the darkness and wrapped around her upper body. They dragged her back toward the tree and she moaned in pain when her head banged against the trunk with a harsh thud. She struggled wildly as vines unwrapped from the tree and slid around her.

They squeezed and squeezed again. She was beginning to understand how a rat felt in the grip of a snake. Her breath wheezed out of her and she made one last strangled cry of fear before a vine snaked around her neck and tightened. Her body shook as her oxygen was cut off. Black roses bloomed in her vision and her eyes bulged as the vines wrapped impossibly tight around her entire body.

She was dying.

She was being murdered by a plant.

Karma for all the innocent house plants she had accidentally killed over the years.

The vine around her neck was torn away and she sucked in a breath of air. She kept her eyes closed, her breath tearing in and out of her throat in harsh pants. The vines were being pulled from her body and she opened her eyes and squinted at the dark shape in front of her. Big blue hands grabbed the vine that was winding across her rib cage and tore it easily in two. Dark green liquid spurted out from the vines, soaking her t-shirt and pants and the vines collapsed to the floor of the jungle as Vida tore away the rest of them holding her captive.

She fell forward. He caught her and held her with one arm as he snapped the last of the vines from her calves and ankles. When she was free, he lifted her into his arms and carried her away from the tree. A few vines were wrapping around his legs, but he broke them easily with just his stride as the muscles in his calves bulged.

"Vida?" Her voice was hoarse. "I – I thought you were dead."

"Why would I be dead?"

"I – because no human can survive here alone."

He grinned, his fangs flashing in the dim light. "I am not human, small flower."

"WHERE ARE WE GOING?" ROSE SQUINTED AT THE TREES around them as Vida walked swiftly.

He was still carrying her, and she really should have been telling him to put her down, but there was something comforting about being in his arms.

"My home."

"Your home? Vida, how did you survive? They said -"

"Shh, human." Vida's arms tightened around her for a brief second. "Do not speak so loudly. The jungle is dangerous at night. You shouldn't have been out here alone."

"Why are you out here at night then?"

"Hunting."

"Hunting what?"

"Food."

There was no derision in his tone, but she still felt stupid.

"You don't have any weapons."

"I have some weapons, but tonight I was checking my traps."

"Oh. Did you, uh, trap anything?"

He shook his head. "Not tonight. You're very lucky that I heard you scream, small flower. The vines of that tree would have choked the life from you."

She shuddered all over and Vida squeezed her thigh. "You're safe now."

"Where is your home?"

"Not far from here."

She lapsed into silence, staring at the hard line of his jaw. She had the ridiculous urge to press her mouth against it. She tore her gaze away and stared at his chest instead. Bad idea. He wasn't wearing a shirt and she studied his smooth skin. God, he was a big man. Big and warm and rather attractive if you looked past the fangs and the horns.

Oh, who was she kidding? The fangs and the horns only increased his hotness factor. She had no idea why, but it was the truth. What would it feel like to have those fangs dragging across her skin? What would it be like to have his big hands touching her? Squeezing her breasts, teasing her nipples, reaching between her legs to –

Rose!

She jerked against Vida and he gave her a curious look before shifting her a bit higher in his arms. Her heart was thudding along like she'd just run a marathon, her nipples were hard peaks and, sweet mother of Mary, was she wet?

Yep. She was definitely wet.

Her face burned, and she resisted the urge to bury her face in Vida's thick throat. Okay, she could explain this. She had almost died not ten minutes ago. The near-death experience, her tiny crush on Vida, and the fact that she hadn't had sex in

89

months, was why she was acting so out of character. She didn't even feel guilty for lusting after Vida when she was engaged to Solomon.

Uh, Rose? Solomon was fucking Marissa. Did you forget that?

She flinched. God, she *had* forgotten for a minute there. She was losing her mind.

Vida stopped and set her gently on the ground. Her shirt and pants were sticky with vine juice and she plucked her t-shirt away from her chest as Vida pointed to the large mass of yellow flowers growing on the stone wall in front of them.

"Follow me, human."

"Follow you where?" She asked. "It's a stone wall."

He took her hand and tugged her toward the wall. Her eyes widened when he pushed aside a portion of the flowers.

"It's a cave."

"Yes." He urged her forward with a hand on the small of her back.

"Is it safe? I mean, are there animals living in it?" She asked.

"It's safe. Quickly, little flower." He was scanning the dark jungle and when the low bird-like whistle came out of the darkness, he pushed her hard into the cave. She stumbled and fell to her knees, wincing at the pain, as Vida let go of the vines of flowers. It was complete blackness in the cave and Rose groped blindly in front of her. Her fingers brushed against Vida's calf and she twitched when his hands circled her waist and he lifted her to her feet.

"Vida? I can't see anything. Can you?"

"No. But I know the way."

She didn't object when he scooped her up and carried her again. She clung to him without any shame and after only a minute or so, she realized she could see a little better. She wasn't sure if her night vision was kicking in, or if there was some light filtering in somehow. She had the vague impression that Vida was walking downhill and the air felt colder.

The tunnel widened, and she stared at the three flickering candles. It was the only light in the darkness. She held Vida's arm in a tight grip when he stopped and set her on her feet. He tried to walk away, and she pulled on his arm. "Don't leave me."

"Stay here, small human. I will not be long."

She watched as he moved to the candles and stooped to pick one up. He moved confidently, lighting candle after candle until the darkness had been banished and she could see again. Her mouth dropped open in shock. The tunnel had widened into a large underground cavern.

"Is that a- a couch?"

"What?" Vida asked. He returned the candle to its rightful spot and watched silently as she staggered over on rubbery legs to the couch. It was dark grey in colour, with thick cushions and green throw pillows set neatly on it. A crocheted granny square afghan was placed neatly over the back of the couch. There were two matching overstuffed armchairs on either side of the couch. A plush green area rug was under the couch and chairs. A coffee table was placed in front of the couch and she stared at the hard cover books that were piled in the middle.

"What the hell is going on?" She whispered.

She made a slow twirl, staring at the bookshelf that was stuffed full of books, the second smaller bookshelf with knick-knacks, photographs in frames and fake potted plants arranged artfully on its shelves.

Behind her was the kitchen, complete with a large oak kitchen table and six oak chairs. A set of pots and pans hung from small hooks in the stone wall and a white rolling kitchen island with four cabinets and two drawers was parked near the table. A green porcelain fruit bowl sat on top of the oak-coloured island counter. Next to it was a steel container that held an assortment of spatulas and serving spoons. A wooden knife block was at the far edge, all of its slots filled with knives. She moved jerkily to the island and opened one of the drawers. It was stuffed full of dish cloths and towels as well as a set of green placemats. The second drawer held a set of silverware.

She opened each of the cupboards, staring at the dish-ware, plastic containers and serving dishes with a numb surprise. She closed the cupboards and swiveled to her right. This section of the cavern was the bedroom. There was a king-size bed, complete with a mahogany frame. The colourful quilt was pushed back and she could see the blue-coloured sheets. Obviously, Vida had been sleeping in the bed.

Matching mahogany nightstands were on either side of the bed and a mahogany wardrobe and dresser were a few feet away. There were candles sitting on both nightstands. On the right one, there was also a book with a pair of reading glasses sitting on top of it.

"Vida, where did you get all of this stuff?"

"It was here when I found the cave. This odd bed is very comfortable. You should try sitting on it." He patted the couch.

"Were there humans here when you found the cave?"

He shook his head. "No, it was empty. Are these things from your world, small flower?"

"Yes. Or at least a place very similar to our world. What I don't understand is why all of this is here? It's like the person packed up their entire house and brought it to this cave. Why would they do that?"

He shrugged. "I do not know."

"Maybe this world is more similar to mine than I thought," Rose said. "Like, maybe it's just this island that's full of-of monsters and stuff. You know?"

He didn't reply, and she ran her hand along the island's smooth counter. "Maybe someone was shipwrecked or something. But, why would they have all of this with them?"

She walked to the bookshelf and picked up a frame. It held a picture of an older couple. They both had necklaces of large pink and white flowers around their necks and they were grinning widely into the camera. Behind them was a large wooden sign with the words, "Welcome to Oahu" engraved into it.

"Is this Oahu a place on your world?" Vida had joined her, and he pointed to the sign on the picture.

"You can read that?"

He gave her a wry look. "I am not the mindless savage your people believe me to be."

She blushed. "I know. I'm sorry, I didn't mean to imply that you were. I just, it's weird that you speak English and read it too."

"Is this Oahu a place you recognize?" Vida asked.

"No. I've never heard of it." She set the frame back on the bookshelf and wandered back into the kitchen. There were two large baskets full of fruit on the ground, another basket of eggs and a large glass serving bowl of dried meat.

"What is that?" She pointed to the meat.

"It's one of the smaller creatures on the island. Very fast with brown fur and long ears. I catch them easily in my traps."

"Ah, it's rabbit."

"How do you know the name of them?" Vida asked.

"I don't, not really. The people we're with, they call them

rabbits. They're not exactly like the rabbits from our world but close enough."

"The men are from your world?"

"No, but I think their world is similar to ours. I think they're from the same world as that woman who came through the orb with you. Wait – how do you know we're with…"

She cocked her head and studied his pants. They were military fatigues and her eyes widened. "Did you come into the camp and steal a pair of pants?"

He grinned, his fangs flashing in the candlelight. "Perhaps."

"How did you do it without them seeing you? They always have someone on watch."

"It was easy to slip by them." Vida didn't elaborate, and Rose frowned at him.

"Why didn't you join us?"

"Why would I?"

"Well, because we have huts and a waterfall for water and bathing in and -"

"I go to the waterfall every day, little flower. This cave is not that far from it. Besides, I have everything I need right here. It is safe from the pink creatures, thanks to the flowers that cover the entrance and it has many more comforts than your huts."

Rose had to admit he had a point. Her hut certainly didn't come with books and a king size bed and a matching set of dishware.

"Come," Vida grabbed one of the bigger candles and crooked his finger at her, "I will show you where you can eliminate and where you can bathe."

"Bathe?" She followed him across the cavern to two tunnel openings she hadn't noticed. He led her down the left one. About twenty feet into the tunnel, it too widened into a cavern. This cavern was smaller with a lower ceiling and she could hear the sound of rushing water.

She stopped abruptly, staring in utter disbelief at the large wooden box sitting in the middle of the cavern. It was at the perfect height for sitting and there was a wooden toilet seat sitting on top of it. A small side table held a large basket full of the smooth broad leaves they used for toilet paper. Completely thrown by the toilet seat, she tamped down her childish giggles as Vida urged her closer to it. The toilet seat was carved from wood and it was a bit crude looking but sanded smooth. The sound of water was growing louder.

"Look, little flower." Vida pointed inside the toilet and she shook her head.

"No, thanks. I don't need to see your, un, waste."

"Look." He insisted. He held the candle over the seat.

She sighed and took a quick look. "Holy smokes, it's a hole in the floor."

It was a decidedly long drop to the water rushing below and she felt a little nauseous at the idea of sitting there.

Vida nodded. "Yes. I believe there is a deeper cavern under this one that is mostly filled with water. Whoever was here before us was very wise to build this over the natural hole. Do you agree?"

"Um, yeah, I guess. Say, how sturdy is this wooden box thing, do you think?" She prodded at the side of the box. It looked and felt sturdy enough but what if it simply collapsed while she was taking a pee. She'd fall through the damn hole. Death by peeing wasn't the way she pictured shuffling off the mortal coil.

"It is sturdy enough."

"Are you sure?"

"Yes. Try it out and see."

"Uh, no thanks. I'm, uh, good for now."

"All right. Come with me."

He turned and headed back down the tunnel. She hurried after him and followed him down the second tunnel. The air was growing steamy and after about thirty feet, the tunnel widened into a cavern. This one held a pool of water and she stared at the steam rising lazily from it.

"Oh my God. It's a natural hot spring." She grinned happily at Vida. "It's not too hot to bathe in?"

"It is not."

"How deep is it?" She asked.

"The middle of the pool is shoulder deep on me."

Anxiety brewed in her belly. "It's over my head then."

He studied her for a moment. "Stay away from the middle and you will avoid drowning."

"Thanks for the tip."

"You should learn how to swim. We are surrounded by water."

"Yeah, I know. Hey, do you think I could take a bath before you take me back to the camp? We only have the waterfall to bathe in and it's very cold."

"I will not take you back to your friends tonight," Vida replied. "It is too dangerous to be in the jungle at night. You will spend the night here with me."

Her mouth went dry and her gaze dipped to his naked chest. "Oh, um, right. Okay. If you're sure you don't mind?"

"Why would I mind?"

"I don't know."

"Have a bath, little flower," Vida said. He lit the candles that were placed around the pool until the air glowed with warm light. "I will prepare food for us."

He left the cavern without looking back.

CHAPTER 7

"**D**o you feel better, human?"

Rose shrieked and slid down in the water. Surprisingly, she'd been half asleep. After nearly being choked to death by a plant, she figured she'd never sleep again. But she hadn't counted on how warm and relaxing the water was. God, she'd missed having a hot bath.

She covered her breasts with her arms, even though they were beneath the water, and stared at Vida as he set down a stack of towels, a pale pink robe and a basket on the ground next to her. "Um, yes, thank you. I was almost asleep. The water is so – hey, what are you doing?"

Vida paused in unbuttoning his pants. "Joining you in the pool."

"What? No, you can't. I – I'm naked."

"It would be strange if you were not."

He unbuttoned his pants and fumbled at the zipper before pulling his pants down. She saw a hint of dark blue pubic hair and looked away immediately, her cheeks a fiery red, and her pulse pounding out a frenetic rhythm.

"Vida, this isn't proper. I don't even know you and being naked together is -"

"Are you worried that I will try and fuck you, human?" The water rippled as Vida sat down in the pool.

She stared at him. "Are you going to, uh, try that?"

"Do you want me to fuck you?"

"I don't even know you."

"Do you need to know me for us to fuck?" Vida rested his arms against the smooth lip of the pool and let his legs float in front of him. The pool was big enough that they were nowhere close to each other, but she kept her arms clamped firmly over her breasts.

"I, no, I guess not. But, I don't want to have sex with you."

"Then you have nothing to worry about."

Unbelievably, hurt rippled through her. She knew she wasn't the best looking woman, but she was in good shape, and she didn't think she was ugly. Before she could stop herself, she blurted, "So, you don't want to have sex with me?"

He arched one dark blue eyebrow at her. "What does it matter if I do or not, human?"

She blinked at him. "It doesn't, and I have a name. It's Rose."

He didn't reply, and she gave him an irritated look. "I was just curious."

"Do you still fight with your mate?"

"How do you know Solomon and I are fighting?"

Vida sunk below the surface of the water. Oh God, could he see her under the water? She crossed her legs and covered her crotch with one hand while keeping the other arm across her breasts.

After nearly five minutes, Vida resurfaced, and she glared at him. "Enjoy the view?"

He grinned, the water sluicing down his blue skin, before shaking his head. "I kept my eyes closed, hum – Rose. Your modesty was preserved."

Again, that weird and completely inappropriate ripple of hurt. Why did it bother her so much that Vida wasn't interested in her sexually? Hell, maybe they weren't even compatible for sleeping together. She knew that he had all the right bits and pieces, she'd read the information reports on him. But just because he had a penis, didn't necessarily mean that he had sex the same way that humans did.

"So, how do you know that I'm fighting with Solomon?"

"He does not seem to be a very good mate."

She hugged herself a little tighter. "He's not my mate anymore."

"Did he die?" Vida asked.

She winced. "No. I went to his hut tonight and I caught him having sex with Marissa, the other lab tech."

Anger and nausea rolled through her and she rubbed briefly at her temples. "He's angry because I released you. Hell, everyone's angry with me because I tried to rescue you and we all ended up on this other world. They blame me."

"I was the one who forced you to take me to the orb."

She just shrugged. "It doesn't matter. They're angry and they have the right to be angry."

"So your mate fucked another to punish you for setting me free?"

"No. Apparently, they were sleeping together before we even went through the orb." She buried her face in her hands as the hot tears dripped down her cheeks. She didn't want to cry in front of Vida. Hell, she didn't want to cry over stupid

Solomon having sex with stupid Marissa, but she couldn't seem to stop.

More tears soaked her skin. "We haven't even had sex in months. I kept trying, but he was always too busy or too tired. I wore sexy lingerie, I offered to give him a massage before sex, but he just didn't want to. I'm so dumb, I actually thought it was because he was tired and busy at work. I never even suspected that he was cheating on me with Marissa. I shouldn't be surprised. She's gorgeous and has a great body. I'm bad in bed, and I knew I was bad in bed, but I kept asking Solomon what he liked and what he wanted me to try and improve on, but he just shut me down. When I walked in on Solomon and Marissa having sex, he looked so-so into it. The noises he was making and the look on his face, that never happened with me. I mean, he would come when we had sex, so I figured he was enjoying himself, and I told myself that it didn't matter if I came or not. What mattered was – oh my god, what am I doing?"

She shut her mouth with an abrupt snap. Embarrassment rushed through her and if she wasn't completely naked, she would have jumped out of the pool and ran. Instead, she kept her face buried in her hands even as she felt Vida move closer.

"Turn around, flower."

She peered through her fingers. Vida had moved until he was sitting right beside her, and she sniffed loudly and wiped at her cheeks. "What?"

"Turn around."

He made a twirling motion with his finger and, after a moment, she turned so that her back was to him.

She could hear him rummaging in the basket beside her. "Tip your head back."

She did what he asked and twitched when he used a cup

to pour warm water over her hair. When it was wet, he reached into the basket again and produced a handful of white gel-like substance.

"What is that?"

"Soap." He smeared some onto her scalp and rubbed it in with his strong hands. She closed her eyes and tried not to moan out loud as he slowly and methodically washed her scalp and the long strands of her hair. It felt amazing, and some of her anxiety disappeared as Vida massaged her scalp.

He rinsed the soap from her hair, using multiple cups of water until the water ran clear, then pushed her hair over her shoulders. He smeared more soap onto his hands and she didn't object when he washed her back with his big, rough hands.

God, it felt so good. She was like a boneless little kitten by the time he was done.

"Little flower?"

"Yeah?" She leaned against his big hands as he cupped her shoulders.

"Would you like me to fuck you now?"

She sat upright, the water splashing into her face. "Uh, what?"

Vida's hands rubbed her back. "Would you like me to fuck you and give you an orgasm?"

"W-why would you do that?"

"Why would I not? You will enjoy it. I promise. I am very skilled at making females climax."

Rose! Say no thank you and ask him to move to the other side of the pool!

"Can you, I mean – are you compatible with humans for sex? You have sex the, uh, normal way, right?"

His low laugh made her blush. "Yes, little flower."

"I – I don't really know you."

"You don't need to know me to fuck me."

She licked her lips, staring at the flickering light from the candle on the wet stone around the pool.

Rosie, say no!

She should say no. She absolutely should say no. Only… she and Solomon were over, and she had almost died tonight, and probably would die at some point, because she was a stupid city girl who had no idea how to survive in a jungle. She hadn't had sex in months, hadn't had an orgasm from anything other than her own hand in over a year, and…and, dammit, she was probably going to die. Why shouldn't she have a little meaningless sex with Vida?

He's not human, Rose.

She pushed that thought out of her head.

What if he can't make you come? Then you'll know for certain that it's you with the problem, not Solomon. Is that what you want?

"Rose?" Vida pushed her wet hair away from her neck and pressed a kiss against her wet skin. "Do you want me to fuck you?"

There was only one way to find out if she was the one with the problem. "Yes."

He spread his legs apart. "Move back."

She scooted back against him. His hands soaped the top of her shoulders, her neck and her upper chest. Within minutes, she was drifting in a sea of warmth and sensation. She leaned against his wet chest, her head lolling on his shoulder. When he tugged on her crossed arms, she let them drop without a second thought.

"Good girl, little flower," he murmured into her ear.

His big hands cupped her breasts. She moaned and arched into them, gasping when his soapy fingers pulled on her nipples. He cleaned her breasts, soaping under them and around them and paying close attention to her rock-hard nipples.

When his hands dropped to her flat stomach, she moaned in disappointment.

"Shh, flower." He nipped at her neck and the little dart of pain only made the pleasure sweeter.

He washed her stomach and her hips and her upper thighs. When one big hand curved around her right thigh and tugged, she parted them eagerly. She could feel his erection pressing against her back and she rubbed against it as his other hand cupped her throat. He held her against him and pressed a kiss against the top of her shoulder.

"Would you like me to wash your sweet pussy for you, little flower?"

"Yes, please," she moaned.

His hand cupped her pussy, his fingers rubbing across the wet lips in gentle circles. She clutched at his forearm as he washed her pussy. She shifted and squirmed, wanting him to touch her clit but he carefully avoided it.

"Vida, please."

She had never heard that almost pathetic whine of need in her voice before.

"Why do you have hair here," his fingers rubbed through the patch of hair at the top of her pussy, before moving lower and stroking her bare lips, "but not here?"

"I – I had it removed." She moved restlessly against him.

"Why?"

"Well, because that's what men like."

He didn't reply and feeling vaguely stupid, she said, "In my world, the women have all of their body hair permanently removed when they're eighteen or so. Most women don't even keep, uh, a little bit of pubic hair."

"How do you remove it permanently?" He was stroking

the lips of her pussy almost absently now and she wished he would touch her more firmly.

"With a machine. You lie on a bed and it scans your body and targets the spots where you want the hair removed. Then it – oh! Oh my God!"

Vida's first finger had slipped even lower and was probing at her entrance. At her startled cry, he moved it away and rubbed her inner thigh. Disappointment welled inside of her and she could hear herself making soft mews of need.

"Please touch me, Vida."

He cupped her pussy again and rubbed with his entire hand. It put delicious friction on her clit and she arched into his hand. His low groan when she settled back against his erection, sent fresh lust through her.

"I'm finished washing your sweet pussy," he said into her ear. "Do you still wish for me to make you come? Still wish to be fucked? Or would you like to get out of your bath and have something to eat?"

"No!" Her cry echoed through the chamber. "No, Vida, please. I need..."

She couldn't say it. It was too embarrassing, but oh God, what if he stopped? What if he didn't give her the relief she needed? She didn't understand what was happening to her. Vida had barely touched her, and she was already way more excited and turned-on than she'd ever been with Solomon.

It was the near-death experience, she decided a little hysterically. It had to be. Nearly dying had heightened all of her senses temporarily – that was a thing, right?

Totally a thing.

There was no way she could be this hot, this needy, for Vida when she barely knew him and hadn't even kissed him, for God's sake.

"Does my little flower need to come?"

"Yes. Yes, please." She clutched his arm with pathetic eagerness.

"My sweet flower needs to spread her legs nice and wide for me."

She immediately did what he asked. He lifted both her legs and hooked them over his, spreading them even further until she was completely open to him.

One heavy arm wrapped around her waist and he cupped her breast, tugging on and playing with her nipple before moving to her other one and doing the same. They throbbed with need and she wished he would suck on them. Before she could ask, his free hand dipped between her legs and she forgot all about her throbbing nipples.

Now it was her pussy that throbbed with an intensity she'd never felt before. Her previous orgasms, when she was able to have one, were pleasant affairs that rippled through her with gentle pulses and left her with a vague feeling of contentment.

But she'd never felt this type of exquisite need before, and she was certain that she was on the precipice of a life-altering experience. When Vida's fingers brushed against her swollen clit, she shrieked and arched against him. A second light caress and she went off like a rocket, her entire body jerking and shaking as pleasure exploded throughout her lower body.

Vida's long finger pushed inside of her and she squeezed compulsively around it as it sent another burst of pleasure through her. He groaned into her ear, his fingers pulling hard on her nipple as she humped his hand through the last of her orgasm.

When she finally collapsed against him, her breathing labored and her pulse pounding in her ears, he kept his finger deep inside of her as he rubbed her nipple with his thumb. He pressed a kiss against the pulse point in her throat.

"You're very tight, little flower."

Was that disappointment in his voice? It was hard to tell in her current orgasm-induced stupor. It couldn't be disappointment. What guy would be disappointed by a tight pussy on a woman?

He pulled his finger free and kissed the side of her neck again. To her surprise, he propped her up against the side of the pool and quickly climbed out. He turned his back before she could even get a good look at his penis. He dried off with a towel and pulled his pants on as she stared at his admittedly impressive looking ass.

"Vida? Aren't we going to, um, have sex now?"

"No, little flower."

"Why not?"

"It's getting late. You need to eat and then rest."

Embarrassment seeped into her and she covered her breasts with her arms when Vida glanced over his shoulder at her. "Can you find your way to the main chamber or do you need me to wait for you?"

She shook her head. "I can find it."

He left without saying anything else and she sunk into the water before rubbing at her temples. She'd just had the best orgasm of her life with a guy who wasn't even human. And she would have gladly fucked him if he hadn't climbed out of the water like he couldn't wait to get away from her

How ugly is your o-face if it's enough to make a guy lose his desire to fuck you, Rose?

She flushed and tried to ignore her inner voice as she climbed out of the water. She dried off with a towel before putting the robe on and tying it securely around her waist.

Shame still heating up her face, she picked up a candle and walked slowly toward the main chamber.

BY THE TIME THE LITTLE HUMAN JOINED HIM, HE HAD HIS need mostly under control. Of course, just the sight of her made his cock twitch. He tried to ignore it as the human gave him an uncertain smile.

"Sit down." He pointed at the odd bed and after a moment's hesitation, she walked toward it. He stared at her ass and the sway of her hips as she walked away from him. His cock swelled, pushing against the confinements of his pants. What he wouldn't give to have her impaled on his thick cock. To watch her wiggle and hear her moan as he brought her to orgasm repeatedly before he found his own relief. The way she had reacted in the pool, the way she had come so explosively from just a few light touches, made him ache to take her to his bed. The way she responded to him almost made him insane with desire.

He'd found the human attractive even before he'd brought her to orgasm. Her scent, her silky hair and her soft, smooth skin were very appealing to him. He couldn't understand why her mate would cheat on her. Her confession that she couldn't orgasm didn't appear to be true.

He turned away and piled some of the meat and fruit into two bowls. He shouldn't have been lusting so much after her. He'd spent the last twenty-five years having sex nearly every day. His people mated often, but sex on an almost daily basis for over two decades was a bit too much even for him. He assumed his body would be grateful for the break. Instead, after a month without sex, it seemed to crave mating even more now.

Or maybe it just craved the little human.

He sighed and adjusted his cock in his pants before picking up the bowls and walking toward the human. The human – Rose, her name was Rose – was too small. The women on his world were large and muscular and more than capable of handling his cock. He'd never had to worry about hurting them.

When he'd first been pulled through the orb from his world to a different world – one ruled by women - the women had also been warriors. Although not as big as his world's females, for the most part they were tall and powerful. Most of them could not take his entire cock, but a few could. The ones who couldn't, he simply fucked them more slowly and carefully.

So do that with the little human. If you go slow, if you get her wet enough beforehand, you might be able to fuck her.

No, he couldn't. He'd felt how tight her little pussy was in the hot pool earlier. He'd fucked virgins who weren't as tight as her.

He handed her the bowl and sat down on the far end of the odd bed – couch, the flower had called it a couch. After a moment, when she didn't eat, he said, "Eat the food, little flower."

"I'm not very hungry." Her face was pale, and she looked tired and a little unwell.

"Do you feel sick?" He was more worried than he should have been.

"No. Just, um, feeling bad about what happened earlier. Vida, I didn't mean to upset you."

"You didn't," he said. "Eat your food."

She stared at the bowl in her lap but didn't eat.

"Flower, you need to -"

"Will you tell me about your world?" Her tiny hands were clutching the bowl tightly.

"Yes. If you try and eat."

She picked up a piece of meat and put it in her mouth obediently.

He ate some of his meat and a bit of fruit before smiling at her. "My world is beautiful. It is made up of many islands such as this one – some bigger, some smaller, and the water that surrounds it is clear and clean. The sky is the most beautiful shade of purple, very close to the colour of our females.

"Your women are purple?"

He nodded, and she studied his blue skin. "Are they…pretty?"

"Yes. They are different looking from the females on your world. Not just the purple skin, but in size and shape. They are tall and strong and excellent fighters."

"Is your world dangerous?" She asked.

"No more than any other world, I suppose."

"Do you have technology on your world?"

"Technology?" He gave her a curious look.

"Um, like computers and machines and electricity."

He shook his head. "No. My world is similar to this one."

"Is that why you've survived here on your own?"

He just shrugged. "Perhaps. My people are used to working for our survival. We have not grown soft and rely on machines as your people do."

She poked at a piece of blue fruit as a dull flush covered her cheeks. "No, I guess not. Do you have a wife or a girl-friend in your world?"

"Do you ask if I have a mate?" He ate more meat, frowning a little when she dropped the piece of blue fruit back in the bowl. "Eat, little flower."

"How do you know it's not poisonous?" She asked.

"The animals eat it."

"Oh." She tasted a small piece of the fruit. "This is good. It's very sweet. It tastes kind of like apricots. Apricots are a fruit on my world."

She ate more of the fruit and he grunted in satisfaction.

"So, uh, do you have a mate on your world?"

"No. Why?"

"I just, um, wondered." Her pale skin was flushing again. He stared at her chest, wishing he could pull open the clothing she wore and watch the flush cover her breasts. Her breasts were small but delectably plump and her nipples seemed very sensitive. He wanted to touch them again, wanted to suck on them until she was pleading in her soft voice for him to make her come.

He forced his gaze away from her chest. "It has been many years since I've seen my world. Even if I'd had a mate, she would have believed me to be dead and found a new mate by now."

"Years?" She gave him a startled look. "You were only at the lab for a month or so. It wasn't…"

Understanding dawned in her eyes. "You were on another world before our world."

"Yes. When the orb sucked me out of my world, it sent me to a world where women ruled."

"Really?"

"Yes. There were very few males born on that world. Males were precious to them. The women lived in tribes and they kept the males as slaves for breeding purposes."

"W-what?" She set the bowl on the small table in front of the couch and gave him a horrified look. "You were a slave?"

"Yes."

"A sex slave."

"Yes."

"Oh my God, that's horrible. How did you escape?"

"It is a long story, but the current Queen was overthrown by the massina. A woman named Quinn."

"What's a massina?"

"It means the head of the queen's guard. Quinn was a human like you who had been brought by the orb, but she was very strong and powerful. The queen was a terrible human who tortured and murdered whenever she felt like it."

"Oh my God," Rose whispered.

"She had murdered the massina's mate in cold blood many years earlier, and Quinn wanted revenge for her mate's death. But, she fell in love with a human who came from the orb, and when the queen also threatened him, Quinn decided they would escape. She knew an orb was coming and she knew I wanted to leave this world, so she included me in her plan to escape."

"I thought you said that the madina overthrew the queen?"

"Massina, not madina," he replied. "The queen learned of Quinn's plan and tried to stop her. It did not end well for the queen."

"Holy shit." Rose stared at her lap for a moment before studying him. "How, uh, how did they decide who got to sleep with you?"

"The women had a claiming ceremony every month. They decided which male they wanted to breed with that month and put their name in for them. They then fought each other for the right to breed with the male. The female who won was given the male for the month to breed with."

The little human was staring at him in mute horror and he gave her a reassuring smile. "They fought with wooden swords, little flower. No one was killed."

"I – did you have a choice who you wanted to sleep with?"

"No."

"Oh my God, that's terrible. So, you slept with a different woman every month regardless of whether you wanted to or not?"

"They gave us a month off in between so as not to wear us out, but I was," he paused, "popular with the queen. She requested me often."

Rose gave him another horrified look. "You had to sleep with the queen? The one who was hurting people."

"Yes. If I had not, she would have cut off my head and fed me to the pigs."

"I'm so sorry," Rose whispered.

He studied her face. She looked sick to her stomach and he was starting to regret being so blunt about the other world. "It could have been worse, small flower."

"How long were you on that world?"

"Twenty-five years."

Her mouth dropped open. "Twenty-five... how old are you, Vida?"

"I am sixty-five."

"Are you kidding me? You look like you're in your thirties."

"We live a long time. It is not unusual for my kind to live over a hundred years."

She stared at him and he pointed at her bowl of food. "Eat some more, Rose."

"I'm not hungry." She pushed the bowl away. "So, you were forced to have sex almost every day with a bunch of different women for twenty-five years?"

"Yes. Until Quinn overthrew the queen. She and the queen's daughter changed the rules. They still had the

112

claiming ceremony, but the men were allowed to decide if they wanted to participate in it or not."

"Did you keep participating?"

"No. Even though it was going to be different, I still wanted to return to my own world. I left in the orb two nights after Quinn defeated the queen, in the hopes it might take me to my world. The human that was with me, was hoping to return to her world."

"Instead, you landed on ours where we tortured and almost killed you," Rose said.

She looked so miserable that he slid closer and touched her arm. "It is not your fault, human."

"Not directly, but I was a part of it." She suddenly twitched and gave him a wide-eyed look. "Did you – did you have children with these women on the other world?"

He nodded. "Yes. Mostly girls, but there were a few boys."

"You left your children on a different world?"

He flinched, and she immediately gave him a chastised look. "I'm sorry. That came out wrong. I was judging, and I shouldn't have. I don't know your situation and -"

"In my world there is a ritual that must be performed between a father and their offspring. If it is not performed within a few days of birth, the child will not bond with the father. It does not matter how much time they spend together."

"A ritual?" Rose said.

"Yes. I exchange takenas with my child."

"What's a takena?"

"It is a living essence within us. Our young are born with their takenas already bonded to their mother's. It happens in the womb. But the child will never love the father unless the father is allowed to bond his takena with the child's during

113

the ritual. The queen would not allow me to perform the ritual with any of my children."

He stopped and stared across the cavern for a moment. "I love my children very much, but they never saw me as anything more than a stranger."

"I'm so sorry." The little human touched his arm and he had the strangest urge to rest his head in her lap. To let her pet him like a catten until he felt better.

Before he could give in to the urge, she let go of his arm and rubbed at her temples again. She looked pale and sick to her stomach.

"Flower, are you ill?"

"Just getting a headache." She couldn't seem to look him in the eye. "Do you mind if I go to bed now?"

"No. Come with me." He tried to take her arm and she pulled away.

"I'll sleep on the couch."

He frowned at her. "The bed is large enough for both of us."

"I know, but I think it's better if I sleep here."

"Why?" He wouldn't – couldn't – fuck the little human, but he liked the idea of having her in the bed with him and in his arms.

"I just – I'd rather sleep here. Okay?"

He could almost smell her anxiety and he hated that he was upsetting her. "All right. Good night, Rose."

"Good night."

He blew out all of the candles except for a few in the kitchen area as she curled up on the couch and covered herself with the blanket from the back of it. He stripped out of his pants and climbed into the bed.

After only a few minutes, he sat up. "Human, are you too cold?"

"No. I'm okay."

He lay back down, staring up at the ceiling of the cavern. He was feeling restless and anxious and he didn't know why.

He sat up again when he heard the human stand up. "What's wrong?"

"Nothing. I – I have to use the washroom."

"Take a candle with you."

She didn't reply but he watched as her slender figure moved toward the candles still lit. She picked up one, the wavering light illuminated her pale skin and blonde hair and disappeared down the entrance to the bathroom.

He waited impatiently for her to return. The flickering light of the candle in the entrance of the bathroom made his tense muscles relax. When the little human uttered a soft squeal and the light was snuffed out, he was on his feet and racing toward her without a second thought.

"Little flower! Where are you?"

"Here, I'm right here." Her voice was disgruntled. "I tripped over my own damn feet and dropped the candle. It went out."

He followed the sound of her voice until he could sense her standing in front of him. She squeaked in surprise when he lifted her into his arms and carried her back to the main cavern. "Vida? What – what are you doing?"

He could feel the coldness of her skin through her clothing. "You are cold, little human. I asked you if you were too cold and you said you were not."

"I wasn't," she said. "I'm just a little cold now. I'll be fine when I get back to the couch and – hey, what are you doing?"

He was sliding her into the bed and he climbed in behind her, pulling her back against his body when she tried to scramble off the other side. "Vida, I -"

"Shh, little flower." He squeezed her waist and nuzzled

115

the side of her neck. "You will be too cold sleeping alone. Relax and go to sleep."

She squirmed a bit more and he tightened his grip on her before rubbing her flat belly with his big hand. "Sleep, sweet flower."

"I can't. I'm too wound up," she muttered.

"Do you want me to make you come again? It will help you relax."

She jerked against him, making the most adorable little sound when he cupped her breast. "I – are you always this, uh, blunt?"

He used his thumb to rub her nipple through the silk clothing, loving the way it immediately hardened for him.

"Does that feel good, flower?" He murmured into her ear.

"I – yeah, but I – oh gosh…"

He had opened her robe to bare her gorgeous breasts and he pulled on each of her nipples until they were swollen and hard. "You have beautiful nipples, flower. So hard and sensitive." He plucked on the right one, grinning in satisfaction when she cried out with pleasure.

"Would you like me to suck on your nipples?"

She gasped, her hand clutching at his forearm as he pinched her nipple. "I – oh God, um, maybe later. Can I ask – oh my gosh, that feels so good – a question?"

"Yes." He pressed his dick against her ass and groaned when she rubbed against him.

"Why did you give me an orgasm earlier?"

"I wanted to show you that you could come. It is your mate's responsibility to please you. If you do not come, it is his fault, not yours. Do you understand?" He nipped at the soft skin of her neck with his fangs.

"In my world, women are supposed to take control of

their own pleasure. To not expect a man to be the one to make them come."

"No, little flower, that is not right." He kissed her neck and licked his way to her earlobe before sucking on it. "There is no need for you to take control. I will bring you pleasure with my mouth and my fingers."

"I want your," he could almost feel the heat of her blush pouring off of her, "cock as well."

He squeezed her breast and toyed with her nipple. "No, little human."

"Why have you changed your mind about having sex? Is it because you've been forced to have sex non-stop for the last twenty-five years?"

He circled her nipple with his thumb. "No. My kind enjoy sex very much."

"Are you afraid I'll get pregnant? I won't. I had my cycle shot only a few days before we got sucked into the orb."

"Cycle shot?" He gave her a curious look.

"It's a birth control shot. It prevents pregnancy."

"You do not wish to have young ones?"

"No, I do. Just not right now. The shot prevents me from getting pregnant only for a year. I didn't want to have a baby before I got married. But, you don't have to worry about me getting pregnant."

He didn't reply, and she pressed her lips together. "Is it because I told you I was bad at sex? Because I can try harder. If you just give me some-some direction, I'm sure I can -"

"It is not because of that."

"Then why?" Her tiny hands covered his, tugging on them until he stopped caressing her breasts. "Please tell me why, Vida."

"My cock is very large, and your pussy is too small and tight. If I try and fuck you, I will hurt you."

117

She swallowed and licked her lips. "Uh, human vaginas can stretch a lot. I'm sure if we go slow and make sure I'm wet, it'll be fine."

He shook his head and squeezed her breast. "You are too small for me, flower."

He watched in amusement as her face flushed with sudden anger and she sat up. "Oh please, you can't be that big. Vaginas are designed to push out babies for God's sake. My mom was small like me and when I was born, I weighed nine pounds and she was perfectly fine. And trust me, she would have told me if I had wrecked her lady parts."

He grinned at her ire and it only seemed to inflame her more. She poked him in the chest. "I get that you're a big guy, and yeah, you probably have a big penis, but I doubt it's like Hulk-sized or anything. Besides, my stupid ex-fiancé had a big dick and I didn't get nearly as wet with him and I still had sex…holy shit."

He had pushed back the covers to the middle of his thighs and even in the flickering candlelight, he could see the shock on her face. He was fully erect, as much from her adorable outburst as from the way her plump breasts jiggled while she lectured him.

She studied his dick in the dim light and he admired her tenacity when she took a deep breath and pasted a smile on her face. "Okay, yeah, you're pretty big. But, I still think we should try. I'm tougher than I look, okay? I can handle some pain. It hurt every time I had sex with Solomon, but I didn't – what's wrong?"

He cupped her face, his nostrils flaring with anger. "He hurt you?"

"Vida, I -"

"He hurt you during mating?"

"I – he didn't mean to. I don't think he even, uh, realized

it. I just wasn't wet enough and – it doesn't matter. The point is, I can handle a little pain, so I think we should at least try and have sex."

He was tempted. Her perfect little breasts, her soft skin and tight pussy were unbelievably tempting. But the thought of hurting the sweet little human who had risked her life to save his, made him feel sick.

"No, little flower, we cannot. Now, lie back and I will make you come so you can sleep."

She glared at him and yanked her robe closed. "No."

"No?" He raised his eyebrows at her.

"That's right, I said no. It isn't fair that I get to have orgasm after orgasm and you don't. So, unless you've changed your mind about having sex with me..."

"I have not."

"Then I guess neither of us are having orgasms." She scooted over to her side of the bed, turned on her side and pulled the covers to her chin. "Good night, Vida."

"Good night."

He laid on his back and stared at the ceiling again. To his surprise, it wasn't long before the little human's breathing evened out and deepened. Unable to resist, he reached over and gently drew her back into his embrace. She turned in her sleep and snuggled up to him, throwing one thigh over his and wrapping her arm around his waist. She rested her head on his chest and he stroked her long silky hair as she drifted into deeper sleep.

Every day, he had gone to her camp and hidden himself in the trees. He had watched and listened as the others had gone about their daily lives. He was adept at blending in with his surroundings and they never knew he was there. Well, once he was almost caught by the one they called Teagan. The human was smart and observant, and Vida admired him. In his world, Teagan would have been their leader, not the one named Patrick who smelled of insanity and deception.

He had learned a lot about this world from listening to the others. He'd been hiding and listening when Rose had admitted she was the one who freed him from his chains. He hated the way the others shunned his flower for it. It wasn't her fault he had trapped them with the orb. He pulled her a little closer, rubbing her back through her robe.

He could admit he was fascinated by her. For one so small, she was very brave. The other two females in the camp were useless. The one spent all her time fucking the leader and the other whined about every chore she was given. His little flower had been helping without any complaints, even when it seemed to be physically too much for her.

As the days had passed, he grew more and more impressed with her. Her friends had abandoned her, she was on a strange new world and it was clear that she was terrified, but she never complained. He had noted the way Duncan and Wallace watched her and it sent weird tendrils of jealousy through him.

He sighed and rubbed Rose's back again. He was already a little too attached to her. It was true that he was worried about hurting her during sex, but it wasn't just that. If he mated with her, he would have to work very hard at not bonding with her. It had been easy enough on the previous world. None of the many women he'd fucked had even stirred any type of bonding desire within him. He had been attracted to the massina, but she had never once indicated any type of attraction to him.

He had no idea why the little human pressed up against him made him want to bond with her, he barely knew her, but he couldn't deny it. He supposed if he tried hard enough, he could have sex with her and not bond, but what if she bonded with him? What if she wanted to become his mate? He was leaving this world as soon as the next orb came along, and he was fairly certain the little human had no desire to jump from world to world. He would have to leave her and if they were bonded...

He shifted in the bed and squeezed Rose's hip when she muttered something in her sleep. He couldn't mate with her and, it was best to not have any contact with her. Tomorrow, he would return her to the others and not go near her again.

She would have died tonight if not for you. Do you really want to leave her with the others? They can't protect her the way you can.

The thought of her nearly dying made him feel sick again. When he'd heard her scream, when he'd seen the vines wrapped around her slender body, something that felt a little like panic had gone through him.

He shook his head and ignored his weird need to protect Rose. The little human was not his concern, returning to his world was all he cared about.

CHAPTER 8

Rose woke the next morning to an empty bed. Vida wasn't in the main cavern nor was he in the bathing cavern. Her clothes were missing, and she tapped her fingers nervously on the rolling island. Should she go look for him or stay where she was?

She was fairly certain Vida would want her to stay in the cave but what if he was injured? What if he needed her help? She paced back and forth. He obviously could take care of himself. He'd survived nearly two weeks in the jungle all alone, why would this morning be any different? Why was she so worried about him?

More importantly, why were you so eager to try and have sex with him last night, Rose? You made a fool of yourself. What is wrong with you?

There was nothing wrong with her. She'd caught her fiancé fucking another woman, and she'd had a near-death experience. Vida saved her life and then gave her the type of orgasm she'd only read about. Of course she would want to sleep with him. It was a completely normal, completely rational reaction for a person to have.

Slut.

She sighed and moved to the clothes dresser. She opened the top drawer and pulled out a pair of pants. They were much too big, and she rifled through the second drawer, looking for anything that might fit so she could go looking for Vida.

"Hello, flower."

She whirled around, relief flooding through her. "Vida. Hi, I mean, morning. Where were you?"

"I washed your clothes and then I cooked some food for you."

She stared at the still steaming body of the rabbit-like creature skewered on the stick he was holding in his right hand. She hurried over and smiled tentatively at him as he set the creature on the cutting board sitting on the island.

"Thank you. Where, uh, are my clothes?"

"Drying outside. I will get them later. Did you sleep well?"

"Yeah, surprisingly I did." Her stomach growled, and Vida grinned. Her pussy actually fluttered at the sight of his fangs and she berated herself internally as he pulled a knife from the block and began to cut up the meat.

While he did that, she set the table with plates and cutlery and poured them both a glass of water from the large water jug. She cut up some of the fruit from the basket using a second knife from the block and another cutting board she found in one of the cupboards of the island.

Her stomach growled again, and she gave Vida an apologetic look. "Sorry. I don't know why I'm so hungry. I hardly ever eat breakfast."

"It is midday."

She paused with the knife held over the piece of green

fruit that was in the shape of a grapefruit and tasted like banana. "It is?"

"Yes."

"I slept until the middle of the day? Why didn't you wake me up?"

"You needed your rest."

He carried the meat to the table and she followed him with the cut-up fruit. "The others must think I'm dead."

He sat down and handed her the plate of meat. "They were searching the jungle for you early this morning?"

"Solomon?" She asked.

Vida shook his head. "No. Duncan, Teagan, Wallace, and Brody."

She wasn't surprised that Solomon wasn't looking for her. But, she was a little surprised that it didn't upset her. Could she really have fallen out of love with him that fast?

Were you ever actually in love with him, Rose?

"Human, you need to eat."

She glanced up at Vida and gave him an apologetic smile before spearing some of the meat with her fork and adding it to her plate. "Sorry. Are the others still looking for me?"

"No. Brian found them and made them return. He said that Patrick didn't want to waste any more time looking for you."

"Of course he did," Rose muttered. "God, he's a bigger asshole than...wait, how do you know everyone's names?"

He didn't reply, and she handed him the fruit. "Have you been spying on our camp the whole time?"

"Perhaps." He gave her another little grin that made her nipples peak against her robe. God, she needed to get control of herself. Vida had made it perfectly clear he wouldn't have sex with her, and she wouldn't be pathetic and beg for it.

She needed to apologize for last night but her stomach

was growling again, and she really was starving. She bit into the meat, chewing happily before swallowing it down and drinking some water. "Oh God, this is so good. Thank you, Vida."

"You are welcome, flower. Eat more."

She did, not noticing the way Vida's gaze studied her every move. She ate some of the blue fruit and then sucked away the juice running down her fingers. Vida made a low noise in the back of his throat and she gave him a curious look.

"What's wrong?"

"Nothing." His voice was hoarse. "Are you enjoying your meal, little flower?"

"Yes," she said. "So much. Where did you cook the meat?"

Vida's hands were clenched around his fork and knife and he was studying her mouth. "There is a shallower cave not far from this one. I use it to skin the animals and cook them."

"Oh." She popped another piece of fruit into her mouth. "You're really good at the whole jungle living thing."

He just shrugged and finally started to eat as she sat back in her chair and studied the cavern. "Man, I wish I knew how all this stuff got here."

"There is something I will show you when I return you to your friends."

"What is it?"

"I don't know," he said, "but I think it may be from the same world as these things are."

"Okay. Hey, would you mind if I had another bath before we left? I want to take advantage of the warm water."

"I do not mind."

"Thank you." She stood. "Um, are you going to join me?"

He shook his head and she immediately felt stupid. She

needed to be apologizing for last night, not trying to tempt him into another round. "Vida, I need to apologize for last night. I was very, uh, upset about Solomon cheating on me, and about almost dying. I acted inappropriately with you because of it and I won't do it again."

He cocked his head at her. "You no longer wish to fuck me?"

Her face flamed red. "Well, um, I just meant that, I mean... you don't want to have sex with me, so why does it matter what I want?"

Before he could reply, she pushed away from the table and headed toward the bathing cavern. "Never mind. I just wanted to say I'm sorry, and that I won't take advantage of you like that again."

"HOLY SHIT." ROSE STARED AT THE VEHICLE IN FRONT OF her. "It's a moving truck."

After her bath, Vida had brought her clothes to her and she'd dressed as he blew out the candles and strapped a machete around his waist. He'd led her through the jungle silently. She was completely lost within minutes, but Vida moved confidently and without hesitation. When he led her past a particularly large clump of bushes and showed her the moving truck, she'd nearly fallen over from shock.

"What is a moving truck?" Vida asked.

Rose moved closer and studied the vehicle. It was starting to rust and over the years, vines had wrapped around the tires and started to crawl up the smooth sides. In ten years, the moving truck would be completely covered by vines and a person could walk by it without ever knowing it was here. It creeped her out a little, the way the jungle was simply starting to swallow it whole like a snake with a mouse.

"Flower?" Vida touched her arm. "Are you cold?"

She shook her head and rubbed away the goose bumps that had risen on her skin. "No. Just creeped out a little."

"What does 'U-Haul' mean?" Vida asked.

Rose studied the lettering on the side of the truck. "In our world, you use these trucks to move your stuff from one house to another. Instead of hiring someone to do it for you, you do it yourself."

"Oh." Vida didn't look like he understood.

She touched the smooth side of the moving truck. "It explains why there's all that stuff in the cavern. The people that lived there before you obviously got sucked through the orb in the moving truck. That's why they had all their stuff with them."

She studied the jungle around them as she wiped the sweat off her forehead. "What part of the jungle are we in?"

"We're near where the orb left us."

"That makes sense," she replied. "They wouldn't have been able to get the truck through the jungle. I can't believe they moved all their stuff from here to the caverns. We've walked a few miles at least, right? How the hell did they get _"

"Hush, flower." Vida's big body had gone stiff. She watched with wide-eyes as he scanned the jungle and automatically moved a little closer to him.

"Vida?" She whispered. "What is it? Is it the pinkies?"

Vida's body relaxed just as Brody rounded the large clump of bushes. "Rose!"

"Brody!"

The redhead threw his arms around her and hugged her

tight, lifting her off the ground before setting her back on her feet. "Oh my God, we thought you were dead."

He kissed her cheek and stepped back as Wallace and Duncan appeared behind them. Wallace winked at her. "Good to see you, Rosie-girl."

He reached to give her a hug and she squeaked in surprise when a big, blue arm wrapped around her waist and pulled her away from him. Vida pressed her against his body, his big hand holding her hip in a tight grip as he stared at Wallace. "Do not touch her, human."

"It's fine. Wallace is my friend." She pulled at Vida's arm, but he refused to release her.

Wallace studied Vida for a moment before grinning at him. "You must be Vida."

Vida didn't reply. Rose gave up on trying to free herself and leaned against him. "Vida, you know Brody sort of, and this is Wallace and Duncan."

"Nice to meet you." Wallace held out his hand.

"Do not touch her. Do you understand?" Vida said in a low voice.

After a moment, Wallace nodded and dropped his hand. Vida turned his gaze to Duncan who met it steadily before nodding as well. Vida's body relaxed, and he loosened his grip on her. She patted his arm.

"They're my friends, Vida." She reached out and took Brody's hand, squeezing it hard. "What are you doing out here?"

"Looking for you," Brody said. "We were out this morning but then that asshole Patrick made us stop looking for you. Said it was a waste of time and that you were dead."

"Watch your mouth, Red," Wallace said.

Brody shrugged. "He's a fucking psychopath and you know it, Wallace."

Wallace didn't reply, and Brody turned back to Rose. "As soon as Patrick went into his hut this afternoon with Talla, I told the others I was going to look for you. Wallace and Duncan said they would come with me."

"Thanks, guys," Rose said. "That was really nice of you."

"Don't mention it, Rosie-girl," Wallace said.

"Why did you run away last night?" Brody asked. He glanced at Wallace and Duncan. "Was it because of what you, uh, saw in my hut last night?"

Wallace grinned at him. "What exactly did she see? Because I happened to be up early this morning and noticed Doc leaving your hut."

Brody blushed, and Wallace laughed before elbowing him. "Doc always did have a thing for the redheads."

"Shut up, Wallace," Brody said without much heat.

"It had nothing to do with you," Rose said. "Didn't Solomon tell you?"

"No. He didn't say anything," Brody replied.

"He wasn't even that pissed at Daryl for letting you run off in the fucking jungle without telling anyone," Wallace said.

"Wallace!" Brody glared at him and Wallace shrugged.

"She deserves to know her fiancé is a dickhead."

"I already know," Rose said. "After I left Brody's hut, I went to Solomon's and caught him and Marissa having sex."

"Are you kidding me? She was banging that cowardly asshole? What the fuck does he have that I don't?" Wallace said to Duncan.

"Jesus, Rose. I'm sorry," Brody said.

"He was having an affair with her before we even landed on this world," Rose said. "Anyway, I kind of freaked out and ran into the jungle. I meant to just go to the waterfall, but I got lost and then was nearly killed by some vines. Vida saved me."

She smiled at the big, blue man, but he was studying the jungle around them.

"You were very lucky, Rose," Duncan said. "Going into the jungle alone at night was incredibly dangerous."

"I know. I won't do it again."

"What the fuck? Is that a U-haul?" Brody had finally noticed the truck behind them. He stepped around Rose and studied it as Wallace clapped him on the back.

"Isn't it something? You got U-haul on your world too, huh?"

Brody nodded, and Wallace glanced at Duncan. "Maybe it isn't from my world then."

Brody walked toward the back. "Is there stuff inside?"

"Nope. We opened up the back doors when we first discovered it about a month after we landed on this rock. It was empty."

"Who took the stuff?" Brody wondered.

"Two options – either the locals emptied it out or it could have been empty when it got sucked into the orb."

"Or maybe the people driving it, emptied it out," Brody said.

"Maybe." Wallace shrugged. "We'll never know for sure."

Rose glanced at Vida. His face was impassive and she strived for the same. She liked Wallace, but she knew he was loyal to Patrick and she didn't want Patrick knowing about Vida's home. He would take it for his own use without thinking twice.

"Is there anything different about the logo on the truck?" Wallace asked Brody. "Anything that would make you think it wasn't from your world?"

"No, I don't think so. Why?"

Wallace shrugged. "Just curious if it really is from my world. Wait… let's check the license plate."

Brody followed him to the back of the truck. Wallace scraped away the dirt from the plate. "North Carolina. It is our world. Unless you have a North Carolina?"

"Never heard of it," Brody said.

"Bingo." Wallace held up his fist and Brody bumped it. "Looks like I win the 'whose world is this from' game."

Brody grinned at him before turning to Rose. "We were talking about differences in our worlds while we looked for you. In their world, Michael Jackson is dead."

"What?" Her mouth dropped open. "Seriously?"

"Yep." Wallace turned and did an exceedingly poor version of the moon walk. "So's Elvis although my mother swears she saw him in the jungle room at Graceland when she visited it in 1983. But between you and me, pretty sure she was hitting the weed hard back in the day."

"Elvis died in our world too," Rose said.

"Cher is still alive in their world though," Brody said.

"No!"

"Yes! And get this…Oprah Winfrey is an entertainment star. She had a talk show and starred in movies and now she has her own television network."

"President Winfrey is a TV star?" Rose blinked at Brody.

Wallace laughed. "Hey, how do you think we felt finding out she's the goddamn president in your world?"

"That's so weird," Rose said.

"You're telling me," Brody replied. "Doc and I have been comparing stuff and it's freaky weird how many things are almost the same but not quite. Like, the governments are run the same way, but -"

"We should get back," Duncan said. "It's going to be dark soon."

"Good point." Wallace pulled off the wreath of yellow flowers he wore around his neck. "Here, Rosie-girl, put this on." Before he could drape the wreath over her head, Vida was baring his fangs at him and pulling Rose back into his embrace.

"I said to stay away from her."

"No, you said not to touch her," Wallace said with a grin.

Vida growled at him and Wallace turned to Duncan. "Did the big blue guy just growl at me? Like an actual growl?"

"Wallace, stop," Rose said. "Vida, it's okay. Just, uh, calm down, all right?" She had no idea what was going on with Vida, but the last thing she wanted was him fighting with Wallace. Vida was big and strong, but Wallace was a damn SEAL.

Vida squeezed her hip. "He is not to go near you."

"I'm trying to help," Wallace said. "Maybe you haven't met the pinkies yet, but these flowers help keep us safe from them."

"I will keep her safe."

Wallace sighed. "Listen, you're big and obviously you've got some skills at staying alive, but the pinkies are -"

"I have seen them. She does not require the flowers, I will keep her safe," Vida replied.

"It's fine," Rose said before Wallace could argue again. "I don't need the flowers."

She smiled up at Vida and he squeezed her hip again before releasing her and taking her hand.

"All right," Wallace said. "Let's make like birds and get the flock out of here."

"HOLY SHIT." DARYL STARED IN DISBELIEF AT VIDA. "HE'S alive." His gaze dropped to Vida and Rose's clasped hands. "Of course you're holding hands with him. You fucking him, Rose? Why not, right? You've had a goddamn hard-on for the blue asshole since the minute you saw him."

"Shut up," Teagan said. He was adding more wood to the fire and he brushed his hands off on his pants.

"You're not the fucking boss of me." Daryl's voice was sullen.

Teagan fixed him with a steady glare. "You're lucky we didn't kick you out of camp for keeping quiet when Rose left last night. Keep your mouth shut or that luck will change."

A flicker of fear crossed Daryl's face and he sat down on the log as Teagan approached them. "Hello, Rose. It's good to see you still alive."

"Thanks, Teagan. This is Vida. Vida, this is Teagan."

"Nice pants." Teagan studied the military pants Vida was wearing.

"At least you know where your pants went," Brian said with a grin.

"Rose?" Solomon hurried out of his hut. "You're alive! Oh thank God."

He tried to hug her, grunting in surprise when Vida shoved him back.

"Do not touch her." Vida put his arm around Rose's waist.

"She's my fiancée." Solomon gave him an indignant look and then stared at Rose. "What are you doing with him? Get away from him."

"He saved my life last night," Rose said.

Solomon cleared his throat. "Well, I'm grateful to him, but that doesn't mean he can just touch you like that. Come with me, we need to talk."

He held out his hand and Rose could feel herself bristling.

Oh, now he wanted to talk? She took a deep breath, now was not the time to be childish. She started forward and Vida's hand tightened on her hip.

"It's fine." She patted his hand. "I need to talk to him alone."

Vida frowned, and she patted his hand again. "It's fine, Vida."

She shivered when Vida leaned down and pressed his mouth against her ear. "Do not allow him to touch you, little flower."

He studied her intently and, weirdly, she couldn't resist giving in to his demand. "I won't."

He relaxed and released her. When Solomon tried to take her hand, she ignored it and walked toward her hut. Solomon followed her into the hut and pulled the fur across the doorway. They stared silently at each other in the dim light.

"What you saw, it didn't mean anything," Solomon finally said.

"How long have you been sleeping with her?"

Solomon looked away. "Not that long."

"How long?" Rose asked.

"I don't know. A while."

"Define a while, Solomon."

"What does it matter?" He gave her a petulant look. "She doesn't mean anything to me."

"I want to know, and I deserve an answer."

He sighed. "About a week after she started working at the lab."

"So, you've been fucking Marissa for over three months now, but she doesn't mean anything to you?" Rose stepped back when Solomon moved closer.

He gave her a look of hurt. "It's you I love. I just – I have

135

needs that you can't take care of and Marissa could. Besides, she came on to me and she was… persistent. I tried to resist."

"You resisted for a whole seven days. Nice work."

Solomon flushed. "Can we try and talk about this like adults?"

"I don't even know what there is to talk about. You cheated on me, it's over."

"Seriously? You're just going to end our engagement?"

Rose glared at him. "Do you really think I'm going to be with you, *marry* you, when you've been fucking Marissa?"

"I told you, I have needs that you can't take care of and -"

"What needs?" Rose snapped. "I practically begged you for sex, Solomon. I repeatedly offered myself to you. I wore sexy lingerie, I offered massages, I bought toys. I did everything I could to think of to try to turn you on, and you still rejected me. You were always too tired or too -"

"You're bad at sex," Solomon blurted.

Rose turned a dull red. "I'm not."

"You are. You think I couldn't tell you were faking your orgasms? Christ, do you know how insulting that is? It got to the point where I didn't even want to touch you. What was the point? I love you, Rose, I do, but I need more than you can give me when it comes to sex."

He took another step toward her, frowning when she backed away. "Rose, listen – I meant to talk to you about having an open relationship before you fucked up and got us all sent to this goddamn world."

"An open relationship?" She crossed her arms over her torso, hugging herself tightly as Solomon nodded.

"Yeah. We'd be together as a couple, and it's you that I love, but I'm allowed to have sex with other women." She didn't reply, and he hurried on. "It's unconventional I know, but it's not as uncommon as you think. I want to be with you, baby, but I need to have my sexual needs met as well. An open relationship is how we achieve that."

Feeling like she'd been run over by a very large truck, Rose said, "So, in this open relationship, you get to fuck Marissa whenever you want, and I can sleep with any of the guys on this island I want?"

Solomon cocked his head at her. "Well, yeah, I guess, but why bother?"

"What do you mean?"

He gave her a self-indulgent smile that set her teeth on edge. "Baby, if I can't make you come, no man can. There's no point in sleeping with other men if you're just going to be faking your orgasms with them too, right?"

She stared at him in silent disbelief. Solomon smiled again at her. "I really think we can make this work. If you keep an open mind and -"

"Vida made me come."

"I – what?" Solomon's gaze narrowed. "What did you say?"

"I said that Vida made me come. Last night, he made me climax. Easily."

"You fucked him?" Solomon's voice was rising, and she made a shushing gesture as she glanced at the doorway of the hut.

"What's the problem? If it's an open relationship, then -"

"He's not even human!" Solomon shouted. "You fucked an alien, Rose. A goddamn alien! What the hell is wrong with you?"

"What's wrong with me?" Rose said. "You're cheating on me and have been for months, but there's something wrong with me? Vida is a good person and -"

"He's not a person! He's a – a thing and he – shit!"

Solomon screamed and staggered back as the fur was

ripped away from the doorway and Vida stomped into the hut. He bared his teeth at Solomon and stepped in front of Rose, blocking her from Solomon's view.

"Get out of here," Solomon said as Teagan and Brody joined them in the hut. "Get out of here, you – you freak."

"Raise your voice to the little flower again and I will rip out your tongue," Vida said. His voice was calm enough, but his entire body was vibrating, and his hands were hard fists at his sides.

"Rose, you okay?" Brody asked.

"I'm fine." Rose slipped around Vida. He immediately put his arm around her waist and drew her back against him.

"Stay with me, flower."

"Maybe you guys should take a break from talking." Teagan was eyeing Vida. "Give everyone a chance to cool down."

"I have nothing else to say to her," Solomon said. "We're finished, Rose. Do you hear me? I'm – I'm breaking up with you."

Rose laughed. It made Solomon turn a bright red and he gave her a furious look, but she couldn't help it. "You're breaking up with me? The minute I saw you dick-deep in Marissa, we were finished. Don't come near me again, Solomon."

"Fine with me, you frigid bitch." Solomon pushed past Brody and walked out of the hut.

Rose released her breath in a shaky sigh as Brody said, "You sure you're okay, Rose?"

"Yeah, thanks, Brody."

"Is there going to be a problem with you and Solomon both being in the camp?" Teagan asked.

Rose shook her head. "No. He'll just ignore me."

"Good. We need to keep things civil in camp, Rose. I get that he -"

"Teag?" Wallace stuck his head in the hut. "Patrick's awake. He wants to talk to him." His gaze flickered to Vida.

"Yeah, okay." Teagan studied Vida. "Patrick is our leader. Don't challenge him or piss him off."

"I am not afraid of your leader," Vida said.

"You should be."

CHAPTER 9

"You were seriously a goddamn sex slave for twenty-five years?" Wallace stared at Vida who nodded.

"Motherfucking shitballs," Wallace said before turning to Brian. "How pathetic is it that I'm kind of jealous of him right now?"

"A little pathetic."

"Fuck, boy," Wallace clapped Brian on the back, "a man can only use his hand so many times before he -"

"Wallace." Teagan's voice was low, but Wallace immediately stopped talking.

Rose chewed at her bottom lip. For the last half-hour, at Patrick's request, Vida had given them a brief rundown of his life. She glanced at Patrick. He was rubbing Talla's thigh absently as he studied Vida.

"Not to be indelicate," Doc said to Vida, "but can your kind get STDs?"

Vida glanced at Rose. "What does STD mean?"

"I have no idea," Rose replied.

Brody grinned at her. "Doc asked me about it the other night. I didn't have a damn clue what he was talking about.

141

They're these weird sex diseases that those guys get." He pointed at Wallace and the others and Wallace held his hands up.

"Whoa, whoa, don't be pointing at me. I've been gonorrhea free since 2003." He held up his fist to Davis who rolled his eyes but fist-bumped it.

"Sex diseases?" Randy took off his glasses and polished them. "You can't get a disease from sex."

"STD stands for sexually transmitted disease." Doc glanced at Brody. "Brody said he'd never heard of them on his world."

"We haven't." Randy was sitting next to Duncan and he nudged him. "Do you have those sex diseases on your world?"

Duncan was sharpening his sword and he shook his head. "No."

"On our world, you can get diseases from having unprotected sex with multiple partners. Some of them are quite deadly and can kill you." Doc said. "They're passed from person to person through sex."

"Holy shit," Daryl said. "For real?"

"Yes." Doc glanced at Vida. "Do they have STDs on your world or the Amazon woman world?"

Vida shook his head. "No, they do not exist on my world or the other."

"You sure?" Doc said.

Vida just shrugged. "Why does it matter?"

"Good old-fashioned curiosity," Doc replied.

"Hey, you got a dick like a human or a fish?" Wallace suddenly asked.

"Wallace!" Rose frowned at him and Wallace shrugged.

"What? It's a legit question. The guy's basically a merman and -"

"Enough." Patrick's voice was a low growl. "Have you run into any of the pinkies yet, Vida?"

"I have seen them from a distance when I explored the north side of the island."

"Shit, you went to the north side? You're either the stupidest or the bravest motherfucker I've ever met." Wallace said.

"Open your fucking mouth again and I'll shove my foot into it. Understand?" Patrick suddenly snarled.

Wallace studied him silently before nodding. "Yes, Sir."

Patrick turned back to Vida. "Have you met the locals?"

"I have seen them," Vida said. "They do not care for strangers."

Patrick barked harsh laughter. "That's for fucking sure. You see where they live?"

"Behind the wall of flowers."

"That's right. Those flowers are keeping them safe from those fucking pink bastards, while we're barely hanging on. Do you think that's fair?"

Vida didn't reply, and Patrick squeezed Talla's thigh until she gasped. "Do you, you big Smurf?"

Vida cocked his head at him. "Another called me Smurf once. I did not like it then and I do not like it now."

"Patrick," Teagan said, "give it a rest."

"Are you in charge, Teagan?" A flush was rising up Patrick's neck.

"Patrick -"

"Are...you...in...charge?"

"No."

"Then shut your fucking mouth." Patrick sneered. "Do you think it's fair, *Vida*?"

"What do you want from me, human?" Vida said.

Patrick stared at him, breathing so heavily that he

reminded Rose of a bull about to charge. He relaxed suddenly, his hand returned to stroking Talla's thigh and he smiled at Vida. "I think we could help each other, Vida. You survived almost two weeks alone in the jungle, but I wonder how much of that has to do with luck? In this world – on this *island* – you need others to survive. You need us. You help me convince the locals that they should share their resources with us and I'll let you stay here with us."

"Convince?" Rose said. "What do you mean by convince?"

Patrick ignored her. "What do you say, Vida?"

Vida stayed silent and Solomon cleared his throat. "He shouldn't get to stay with us."

Patrick turned his gaze to him. "What did you say?"

Solomon glanced at Daryl and Peter and Randy who were sitting together. "He and Rose are the reason we're even on this damn island. They're the reason that Leslie and John are dead. I think they both should be kicked out of camp."

"I agree." Daryl said.

"Me too." Marissa took Solomon's hand and squeezed it.

"Peter and Randy? What about you?" Solomon said. "Do you vote yes or no to kicking them out of the camp?"

"Vote?" Patrick stood and stretched lazily before moving to the table and pouring himself a cup of water. He drank it and then leaned one hip against the table. "What gave you the idea that you get a vote on anything that happens here?"

Solomon flushed before straightening his back. "I just think that since they were the ones responsible for -"

"Don't think." Patrick's voice was soft. "Don't think, don't speak, hell, from this moment on you don't even piss without my permission. Is that clear?"

Solomon stared at him and after a moment, seemed to crumple into himself. "Yes."

"Yes, what?"

"Yes, Sir."

"Good." Patrick chewed on a piece of dried meat. "It's getting late. The Smurf, excuse me, *Vida*, will stay with us tonight, eat our food and enjoy our protection. It will give him a taste of what he can gain from partnering with us."

He winked at Vida. "We'll pick up this discussion in the morning."

"I do not wish to stay the night." Vida stood, and Rose jumped up when Patrick glanced at Teagan and Wallace. The two men stood and placed their hands on the guns sitting in the holsters around their waists.

"It's awful rude to turn down a man's hospitality," Patrick said.

Rose glanced at Duncan. He was holding his sword loosely in one hand, but his entire body was tense. She couldn't tell if he would back Patrick up or not, but she knew for certain that the rest of the men would. They might think Patrick was a couple of screws loose, but they would do what he told them to.

"You are not my leader," Vida said. "I will not follow your rule."

That red flush was creeping up Patrick's neck again and feeling sick with fear, Rose grabbed Vida's hand and squeezed it. "Vida, please. Will you stay for me?"

He stared down at her and she tried to smile at him. "Please? It's going to be dark soon and I would feel much better if you spent the night with us."

Vida touched her hair and nodded. "I will stay for you, flower."

"Thank you." She was weak with relief.

"Then it's settled. Vida stays." Patrick grinned broadly at them. "Who's on cooking duty tonight?"

WHAT ARE YOU DOING, ROSE?

She ignored her inner voice as she picked her way across the clearing toward Vida's hut. She almost screamed when she passed Teagan's hut and he appeared in the doorway. He took her arm and pulled her to a stop.

"No leaving the camp again, Rose."

She smiled at him. "I'm not. I just wanted to speak with Vida for a moment."

"You trust him, don't you?"

"I do. You should too. He's a good man, Teagan."

"Man?" He gave her a wry smile.

"You know what I mean."

"You haven't known him very long."

"No, I haven't," Rose said. "But I know he's good and honourable. Just like I know that Patrick is batshit insane."

"Keep your voice down." Teagan glanced at Patrick and Talla's hut before staring up and into the trees. Duncan was on watch and he nodded to Teagan before turning his gaze back to the jungle.

"You should be leading this group, not him." Rose lowered her voice. "You know he's crazy, right?"

Teagan released her arm. "Good night, Rose."

He stepped back into his hut and she hesitated before continuing toward Vida's. She was just going to say good night and see if he needed anything. Some water or a blanket maybe. It got cold at night and he was used to being in the cave. He might be too cold in the hut.

You gonna offer to warm him up with body heat?

She blushed a little. So what if she did? She was single, and she was attracted to Vida. There was nothing stopping her from sleeping with him if she wanted.

Except for the fact that he won't fuck you. Or have you forgotten that part?

She hadn't forgotten. She wanted to forget it, but it was kind of impossible. She stopped in front of Vida's hut. She could change his mind. He wanted her, that was obvious. It would be easy to seduce him into having sex.

Do you think maybe you should be a little freaked out by his sudden weird possessiveness? The guy gives you one orgasm and now he's acting like you belong to him. That's not normal, Rose.

Maybe it was normal on Vida's world. Maybe they just didn't like other men touching the women they were having sex with.

You're not having sex!

She shoved her inner voice out of her head and ducked into Vida's hut. The hut was lit with only two candles and the light was dim, but she could clearly see Talla and Vida standing near the pile of furs. Could clearly see when the gorgeous woman pulled off her shirt and dropped it to the floor. She was naked beneath it and Rose's mouth dropped open when Talla cupped her breasts.

"Well, what do you say? Is this what you want?"

"Are you fucking kidding me?" Rose said.

Talla made a soft shriek and grabbed for her shirt, struggling into it as Vida said, "Flower, what are you doing here?"

"Making a fool of myself, again." Her throat burning and hot tears pricking at her eyes, Rose backed out of the hut. She turned and ran across the clearing to her own hut. Her stomach hurt, and her chest felt tight, and she was stupidly disappointed.

She dropped onto the furs and buried her face in them. She was an idiot. Of course, Vida would sleep with Talla. She was tall and gorgeous and probably had a vagina as big

147

as a house. She'd have no problems taking Vida's cock. Hell, he was probably sticking his dick in her right now. Probably —

"Flower?"

She shrieked into the furs and sat up, staring wildly at Vida as he entered her hut. "Go away, Vida."

"We need to speak."

"There's nothing to say. You can go back to your hut and bang stupid beautiful Talla with your dick until it's bleeding for all I care. But you'd better hope Patrick doesn't find out or he'll kill you."

"Why would I bang my dick on her until it bleeds?"

He sat down next to her on the furs and she gaped at him. "What?"

"You said bang her with my dick until it is bleeding. That is not pleasurable."

She scooted away from him when he tried to put his arm around her. "Banging is another word for fucking."

"Strange." He studied her for a moment. "I do not wish to fuck Talla."

"Right. She was just in your hut and naked because it's a warm night."

He sighed and scratched at the skin around his horns. "Her mate Patrick sent her to my hut to fuck me."

Rose's mouth dropped open. "What? She told you that?"

"Yes."

"Why would Patrick do that?"

"Patrick's female -"

"Talla."

"Patrick's female Talla said that Patrick told her it was to sweeten the pot. I did not know what that meant, and she did not either."

Rose rubbed at her temples. "It means he offered sex with

148

Talla as another incentive to try and convince you to help him with the locals."

"I have no wish to sleep with Patrick's female."

She stared up at him. "You-you don't?"

"No, flower, I do not. I sent her back to Patrick."

"Because I showed up."

"No. I would have sent her away anyway."

This time when he reached for her, she didn't pull away. He lifted her into his lap and stroked her long hair. "It is not her that I am attracted to."

"But you won't have sex with me."

He nuzzled her neck. "I cannot, little human. I will hurt you."

"You don't know that," she argued. "We can try."

He shook his head. "No. But I would like to make you come again. Will you allow me to do so?"

She should say no. It wasn't fair to Vida that she kept having orgasms and he didn't. After faking her orgasms so much with Solomon, she knew a little something about the frustration of watching your partner come while you didn't.

You don't have to have sex to make Vida come, you twit.

Shit, she *was* a twit.

———

VIDA STUDIED THE SMALL HUMAN SITTING IN HIS LAP. HE'D been feeling anxious and unsettled since the moment they'd entered the humans' camp. He'd had to fight his urge all evening to simply pick up his flower and carry her back to his den.

Being close to Rose, having her soft body touching his, gave him his first measure of relief since they had joined her friends. He stroked her thigh, resisting his desire to cup her

149

pussy and push her into accepting his offer to bring her to orgasm.

When she stayed silent, he couldn't stop from asking her again. In fact, he was afraid he was very close to begging her to let him touch her. "Flower? Will you allow me to make you come?"

"Yes," she said. "I want that, Vida."

Relief flooded through him and he smiled at her. "Good."

He reached for her shirt and she squeezed his arms. "Does your kind – I mean, your people – do they kiss?"

He stared blankly at her for a moment before giving her an apologetic look. "Forgive me, little human. I have forgotten that humans enjoy mouth kissing when they mate."

"So, your kind doesn't like to kiss?"

He didn't want to tell her the truth. His kind occasionally kissed, but never during mating and never with tongue the way the humans seemed to enjoy. Kissing for his kind was seen as more of a sign of affection rather than desire. Truthfully, he had always been a bit baffled by the human's desire to kiss so intimately while they mated. The warrior women on the previous world had quickly taught him how to kiss, but he'd kissed them only when they asked or reminded him to do so.

"Vida?"

He sighed. He couldn't and wouldn't lie to her. "We kiss on occasion, but not when we are mating."

"Oh. Okay. I, um, won't kiss you then."

He stroked her blonde hair again. "The women who held me captive enjoyed kissing during mating. They taught me to kiss them while we mated. I will do so now, with you."

She shook her head immediately. "No, absolutely not. You were forced to do things you didn't want to for twenty-five years. I'm not going to do that to you now."

"I do not mind."

She made a sound that was almost a laugh. "Kissing me because you don't mind, would be worse than kissing me because I forced you to kiss."

"I do not understand."

"I know," she said. "I'm fine without kissing."

"Are you certain?" He studied her face and she looked away before nodding.

"I am."

He believed she was lying, but she pulled her shirt over her head and he was immediately distracted by her soft pale skin. He ran his fingers over her upper chest before tugging on the strap of the undergarment she was wearing. "What is this?"

"It's called a bra."

"Why do you wear it?"

"Well, women wear it for different reasons. It's mostly worn to support your breasts."

"Do all women on your world wear one?"

She shrugged. "Just depends on the woman I guess. My breasts aren't very big so I could go without one, but for women who have larger breasts, a bra supports them when they're running, that sort of thing."

"I do not like it." He tugged at the strap again and she laughed.

"Most men don't."

"How do you remove it." He pulled at the front of it and she tugged his hands away.

"It has hooks in the back." She reached behind her and after a few seconds, the bra loosened. She took it off and he stared at her breasts.

"You have beautiful breasts, little flower."

"Thank you." She gave him a shy smile. "You said your females look similar to us, right?"

He nodded. "Mostly. They have horns and fangs like we do and as I said before, their skin is purple. They are larger than most human women. They are warriors like us and excellent fighters."

"Oh. So, I'm the exact opposite of what you're used to."

"Yes." He traced his finger between her breasts and she shivered delicately. "But I like your pale skin, little flower." He circled her nipple with his finger, smiling when it hardened. "I like your pink nipples."

"Vida, please," she whispered.

He bent his head and licked her collarbone before cupping her small breast. It fit perfectly in his hand and he squeezed it gently. He kissed her neck and nipped at her soft skin. She gasped and arched into his hand before running her hands over his naked chest. He groaned when she slipped her hand beneath the waistband of his pants and grasped his cock.

"Lie back, Vida" she whispered.

"We cannot mate."

"I know." She pushed on his chest with her free hand and after a moment he relaxed on the furs. The little human leaned over him and he cupped her head when she kissed a slow path across his chest. God, her lips were so soft and her hand rubbing his dick felt amazing.

She pulled her hand free and unbuttoned his pants, pulling the strange metal teeth apart with an ease he hadn't mastered yet. "What is that called?"

"What? This?" She tugged on the metal.

He nodded, and she grinned at him. "It's a zipper. You don't have them on your world, huh?"

"No."

"Hips up, big guy."

He lifted his hips and she pulled his pants down his legs and off his feet. She tossed them into the pile with her shirt and bra, and he sucked in his breath when she pressed a kiss against his knee.

"I know you don't want to have sex with me, but that doesn't mean I can't use my mouth, right?" She said before kissing his thick thighs.

His cock swelled, and his pulse thudded erratically. "You wish to suck my cock, flower?"

He loved the way her pale skin turned pink when she was embarrassed. "Yes. If, um, your kind does that? They do, right?"

"Yes. But the women who held me captive preferred fucking, so it's been many years since I've had my cock sucked."

"Seriously? They never gave you oral sex?"

He shrugged. "They did not want to waste my seed."

She sat up. "But, they could still do a blowjob without you wasting your seed."

"They did not trust that I could stop my orgasm. What is a blowjob?"

She grinned at him. "It's just what we call oral sex."

"Oh."

She took his cock in her hand and rubbed. He groaned, his hips arching upward, and she smiled at him before leaning down and licking the head of his cock.

"Fuck!" The human's curse word fell from his lips like a prayer.

Her smile widened. "Do you like that?"

"Yes." He reached down and curled his big hand into her hair. "Do it again."

She licked his cock again and his hand tightened in her hair. "Your tongue is very soft. I like it – fuck!"

She had slid her mouth down over his cock and his hips

bucked against her mouth. She pressed one tiny hand against his hip and wrapped the other around the base of his cock before sucking hard.

Her hot, wet mouth felt amazing and after so many years of not having his cock sucked, he was almost immediately ready to come. He moaned and panted, his hips rising and falling as she sucked and licked. He was too big for her to take all of him in her mouth, but he appreciated the effort she was making. She sucked hard and fast and the base of his spine began to tingle.

"Flower," he moaned, "I am close."

She sucked harder in response and he threw his arm over his mouth, muffling his harsh shout of pleasure as his balls tightened and his cock swelled, and he came with another low roar. She did her best to swallow all of it, but he could see some dripping from the corner of her mouth. She sat up and wiped her mouth with her fingers. Panting and twitching from the pleasure that was still coursing through his body, he watched as she held her hand closer to her face. She had a single candle burning next to the furs and she squinted in the flickering light.

"Is your come purple?"

He nodded, and she giggled before licking her lips. "Weird. It also tastes really sweet. Like… cotton candy."

He had no idea what cotton candy was, but he jerked and cried out when she leaned over and licked away the bit of come that still coated the head of his softening cock.

"Sorry, I know you're sensitive." She grinned. "It just tastes really good."

She studied him as he came down from the high of his orgasm. He was very tired, and he couldn't stop his yawn. He hadn't slept well last night and the combination of that and his orgasm had him barely able to keep his eyes open. He struggled against his weariness. He needed to pleasure his little flower. Needed to touch her until she was wet and begging and then he would fuck her and...no, he couldn't fuck her. He yawned again as his eyes slipped shut. He would just make her come and then they would both sleep.

She was moving next to him and he muttered. "Your turn, small flower."

"Go to sleep, Vida."

"No." His voice was thick with sleep. "I will make you come first and -"

Another yawn, so large it felt like it was splitting his face in two.

She laughed softly and blew the candle out before pulling a fur over their bodies and resting her head on his shoulder. "Go to sleep."

He mumbled one last protest before sleep took him.

CHAPTER 10

R ose sat up with a gasp. She was alone in the pile of furs and she felt a moment of panic before she caught sight of Vida standing in front of the doorway.

"Vida?"

"Good morning, little flower."

He returned to the furs and sat beside her.

"Is it morning?" It wasn't dark in the hut, but it didn't look like the sun had risen yet either.

"Almost. The sun will rise soon."

He reached out and cupped her naked breast. "Did you sleep well?"

"Yes." She bit her bottom lip as he rubbed her nipple into an aching hardness. "Did – oh – did you?"

"Yes." He leaned down to press a soft kiss against the swell of her breast.

"Your skin." She touched the skin around his left horn. It was dry and cracking, and flakes of skin rubbed off when she ran her fingers over his forehead. "You're crying out."

He straightened. "I was about to go to the waterfall for a quick swim, but I will pleasure you first."

"That's okay. You should rehydrate."

He frowned at her. "I was selfish and fell asleep last night instead of pleasuring you. I will not be so selfish again."

"You were tired, not being selfish," she said. "Besides, I wouldn't mind going to the waterfall and, uh, freshening up a bit first."

He studied her before leaning down and pressing his nose to her throat. He inhaled deeply. "You smell fresh to me."

She laughed. "Thank you, but I'd still prefer to have a bath first."

"All right."

She was still wearing her pants and she grabbed her shirt. She left her bra on the floor of the hut and put her shirt on before slipping on her shoes. Vida was barefoot and she gave him a curious look. "Doesn't it hurt to walk around barefoot?"

He shook his head. "My kind do not wear shocks."

"Shocks?"

He pointed to her shoes and she smiled. "Oh. No, it's shoes. They're called shoes."

"Shoes." He repeated before holding out his hand. "Come, flower."

She broke off a chunk from her ration of soap and stuck it in her pocket. She took his hand and followed him out of the hut. The air was misty, and it was so quiet she could hear the rustling of animals in the trees behind their hut. She stepped a little closer to Vida and he squeezed her hand before leading her across the clearing.

There was a soft whistle above them and she looked up at the lookout. Teagan was on watch and he arched one eyebrow at her. "Where are you two going?" His voice carried easily in the silence.

"Just to the waterfall for a swim," Rose said. "We won't be long."

Teagan nodded, and she checked the buckets on the table as they passed by them. Only one was empty and she grabbed it and smiled at Vida when he took it from her. "Thank you."

They stopped at the outhouse and Vida waited patiently for her to use it before he used it himself. When he was finished, they walked into the jungle.

"Do you know how to get to the waterfall from here?" She asked. She'd gone to the waterfall numerous times and she was pretty certain she knew her way, but after getting lost two nights ago, she was feeling nervous.

He nodded. "Yes."

"You have a good sense of direction, huh? I can't find my way out of a wet paper bag."

"Why would you be in a wet paper bag?" Vida asked.

She grinned at him. "It's just a saying It means that you get lost easily."

"Then why not say that you get lost easily?"

She thought about that for a moment. "Humans say weird things sometimes, I guess."

They were almost to the waterfall when Vida stopped abruptly. He put his finger to his lips and pushed her back until they were hidden in the thick foliage. She pressed up against the reassuring bulk of his warm body and he put his arm around her. They waited silently for a few minutes and her eyes widened when the animal appeared from the direction of the waterfall. It was massive in size with paws as big as her head. It looked like a tiger, but it was navy blue with lighter blue stripes that almost matched the colour of Vida's skin. Water was still dripping from its mouth and when it yawned, Rose could see large, razor sharp fangs. When it bent its head and snuffled at the ground, it revealed the two-inch hole in the top of its skull. It lifted its head and sniffed the air before taking a deep breath and blowing it out through the skull hole. A fine mist sprayed out of the hole and the animal made a low purring sound.

Something rubbed up against Rose's leg and she glanced down. Her mouth went dry when she saw the baby version of the blue-striped animal standing next to her. It stared up at her with its amber coloured eyes, and she didn't object when Vida put his hand across her mouth.

The baby sniffed her leg through her pants before licking the material. She stood stock-still, her heart banging against her ribcage, as the baby batted at the laces on her shoes. Its mother made another low purring noise and the baby called to her, it's purr high-pitched and squeaky. Rose remained frozen to the spot as a second baby appeared next to Vida. This one sniffed at Vida's foot before licking it. It sneezed and shook its head before spying its sibling. It bounded clumsily over their feet and attacked its sibling with enthusiasm. The bigger one bit its sibling on the ear and it screeched and hissed before swiping at its sibling's belly with its paw and then headbutting it.

The mother called again, and the two babies broke apart before pushing through the foliage to join their mother. She purred and licked both of their heads, nuzzling them affectionately before disappearing into the jungle. The two babies chased after her and Rose leaned against Vida as he took his hand from her mouth.

"Are you all right, flower?"

She nodded and pressed her hand against her rapid heartbeat. "Yeah. Small heart attack, but I'm good."

He squeezed her waist as she said, "I think that's what Wallace calls a blowcat."

Vida just shrugged before leading her out of the thick bushes and back on the path toward the waterfall.

The sun had risen, and she lifted her face to its warmth as Vida set the bucket down next to the pool of water. He stripped off his pants and waded into the pool. She watched as he walked forward until he suddenly dived under the water and disappeared.

She glanced around before slipping out of her pants. She took the soap from the pocket and folded the pants neatly before lying them on a rock. Wearing just her shirt and panties, she waded into the water, steeling herself against the cold.

"Shit, that's cold." She forced herself to move deeper into the water until it was about chest high. The roaring sound of the waterfall was very loud, and she took another nervous look around. There was no sign of the pink creatures or the blowcat, and she pinched her nose shut before ducking under the water. She popped back up immediately, shivering and muttering curses under her breath. She thought longingly of the hot springs at Vida's cave before scrubbing soap into her scalp. There was still no sign of Vida and she scanned the water around her. It was remarkably clear but she saw no flashes of blue. She knew the drop off was only a few feet ahead of her and she moved back a little. Drowning wasn't exactly her idea of a good time.

She washed her hair and then tipped her head back, rinsing the soap out with one hand before washing her arms. It was a pain in the ass to bathe in her shirt and panties but forgetting the fact that she normally had one of the men with her and didn't fancy showing off the goods to them, she also didn't like the idea of running through the jungle naked if she had to leave the water suddenly. She washed the rest of her body quickly, stomping her feet as she washed her upper body to try and bring some warmth back to them.

The water rippled next to her and she gasped when Vida emerged. Water streamed down his body and he grinned happily at her. "Hello, flower."

"Hi. Do you feel better?"

"Yes. Are you finished bathing?"

"I am. Here." She handed the soap to him and watched as he washed his upper body. When his hand dipped under the water, she moved a little closer and watched as he cleaned his dick and then his upper thighs.

"Why are you still wearing your clothing?" Vida asked.

She shrugged. "If there's trouble, I don't want to have to run naked through the jungle."

"I will keep you safe if there is trouble," he replied.

"Thank you. Do you want me to wash your back for you?"

There was only a sliver of soap left but he handed it to her and turned around. The water was only about waist deep on him and she admired the way his blue skin gleamed in the sunlight. She touched his back. He was incredibly warm despite the coldness of the water and she had to stop herself from crowding up against him to leech some of his warmth. Instead, she soaped her hands up with the last of the soap before washing his back. She took her time, running her hands over the large muscles of his back.

She considered cupping his ass and giving it a squeeze but wondered if that might be a bit too forward.

Too forward? Uh, Rosie-girl? You had his cock in your mouth last night, remember?

She remembered all right. God, just thinking about it made her mouth water. His come was so damn sweet. Great, now she was addicted to Vida's semen.

"All done." She squeezed his hip and he sunk down and rinsed the soap off before standing again and turning to face her.

"Time for your swim lesson, flower."

"What?" She gave him a startled look and automatically backed away.

He reached out and snagged her around the waist, drawing her into his embrace. "You live on an island now. You must learn to swim."

"I know, but I…"

"But what?"

"I'm afraid."

"You do not need to be afraid. I will not let any harm come to you."

She licked her lips. "I – okay, I'll try."

"Good." He lifted her and placed her on his hip like she was a little kid. "Ready?"

"I don't want to go underwater," she said in alarm.

"You won't. Trust me, flower."

She took a deep breath and wrapped her legs around his waist. She clung to his shoulders as he waded toward the drop-off. Panic flooded through her.

"I – I've changed my mind," she said. "Please, Vida. I don't want to do this."

He stopped just before the drop-off and squeezed her thigh. "I will not let you drown, sweet flower."

"I don't want to go past the drop-off," she whispered. "Please."

"All right." He tugged at her legs. "Let go."

"Do I have to?"

He nodded, and she untangled her legs from around his waist. She couldn't touch the bottom and she resisted the urge to wrap her legs around him again but squeezed his shoulders tightly with her cold hands as he faced her.

"I'm going to teach you how to swim in place." Vida kept his hands around her waist. "You must relax."

"I'm relaxed."

"You are not relaxed. Tilt your head back and stare at the sky."

"Don't let go of me."

"I will not."

"Do you promise?"

"Yes."

She eased her head back, keeping her ears above the water line so she could hear Vida. She stared at the sky as Vida squeezed her waist.

"Breathe deeply, little flower."

She took a few deep breaths and Vida made another sound of approval. "Good. Kick your feet back and forth slowly."

She did what he asked and after a few moments, he said, "Very good. Let go of my shoulders and move your hands like this.

She lifted her head as he pulled her closer, so his arm was wrapped around her waist. He used his free hand to make a sideways back and forth motion in the water.

"Move both hands like that?" She asked.

He nodded and pushed her back before holding her around the waist with both hands again. "Ready?"

"I think so. You won't let go of me, right?"

"No, sweet flower. Trust me."

"I-I do." She took another deep breath and let go of Vida's shoulders. She moved her hands back and forth under the water and Vida smiled at her.

"Very good. Do not forget to kick your feet."

She kicked her feet and waved her hands and after a few minutes, Vida said, "I'm going to remove one of my hands. Are you ready?"

"I – okay."

"Keep kicking and moving your hands." He waited another ten seconds and then moved his left hand away. "Keep moving, little flower."

She was starting to pant from the exertion, but she nodded and kept kicking her feet and waving her hands. At least she was feeling warmer now.

"You are doing very well," Vida praised. "I am going to let go."

"I'll sink." She could hear the panic in her voice.

"No, you will not." He cupped her face and rubbed her cheekbone with his thumb. "Trust me, Rose."

She shivered at the sound of her name on his lips and he smiled at her, his fangs gleaming in the sunlight, before releasing her waist. She had another brief moment of panic that she fought her way through by kicking her feet a little harder.

She dipped a little lower in the water, but she waved her hands and kicked her feet and to her astonishment, didn't sink below the water. After about a minute, Vida reached out and drew her into his embrace.

She hooked her legs around his waist and cupped his face. "I did it!"

"Well done, flower," Vida said.

She was nearly giddy with excitement and without thinking about it, she leaned closer and kissed Vida on the mouth. He stiffened, and she immediately stopped kissing him.

"I'm sorry, Vida. I shouldn't have kissed you. I just forgot, but I won't do it again. I prom -"

Vida pulled her close, his hand cupping the back of her head and she made a soft squeak when he pressed his mouth against hers. He licked at her mouth and she parted her lips. He slipped his tongue into her mouth and kissed her deeply.

For someone who didn't kiss, he was amazing at it.

She touched his fangs with her tongue and then moaned when he captured her tongue between his lips and sucked hard. She forced herself to pull back.

"Vida, you don't have to kiss me. Really. I know it's not something you enjoy and -"

"Feel how much I enjoy your kisses, flower." He cupped her ass and pressed her against his erection before kissing her again. "I like the way you taste. Will you deny me your kisses?"

"No, but I don't want you to think you have to kiss me."

"I do not." He kissed her a third time, this time cupping her breast and flicking at her hard nipple with his thumb. She moaned and rubbed her pussy against his cock. She wanted him so much. He kissed his way down her throat as he squeezed and caressed her breast. He was sliding his hand into her panties when he suddenly stopped and stared into the trees that surrounded them.

"What's wrong?"

"The winged one is watching us."

"The what?" She scanned their surroundings. "Who's watching us?"

"The fat one with wings."

"Arden? I don't see him."

She squinted in the direction that Vida was looking but still couldn't see the fairy.

"He is there." Vida carried her back through the water until she could touch the ground again. "Tomorrow, I will give you another swimming lesson."

"Thank you." Her body was going numb and her teeth were starting to chatter.

Vida touched her mouth with his thumb. "Your lips are turning blue, flower."

He picked her up and carried her out of the water to sit on a large flat stone near the water's edge. "Sit here and let the sun warm you for a bit."

"Will you sit with me?"

"Yes." He joined her, and she squeezed water from her shirt as he lounged naked beside her. The hot sun warmed her quickly and she grinned at Vida.

"You're pretty comfortable in your skin, huh?" She glanced at his cock. It was still half-hard and she had to resist the urge to lean over and take it into her mouth. Having Arden watch her give Vida a blow job wasn't high on her list of fantasies.

"The one named Patrick is mad," Vida said bluntly. "You are to stay away from him. Do you understand?"

She nodded. "Yeah, I know."

He sat up and cupped her face. "You are never to be alone with him. Promise me."

"I won't. I promise." She studied his face before touching his cheekbone with the tips of her fingers. "I like you, Vida."

He smiled, revealing his sharp fangs. "You please me as well, small flower."

She laughed. "Thanks."

Vida slid off the rock and put his pants on before filling the bucket of water. "Come, we should return to the others."

She put her pants on and slipped into her shoes. She took Vida's hand and he squeezed it. "The others are here."

She looked up as Duncan and Teagan came out from the trees. She turned to Vida. "Holy crap. You have hearing like Superman."

"Who is this Superman?" Vida asked.

Before she could reply, Teagan and Duncan had joined them. Teagan's face was even more solemn than usual, and fear spiked in her belly. "What's wrong?"

"Nothing's wrong," Teagan said. "It's time for breakfast."

"You came to the waterfalls to tell us it was time for breakfast?" Rose said.

"Time to go back to the camp, Rose," Teagan replied.

"What if we say no?" Rose asked.

"You and Vida are safer with us than on your own. You know that."

Rose glanced up at Vida. She had no doubt of Vida's strength and his courage, but Teagan was right. They were safer with the camp, despite Patrick's obvious lunacy.

"He's right, Vida."

"I will keep you safe, flower."

"Vida, the jungle is very dangerous. It's better if we stay with others. We should be helping to keep each other safe. Do you understand?"

Vida nodded but she had no real belief that he would stay at the camp much longer. It didn't matter. If Vida left, she would go with him. She believed they were safest in the camp, but she would rather take her chances alone with Vida than stay with the others. Patrick was too unstable, most of the others hated her, and Solomon was having sex with Marissa. She didn't want to face any of that without Vida.

Hey, Rose, do you think maybe you're getting a little too attached to a guy you just met? What do you know about Vida, really, other than he can make you come? Also, Vida's into you now, but he thinks you can't fuck him. How long do you think it will take before he gets tired of you, just like Solomon did? You can't hunt, you can't protect yourself, you have no idea how to survive in a jungle. The only benefit you provide to Vida is sex, and he believes it's impossible.

She took Vida's hand and squeezed it as they followed Teagan and Duncan back toward camp. She would just have to convince Vida that she could have sex with him. And if it did hurt, she'd make damn sure he didn't realize it.

CHAPTER 11

"So, are you and the big blue guy a thing or what?"

Rose picked up a small carving of an elephant that was sitting on the ground near Brody's furs. "Are you and Doc a thing?"

Brody grinned. "Nah, we're just banging every night."

She jumped up from his furs and gave them a suspicious look. "You could have warned me before I sat on your bed. And having sex every night is probably a thing."

"Is it?"

Rose ran her finger over the elephant's smooth back. "I think so. Where did you get this?"

"Scott made it for me."

"Scott?"

"Doc. His real name is Scott."

She smiled at him. "You have sex every night, he told you his real name and he's giving you gifts. Forget *thing,* you two are a couple."

"Maybe we are." Brody stared at the wooden elephant in her hand.

"Good. I'm happy for you, Brody."

"Weird to think that I had to be sucked into an orb and stranded on an island in the middle of fucking nowhere to finally find a decent guy, huh?"

She laughed and placed the elephant on Brody's pillow. "Love happens in the strangest of places."

"You in love with the blue guy?"

"His name is Vida."

"Sorry, are you in love with *Vida*?"

"I barely know him." Rose crossed her arms over her torso. "You can't fall in love with someone you've only known for a few days."

"Fair enough. So, it's just boning then?"

She didn't answer, and Brody touched her arm. "Hey, Rosie, look at me."

She stared up at him and he squeezed her shoulder. "What's wrong?"

"Vida and I aren't a couple."

"You sure he knows that? He acts like you belong to him. He won't let anyone else get near you, and I heard him telling you not to let Solomon touch you."

She shrugged. "He's just, um, overprotective."

"I think it's more than that."

"It's not. We're not even having sex."

"Seriously?" Brody blinked at her. "Why not? Is it Solomon? Because fuck that guy, Rose. He doesn't deserve you. You're into Vida, I can tell, and he's definitely into you."

"We've done some stuff," she admitted before pacing back and forth in Brody's hut. "But, um, Vida's a big guy which means he has a…"

"Big dick?" Brody said with a grin.

Now it was her turn to blush. "Yeah."

"Nice." He held up his fist. "Don't leave me hanging. Bump it, girl."

She fist bumped him before resuming her pacing.

"If Vida's got such a big one, why do you look like a woman who's dating a small-dicked man?"

She laughed. "God, you're so crude, Brody."

He just grinned at her. "Spill it, Rosie."

She picked at a small scab on her forearm. "Vida says I'm too small to take his, you know…"

"So what, you tried and it didn't fit?"

"He won't even try." She gave him a look of frustration. "He says he'll hurt me if he tries."

"He knows women push babies out of their vajayjay, right? Wait… do his women even have muffs like human women?"

"They do. They look like us, he says, only with horns and fangs and purple skin. But, they're bigger and they're warriors who can fight. Basically, everything I'm not."

"He still seems attracted to you."

"He is, and he says he wants to have sex with me, but he won't risk hurting me. He won't allow us to," she paused, "mate as he calls it. It's frustrating as hell."

"You need to change his mind."

"I've tried. It doesn't work. And it's not like I can pin him down and have sex with him when we're, uh, making out. He's got more muscles in his baby finger than I do in my whole damn body."

"Middle-of-the-night sex."

"I'm sorry?" She stopped pacing and stared at Brody.

"You need to do middle-of-the-night sex. Listen, you know how you sometimes half wake up in the middle of the night to find your man's dick hard against your ass? Maybe he's sleeping, or maybe he's only half awake too, but next thing you know, you're having a round of sex when you're both only sort of with it. That's what you do to Vida. Get his dick into your happy place before he's even fully awake."

"Do you really think that would work?"

Brody nodded. "Yes."

"It's worth a try," Rose said thoughtfully. "Maybe he'll realize that -"

"Hey, babe? Did I leave my shirt in…oh, sorry, I didn't realize you were still talking with Rose." Doc stopped in the doorway of the hut. "I didn't mean to interrupt."

"You didn't," Rose said. "I was just leaving to find Vida."

"He's gone."

Rose's heart dropped into her stomach with a hard, heavy, hollow thud. "He's gone?"

Doc nodded, and she swallowed down the bile before staring mutely at Brody.

"It's okay, Rosie." Brody gave Doc a look of alarm and the blond man joined them.

"Rose? Do you feel faint?" He pressed his fingers against the pulse in her wrist. "Your pulse is racing. You should sit down."

"I'm fine."

She wasn't fine.

Vida had left her.

Vida had left her without even saying goodbye.

"Did he tell you to say goodbye to me?" She croaked. Her throat was dusty-dry.

Doc gave her a strange look. "He's just gone hunting with Teagan, Wallace and Duncan. They'll be back in a few hours."

Relief rushed through her. It was enough to make her knees wobble and both Doc and Brody grabbed an arm to steady her.

"Maybe you should sit down." Doc felt her forehead.

"No, I'm okay. I just thought…it doesn't matter. I'm fine."

"Vida did give me a message to give to you. He said he didn't want to interrupt you while you were talking to your friend."

"What did he say?"

Doc glanced at Brody. "To remember that the other males in the camp were not to touch you."

"Uh oh," Brody grinned, "we're gonna get the big blue guy beating the hell out of us."

"Oh, he made sure to mention that we were allowed to touch her as we were laying with each other, and had no interest in his small flower's vagina," Doc said with a cheeky grin.

Brody burst into laughter as Rose turned bright red. "Oh my God. Oh my God, I'm so sorry. Vida didn't mean… that is, he's very blunt and not socially…"

"It's fine," Doc said as he released her arm. "He's not wrong. Listen, I'll let you and Brody finish your discussion."

"No, we're done. Thanks, Doc. I'll give you guys your privacy." Rose moved past them, her stupid legs still felt a little trembly, and out into the humid air of the jungle. She breathed deep and sat down on one of the logs around the campfire. She stared at the burning coals, her heart still thumping away in her chest like a frightened rabbit.

Her reaction to thinking Vida had left her was alarming, but she hadn't been able to control it. She rubbed at her forehead. Shit, what was happening to her?

"WHY DO YOU WANT TO GO WITH US?" PETER FROWNED AT her before picking at the acne on his face.

Rose ignored him and smiled at Brian. "Do you mind, Brian? I feel like it's a good idea for me to better understand how the traps work."

Brian shrugged and picked up a second spear from the pile leaning against an empty hut. He handed it to her. "Fine with me. Let's go."

"She'll just slow us down," Peter said. "Let her stay in the camp and do the woman stuff."

Before Rose could reply, Davis made a loud snort from where he was hanging wet clothing on the clothesline. "Are you fucking serious? You're gonna pull that macho, chest-beating, women stay in the camp bullshit? If Rose wants to learn the traps, then she can fucking learn the traps. Everyone on this fucking sandtrap works together."

"Thanks, Davis."

"Don't mention it, Rosie." He gave her a quick salute before returning to hanging wet clothes.

Peter gave her a sullen look. 'We wouldn't even be in this fucking mess if it wasn't for you."

"Yeah, I know," Rose said wearily. "It's all my fault. Do me a favour and give it a rest just for an hour or so, would you, Peter?"

"Whatever." He followed Brian into the jungle and Rose followed him. She readjusted the wreath of flowers around her throat and gripped the spear in her right hand. Not that she had any real confidence in using it. Before she'd nearly died in the jungle and been rescued by Vida, both Brian and Duncan had given her some lessons with the spears, but she would be the first to admit that she wasn't very good at it.

She peered around as she followed Brian and Peter. She wouldn't admit this, but she was only going into the jungle in the hopes of finding Vida and the others. They'd been gone much longer than their usual hunting expeditions, and her stomach was churning with worry. What if the pinkies had found them? What if they'd stumbled onto a blowcat with babies? What if – her stomach heaved – it was a trap set by Teagan, Wallace and Duncan and they had killed Vida?

They wouldn't. You know they wouldn't. They're good men.

Yeah, they were. But they also followed Patrick's rules.

Patrick isn't going to kill Vida. He needs his help.

He did, but Patrick also was clearly off his rocker.

Worry gnawing at her stomach, she gripped her spear a little tighter and followed Brian and Peter deeper into the jungle.

———

"SHIT." BRIAN BENT AND STUDIED THE BROKEN TRAP. IT WAS made from sturdy but flexible tree branches and he swiped his finger across the jagged edge of one broken branch. It came away red and Rose took a nervous look around.

"Is that blood?" Peter asked.

"Yeah. Something's been breaking our traps and grabbing the animals in them." Brian stood and pushed at the trap with his foot as Peter moved to the second trap that was at the base of a large clump of bushes that were almost twenty feet high. "We think it's the bears."

"They have bears on this island?" Rose said.

"Not quite. I mean, they kind of look like a cross between a bear and a rhino," Brian said.

"Wait, are they the things that Wallace calls brinos?" Rose asked.

Brian nodded. "Yeah, not very original, I know. We really gotta stop letting him name stuff."

"What are you talking about?" Peter dropped the second trap. "This one is broken all to shit too."

"Brinos," Rose said. "Wallace told us about them the second or third night we were on the island. They look like bears, but they have skin like a rhino and a big horn sticking out of their chest with a smaller one above it. Right?" She glanced at Brian for confirmation.

"Yeah. They usually don't bother much with us. We thought they ate mostly fish, we've seen them wade into the ocean and catch them. Although Duncan saw one take on a blowcat and win, and he said the thing feasted on the blow-cat's guts afterwards."

"Maybe with the sharkgators so close to the shores for breeding, they don't want to go into the ocean," Rose said.

Brian thought that over for a minute. "It's a good theory. But if they keep breaking our traps, we'll have to take them out. These traps aren't easy to make, and Duncan is still the only one with any real skill at making them. Shit, the stuff that guy knows about trapping and surviving in the wilderness is impressive. We'd have been dead a long time ago if it wasn't for him."

"Yeah, well, I'm starting to think you guys might be bull-shitting us with your blowcats and brinos." Peter kicked at the trap again. "We haven't seen anything like that and we've been on the island for almost three weeks."

"I saw a blowcat this morning," Rose said. "Vida and I saw it and her babies on our way to the falls."

Brian just rolled his eyes. "Whatever, dude. What possible reason could we have for making this shit up?"

Peter shrugged. "I don't know. I don't even know you, do I? For all I know, this whole sucked into an orb thing could be a hoax, and we're on some island in the middle of our own world as some sort of fucked up social science experiment."

"Are you serious?" Rose said. "Peter, you worked at the lab for two years. You saw how the orb worked, you saw -"

"Maybe we saw what they wanted us to see," Peter said.

"How do you explain Vida, then? Or the other creatures you saw come out of the orb? Or the fucking pink thing that ate John's face off?"

"Maybe they're drugging us. Maybe they're pumping us full of shit that makes us all mass hallucinate."

"You're talking crazy, Peter," Rose said.

"Yeah, right. Because tigers that blow acid from their foreheads and bears that have horns like rhinos is so fucking sane. Just think about it for a minute, Rose. If people really -"

"Peter? What's wrong?" Rose took a step toward him as his face paled.

"Rose," he whispered. Blood dripped out of his mouth and Brian's hard hand wrapped around her arm, preventing her from moving forward.

"Help me," Peter whispered. "Please..."

There was a loud cracking noise and blood gushed from his mouth like a waterfall. A horn tore through his chest, the end of it covered in flesh and blood. Peter made a strangled noise of pain as paws, their skin a scaly grey colour and tipped with long, black, razor-sharp claws, gripped his arms.

The creature stepped out of the bushes, the horn on its chest protruding further out of Peter's chest as it yanked the man back against its giant body. Another glut of blood poured from Peter's mouth and he took one last gurgling breath before dying. His head lolled back and the creature bit into his face with a loud crunch, tearing off Peter's nose and chewing it down happily.

Rose's gorge rose, and she barely felt Brian's hand on her arm as another brino stepped out of the bushes. It tried to tear

Peter's arm off, and the first brino snarled at it before dragging Peter's body into the bushes.

"Brian," Rose whispered through numb lips as the second brino studied them with it's beady eyes. "What do we do?"

Brian lifted his spear and threw it with a hard whistling grunt at the brino. It struck the creature in the stomach just below its horn. Despite the speed of Brian's throw and the sharpness of the spear, the tip barely penetrated the brino's skin.

"Fuck," Brian said when the creature plucked the spear from his stomach before dropping it. It sniffed the air as Brian grabbed Rose's spear from her ice-cold hand. The brino took two lumbering steps forward. Rose could see bugs crawling across its leathery skin as it sniffed the air again.

"Rose?"

"Yeah?"

"Run."

Brian's hand gripped hers and they turned and ran. She could hear the brino behind them, hear its harsh pants and grunts, and made a terrified squeal when she felt its hot breath on her back.

"Faster!" Brian bellowed.

They put on a burst of speed and sprinted across the jungle. Brian dragged her over a fallen log and hauled her to her feet when she stumbled and fell. "Keep moving!"

They raced through the jungle. The grunts of the brino were quieting, but Rose didn't dare look behind her. She'd fall for sure if she did. When Brian made a sharp left and yanked her into a large clump of bushes, she threw her hand over her mouth, trying to quiet her rapid panting as Brian wiped the sweat from his face.

He put his finger to his lips and she nodded and tried to catch her breath as Brian gripped her spear tightly and cocked his head. They listened intently for almost five minutes before Brian relaxed a little.

"I think we lost it," he said.

She took a deep, trembling breath. "Peter's dead."

"Yeah," he said. "You okay?"

She nodded. "I think so. You?"

"Yeah. A little freaked out but -"

A paw appeared, and the long black claws sunk into Brian's shoulder. He gave Rose a weary look of resignation. "Fuck me sidew-"

He was yanked out of the bushes, her spear falling from his hand. Rose screamed and scooped up the spear before pushing her way free of the clinging branches. She stopped, staring in horror at the brino as it lifted Brian off the ground and drove its horn deep into his belly.

"Brian!" Rose screamed and darted forward, thrusting the spear into the creature's side. It roared with anger and pain and she stumbled back. It dropped Brian to the ground, and Rose made a moaning cry when she saw the intestines hanging out of the wound in his stomach. The brino yanked the spear from its flesh before snarling viciously at her.

"Rose."

Her terrified gaze flickered back to Brian.

"Run." He reached out with one hand and grabbed the creature's leg when it started to move toward her.

"Brian, no, I won't leave you," Rose moaned.

"Run," Brian wheezed. He sank his nails in the creature's hide. The creature stared down at him and Brian gave him a blood-coated grin. "C'mon, motherfucker. Finish the job."

The creature dragged him to his feet, sniffing at the blood pouring from Brian's mouth.

"Go, Rose. Now," Brian groaned. The creature bent his

181

head and tore Brian's throat out with a sharp jerk of his mouth.

Rose turned and fled.

SHE WAS GOING TO DIE. IF THE BRINO DIDN'T GET HER, IF THE blowcats or the pinkies didn't kill her, then the fucking plants would. She was a dead woman walking and it didn't matter how positive she tried to be, she had just watched two men die in front of her. She didn't stand a chance and she'd might as well just find the nearest killer plant and let it strangle her to death. It would be faster and –

Rose, stop! Just fucking stop.

The coldness of her inner voice drew her frantic stumbling race through the jungle up short. Panting and gasping, she checked the tree next to her for vines before leaning against it. She strained to hear past the sound of her own labored breathing and pounding heartbeat. The jungle was alive with noise and for all she knew, one of them could be the brino lumbering its way toward her.

Just shut the fuck up and stop panicking like a pussy for one goddamn minute.

Her inner voice was pissed.

She shut the fuck up and took breath after breath, drawing the humid air deep into her lungs before releasing it. After a few minutes both her panic and her heartbeat subsided to a more manageable beat and she studied the jungle around her.

She was lost again. Understandable, considering she'd been running for her damn life, but not helpful. She'd always had a poor sense of direction and being surrounded by trees and killer plants and giant creatures that were a hellish mix of bear and rhino wasn't exactly helping her get her bearings. She'd never find her way back to camp.

Find the river.

She blinked and stared up at the glimpses of bright blue sky. Sweat trickled down her neck and into the collar of her t-shirt. Small insects buzzed in her ears and she slapped absent-mindedly at her arm.

Why the river?

Her inner voice made a sound that was a cross between irritation and laughter.

Follow the river to the waterfall, idiot.

Her eyes widened. Of course. The river flowed into the waterfall. If she found the waterfall, she could find her way back to the camp from there. Only one small problem, she needed to find the river.

Close your eyes and listen.

She closed her eyes and held her breath, straining to hear. There was nothing but the heavy buzz of insects. Disappointment trickled through her. Did she really think she'd hear the river? It could be anywhere and –

Just shut up and listen.

She listened.

After a few moments, she opened her eyes before turning to her right. She thought she'd detected the faint sound of water coming from her right. She barked harsh laughter that made the birds in the trees above her squawk in alarm before taking off in unified flight. She sucked in some air and picked her way through the trees. Maybe she was wrong. Maybe the river wasn't in this direction, but she couldn't just stand around and wait for a brino or a blowcat or a pinkie to show up. She needed to keep moving and hope she found Vida and the others, or the river.

She'd only been walking for about fifteen minutes when

the shrill cry made her freeze. Goosebumps popped up on her arms and the hair on the back of her neck stood up.

"What was that?" She whispered.

There was another cry – it was full of heartbreaking fear – and she cringed before quickly making her way toward the noise.

"You're being an idiot, Rose," she muttered to herself.

Yeah, she was, but as another piercing cry echoed through the jungle, she broke into a jog. The fearful cry was tugging at every goddamn heartstring in her body. She couldn't –

Oh God.

She had almost jogged right into the dead body of the blowcat. As it was, she was standing on some of the intestines that were ripped out of its body and lying near it's back legs. Her stomach churned, and she clapped her hand over her mouth as she gagged. She stepped back, wiping the bottom of her shoe on the ground and trying not to barf. The blowcat had been torn open from chest to groin and she could see that most of its internal organs were missing. She had no idea what had killed it and she really didn't want to know.

Flies buzzed around the blowcat's dead body and its milky eyes stared accusingly at her as she stepped around it. There was another wailing cry and she pushed past a bush, her breath catching in her throat.

The baby blowcat was crying continuously now, it's small fuzzy body wrapped in vines that were dragging it relentlessly backwards. It cried pitifully and dug its nails into the jungle floor as the vines tightened around its body. Without thinking, she lunged forward and began to tear at the vines. These ones were smaller and thinner than the vines that nearly killed her and she tore them in two easily. She worked swiftly, constantly jerking her legs back and forth to tear apart the vines that were wrapping insidiously around her legs.

When the baby was free, she picked it up and stepped away from the vines swaying blindly in the air around them. She carried it a safe distance away from the vines and petted the top of its head as the baby stared unblinkingly at her.

"It's okay, baby," Rose crooned. "You're safe now."

She petted it again, avoiding the hole in its forehead. A smile of delight crossed her face when it broke into a raspy purr.

"That's right. You're a good baby. I'm sorry about your mama, but don't you worry, I'm going to take good care of..."

The vine, this one thicker and larger than the others, wrapped around her waist. Her eyes widened, and she yanked at it with one hand before trying to run. The vine tightened immediately as more vines came slithering out from the bush to her left.

"Are you fucking kidding me?" She shouted as the vines wrapped around her waist and hips and thighs and pulled her forward. A vine wrapped around the baby blowcat's back leg and tried to yank it from her grip. The baby howled, and Rose screamed when it dug its sharp claws into her shoulder in a frantic bid to cling to her.

"For fuck's sake!" Rose shouted as she tore at the vines with one hand and clutched the baby blowcat with the other. She could feel blood soaking into her t-shirt as the razor-sharp claws of the blowcat sunk deeper into her flesh. She glanced up and the pain in her shoulder became meaningless.

She stared in silent horror at the monstrosity in front of her. The bushes had parted to reveal the head of the plant and she shrieked before tearing at the vines with strength brought on by pure panic.

"It's a fucking Venus fly trap!" She shouted before struggling to back away. The vines tightened around her legs and she was knocked to her back on the ground. The baby blowcat clung to her, screaming into her ear as the vine around it's back leg tightened until she could see the baby's flesh bulging under its fur.

She was dragged forward, shrieking and writhing, to the plant's mouth. She wasn't wrong about the plant looking like a Venus fly trap. If Venus fly traps were seven feet tall and had long waving tentacles covered in thousands of small black spiders sticking out of their mouths. The plant's teeth glistened with saliva as the spiders scuttled and scurried up and down the swaying tentacles jutting from the plant's mouth.

"Fuck!" Rose screamed as the plant dragged her closer. Her shoulder bumped against an exposed root and as she was dragged by it, she reached out with her free hand and grabbed it. She was brought up short, the muscles in her arms straining as the vines around her waist and legs yanked viciously.

The blowcat wailed and howled in her ear, it's warm breath washing over her neck as her fingers began to loosen from the root.

"No! Goddammit no!" Rose shouted.

It was no use, she could feel her grip slipping and she screamed again in fear and rage as her fingers lost their tenuous grip on the root. A hard hand caught her wrist and Wallace grinned down at her.

"Hey, Rosie-girl."

"Wallace!"

"Hold on, Rose." Duncan and Teagan ran past her and they hacked through the vines with Duncan's sword and Teagan's machete. The vines pulled harder in response and she gave Wallace a panicked look when she was dragged forward. He dug his heels in, vines were already starting to wrap around his legs, and wrapped his other hand around her upper arm.

He held on grimly as Rose's body lifted a few inches off the ground. She cried out, feeling the stretch in her spine and her legs as she was pulled in two different directions.

"Fuck, kill it before she gets torn in goddamn two," Wallace roared at Duncan and Teagan.

Duncan darted past the vines and thrust his sword deep into the plant's gaping mouth. All of the vines relaxed at once and Rose fell to the ground with a hard thump, banging her head.

She sucked in a deep breath, wincing when the baby blowcat retracted its claws before resting its head on her shoulder. It meowed softly, and she petted it with one shaking hand as Wallace collapsed on his ass next to her and wiped away the sweat from his forehead.

"Fuck, I hate those goddamn plants."

"You okay, Rose?" Teagan helped her to her feet, eyeing the baby blowcat she held in her arms. "Where did you find that?"

"Its mother is dead behind those bushes," Rose replied. "It was being strangled by the vines so I..."

"So you rescued it?" Teagan raised his eyebrow at her.

"It's just a baby," she said defensively.

"You almost died trying to save it."

She flushed and held the baby a little closer before repeating, "It's just a baby."

Duncan had moved behind her and he studied the back of her shoulder. "She's bleeding."

Rose winced when he touched her back as Teagan said, "Why are you in the jungle alone again?"

"I wasn't. I was with Peter and Brian. We were attacked by two of those brino things."

187

Teagan stiffened. "Where's Brian?"

"I'm sorry. He – he didn't make it. Peter was killed first, and Brian and I ran and hid but the second one found us, and it-it killed Brian. I tried to help him, but he told me to run." She touched Teagan's arm. "I'm so sorry, Teagan."

"Fuck," Teagan muttered. Sweat was dripping off his forehead and he wiped it away before glancing at Wallace. "You okay, man?"

Rose knew Brian and Wallace had been close. The cheerful look on Wallace's face had dropped like a stone and he looked pale and sick to his stomach.

"Motherfuck," Wallace said. "Brian saved my life in Mosul."

"I know." Teagan squeezed his arm.

"He didn't deserve to die on this motherfucking rock in the middle of goddamn nowhere." Wallace's voice was rising. "He sure as shit didn't deserve to die because of some bullshit half bear half rhino motherfucker."

"He didn't, but you gotta keep your shit together, man," Teagan said. "We need to get back to camp."

"Where's Vida?" Rose asked suddenly. "Brian said he was with you guys."

"He -"

"Oh fuck me up the ass with a motherfucking dildo," Wallace snarled.

"What – shit!" Teagan shoved Rose behind him.

She peeked around his broad body, holding the now-sleeping blowcat in her arms. Panic infused her entire body when the pinkie stepped out from behind the tree. The creature stared unblinkingly at them as Duncan and Wallace moved to stand next to Teagan.

"Rose, move back slowly into the trees," Teagan said in a mutter.

"I'm not leaving you guys," Rose said.

"We'll be right behind you, Rosie-girl," Wallace replied. "Go."

"No, I won't -"

"Go now." The tone of Teagan's voice made her start to back away immediately. She took a quick look behind her and stumbled to a stop as fresh panic wormed its way into her chest.

"Keep moving, Rose," Teagan said as he studied the pinkie in front of them.

"I can't. There's another one behind us."

"Well, we're fucking dead," Wallace said. "Nice knowing you all, ya assholes."

"Use your guns." Rose turned and backed up until her back was pressed against Teagan's. She stared at the pinkie who had cocked his head and was studying the flowers around her throat. She shuddered all over. "They can't survive bullets, can they?"

"We ran out of bullets a week after we fucking got here," Wallace said. "Teag, we gotta try and make a run for it."

"We can't outrun them, they're too fast," Duncan said. "The flowers will keep us safe."

Like Rose, they were all wearing wreaths of the yellow flowers. Wallace pulled out a long and wickedly sharp dagger from his belt.

"So, what? We all just stand here until the end of fucking time?" He asked.

"Just shut up and let me think," Teagan replied.

Duncan and Wallace stepped in front of Rose. Duncan had a knife tucked into the back of his belt and Rose plucked it out and held it tightly. Duncan glanced at her and she gave him a short nod and placed the baby blowcat at her feet. It blinked sleepily at her before curling into a ball and tucking its face into its body.

The three humans and the two creatures stood in silence for nearly five minutes. Sweat dripped down Rose's back and she swatted away an insect buzzing near her mouth. Her throat went dry when the pinkies stared at each other over their small group and then walked forward

"Hey, Duncan? The flowers aren't fucking working," Wallace said as the pinkies moved toward them simultaneously, their mouths opening and their jaws distending as their mottled green teeth protruded. "You go for its guts, I'll go for – holy shitballs!"

There was a familiar low growl and Rose pushed past Duncan and Wallace, her heart galloping into high gear.

"Vida!" She gasped.

The big blue man was standing behind the pinkie. It was fast, but Vida was faster. He wrapped one big hand around the pink creature's forehead and the other around its lower jaw. It made a high-pitched squeal that made Rosie's teeth ache. Vida, his face serene, twisted the pinkie's head to the left. Its neck broke with a quiet snap and the creature fell to the ground. Vida stepped over it without a second look and walked toward them.

"Holy shit. I mean...holy...shit," Wallace said.

Vida walked by their small group. He was headed toward the second pinkie and Rose's eyes widened when the creature suddenly turned and fled into the jungle.

"Son of a motherfucking biscuit," Wallace said. "The giant fucking Smurf just killed a pinkie and scared the other one off."

"Do not call me Smurf," Vida said.

"Sorry, big guy." Wallace glanced at Teagan who was studying Vida. "Did you see him just crack that fucker's neck like it was a fucking egg? Shit, he's fucking faster than the pinkies."

Teagan nodded. Duncan slid his sword into the sheath around his waist and took the knife from Rose's hand. Rose took a few hesitant steps toward Vida. He smiled at her and held out his hand. "Come to me, small flower."

She ran forward, ignoring the pain in her back, and wrapped her arms around Vida's waist. He hugged her and she tried not to wince, but he immediately pulled back and turned her around.

"You are bleeding." There was alarm in his voice. "Why are you bleeding?"

"The baby blowcat – I tried to save it from a plant and it dug its claws into me, but I'm okay and I – are you okay?"

"Why would I not be?" He cocked his head at her.

"You just – you killed a pinkie," she whispered.

"It was threatening my sweet flower," he replied. "You should not be wandering in the jungle alone."

"I wasn't. I was with Brian and Peter, but we were attacked, and they died." Her voice broke and Vida bent and pressed a kiss against her mouth. She took a deep breath and studied the guns tucked into Teagan and Wallace's waistbands. "Are you seriously out of bullets?"

Wallace nodded. "Yeah. Doc was the only one carrying his kit when we got sucked into the orb and his kit had med supplies. The rest of us just had our Glocks."

"Why wear the guns then?" Rose asked.

"Habit." Teagan turned to Vida. "Did you find it?"

"I followed the trail of the wounded beast and put it out of its misery. I hung it in a tree, but we should return to it before other animals go after it."

"Wounded beast? Did you kill a brino?" Rose asked.

Duncan shook his head. "No. It's one of the creatures of

the forest that eats the plants. It has antlers and is similar to deer on my world."

"Our world too," Wallace said. "We were lucky to find one. There aren't many of them on the island. I think the pinkies go after them when they can't get humans. The blue guy's right, we need to go back and grab it before some fucking blowcat yanks it out of the tree. Speaking of which…"

He studied the sleeping baby at his feet and Rose hurried over and picked it up. She held it against her chest as Wallace glanced at Teagan. "We can't take it with us, Rosie-girl."

"It'll die if we abandon it," Rose said. "I'm not leaving it."

"Teag?" Wallace turned to the big man.

Teagan studied Rose for a moment. "She's right. She can bring it with us."

"Oh great," Wallace said with a grimace, "now we're raising blowcats. Awesome. Fan-fucking-tastic. Patrick isn't going to shit the bed over this at all."

"Leave Patrick to me," Teagan said. "It might be handy to have a trained blowcat in camp. They're -"

"Something is coming." Vida crossed to Rose and pulled her against him.

"More pinkies?" Teagan asked.

Vida shook his head as the bushes in front of them shivered. A man, he was wearing a loincloth and a wreath of flowers around his neck and nothing else, stepped out. He held a spear in one hand and a dagger in the other. His thick black hair was short, his skin tanned from the sun, and his eyes were dark brown. He studied them without fear.

"Shit," Teagan said as more of the islanders stepped out of the bushes. They were completely surrounded by over a dozen of them and Wallace glanced at Teagan.

"Do we fight?"

"No."

The leader stepped forward and prodded at the dead pinkie with his bare foot before turning to stare at Vida. He said something in his native language and another of the islanders moved toward Rose. Vida growled at him and the man hesitated before speaking rapidly to the leader.

The leader nodded and pointed at the sleeping blowcat. Rose held it a little tighter as three of the locals gathered around the leader. They spoke quietly for a few minutes before the leader nodded again. He pointed at their group then pointed into the jungle and made a 'come' motion with his hand.

"They want us to go with them," Duncan said.

"Yeah, thanks, Captain Obvious," Wallace replied. "Teag, do we go?"

Teagan stared at the locals behind them. They were moving forward slowly, their spears pointed at them. "I don't think we have much choice."

CHAPTER 12

R ose held Vida's hand in a tight grip. He had taken the baby blowcat from her and was holding it in one arm. It slept on, oblivious to the hundreds of people staring at it in a combination of awe and fear.

"Why aren't they killing us?" Wallace asked.

"I have no goddamn idea." Teagan studied their surroundings. The locals had led them through the jungle to the west side of the island and the giant stone wall. Its surface was completely covered in yellow flowers. They had followed the wall to massive wooden doors, even they had vines of flowers growing up them. One of the men had whistled piercingly and, after a few moments, the giant doors groaned open.

Beyond the wall was an enormous clearing in the jungle. Numerous huts populated the space and there were hundreds of islanders milling around the clearing. Furs were stretched out in the sun, cooking fires were dug out in front of most of the huts, and Rose could hear the gentle noise of the ocean.

"The village sits on a cliff," Vida told her. "The wall curves around to the cliff on both sides. They are protected from their enemies by the wall and the ocean."

"Fucking brilliant," Wallace said. "How do you know that?"

Vida shrugged. "I explored the island when I first got here."

"We did too and almost got killed by these guys for even getting close to their wall."

"I am faster and quieter than you," Vida said.

Wallace nudged Duncan. "I want to argue, but the guy ain't wrong, you know?"

"Quiet," Teagan said.

A man was approaching them. He was tall and lean, and his dark hair was on the longer side. Like the others, he wore a loincloth and nothing else. Wooden beads were strung around his neck in long loops and a scar slashed across his naked chest. He stopped in front of them, studying the blowcat that was in Vida's arms.

Rose's mouth dropped open when he said, "My name is Gormet."

"You speak English," Teagan said. He sounded as surprised as Rose felt. "How?"

"A man named Walter taught me and some of the others in my clan, your language. He came from the orb with his mate Freida, just as you did."

"Where's Walter now?" Teagan asked.

Rose had a bad feeling that both Walter and Freida were dead. After all, Vida was living in what was obviously their home.

"Dead. As is his mate."

"Killed by the pinkies or something else?" Teagan said.

"Neither. Simply old age. We burned their bodies as is our custom and they live forever beyond the great gates now."

"So, why aren't you killing us?" Wallace asked.

"Wallace," Teagan snapped.

"What? It's a valid question. They've always tried to kill us in the past."

Gormet stared at Wallace for a moment before pointing at Rose and Vida. "She attempted to save the young of the mighty voprea, and he killed one of the elidas."

"We call them the blowcats and the pinkies," Wallace said with a grin.

Gormet considered this for a moment. "I do not understand either of those words. Voprea means striped one in our language."

"What does elida mean?" Duncan asked.

Gormet's gaze slid to him. "Death."

"Figures," Wallace replied. "So, what? Now that we've killed death, we're considered gods to you people, is that right?"

"Not you," Gormet replied before his gaze shifted to Vida.

"Ouch," Wallace said. "Hey, Rosie, looks like you're banging a god now. That's quite the step up from that douchebag Solomon."

"Shut it, Wallace," Teagan said.

"Yes, Sir." Wallace gave him a cocky grin but lapsed into silence.

Gormet moved close to Rose, stopping when Vida put his arm around her waist and growled at him.

"Is this your mate, female?"

"Um, well…" Rose flushed bright red.

"Yes," Vida replied. "Neither you nor your clan will go near her if you wish to live."

A brief smile crossed Gormet's face, but he didn't move closer to Rose. "Why did you attempt to save the voprea, even at risk of your own life?"

"Because it was a baby and it needed help," Rose said.

"The poor thing's mama was dead and... I don't know, it seemed like a good idea at the time."

"Until you nearly got eaten by a giant, nightmare-inducing plant." Wallace couldn't resist joining in again. "What was up with those goddamn spiders by the way? Did you see those things?"

"Wallace," Teagan warned.

"Mouth shut, right...sorry, Teag."

The baby was starting to wake up and when it made a low and raspy purr, the locals who had gathered around them in a loose circle, all gasped in excitement. They spoke rapidly to each other in their own language until Gormet held up his hand and they lapsed into silence.

Vida set the baby down and it studied its surroundings before rubbing up against Rose's leg and purring loudly. It sauntered toward Gormet and they watched as the leader's eyes widened. When the baby rubbed against him, he reached down and petted it, a look of reverence on his face.

He turned and spoke to the man on his left. The man nodded and disappeared into the crowd. The baby blowcat sniffed at a few of the local's feet, each of them stood in stunned silence, and when he batted at one woman's calf, she giggled in unabashed delight.

The man returned carrying a leg of raw meat. Rose wasn't sure what creature it was from and her stomach curled a little at the blood dripping onto the ground. The man set it in front of the baby and they watched as it attacked the leg with fierce determinedness, ripping and biting into the flesh.

Gormet turned toward them again. "You have brought us a great gift, and for that we will spare your lives. You will join us in celebrating the life of the voprea and the death of the elida. We will give you a bed for the evening and food for your belly."

"Thank you, but we should be returning to our home before it gets dark," Teagan said.

Gormet shook his head. "This is not a choice, big one."

"THANK YOU." ROSE SMILED AT THE WOMAN WHO WAS applying a thick green paste to the wounds on her back. She had no idea what it was, but it soothed the pain and stopped the bleeding. The woman had helped her remove her shirt before rinsing the puncture wounds with water and applying the paste. The woman added another layer before stepping back and washing her hands in a bucket of water.

She said something in her native language and Rose glanced at Vida. Gormet had invited all of the men to join him around the largest fire in the center of the village, but Vida had refused. He had followed Rose and the woman to the hut instead.

"I have no idea what she's saying," Rose said.

"Nor do I, flower."

The woman cocked her head at them before pointing to her paste-covered back. "No wash." She held up one finger. "One day."

Rose nodded. "Got it. Leave the paste stuff on for one day."

She went to put her shirt back on and the woman shook her head and pointed to the paste. Most of the women in the village wore just a loincloth like the men did, but Rose had seen a few with fabric wrapped around their upper half like a tube top. The woman tried to pull her shirt away and Rose shook her head and clutched it tight against her naked breasts.

"No, I can't go topless."

The woman eyed her for a moment before sticking her

head out the door of the hut and yelling something in her language. After a few moments, another woman entered the hut. She was holding a piece of fabric in her hand and she and the other woman wrapped it around Rose's small breasts before tucking and securing it at the back.

"Thank you," Rose said.

The woman stared at her before grinning. "Welcome."

The second woman was staring at Vida's naked chest and when she pressed her arm against Vida's stomach, studying the difference between his blue skin and her tanned skin, a surge of jealousy went through Rose. She moved toward them, taking Vida's hand and feeling mildly ridiculous when she had the urge to push the woman away. Vida put his arm around her waist and the islander smiled before leaving the hut.

The other woman crooked her finger at them and Rose and Vida followed her to the main fire. They sat next to Teagan who studied the paste on her back. "How do you feel?"

"Better. I don't know what this is, but it took the pain away," Rose replied.

"Many healing plants in the jungle," Gormet said. He was smoking a pipe and he took another deep inhale before handing it to Wallace. Wallace shrugged and inhaled his own lungful of smoke.

He blew the smoke out. "It's like a combination of weed and tobacco. Teag?"

Teagan shook his head and Wallace glanced at Duncan. "Duncan, you want to try it?"

"No."

"Rose? Big guy?"

They both declined, and Wallace handed it back to Gormet. He was speaking to another local and Teagan turned to Rose and Vida. "Here's what we've learned. The locals think the blowcats are some kind of ancient gods. They worship them, have an alter where they make sacrifices to them, that sort of thing."

"What kind of sacrifices?" Rose asked nervously.

"Smaller animals," Teagan said. "Anyway, the fact that you tried to save one of the babies and Vida killed a pinkie, has us in their good books."

"Walter had many of these good books," Gormet said. "He tried to teach me to read them but..."

He shrugged and took another hit off the pipe in his hand.

"I wonder where all of Walter's shit got to," Wallace said. "Unless they've got it tucked away in one of their huts."

He scanned the huts as Rose glanced at Vida. She was surprised when Vida said, "I found the human's home on the island and have made it my own."

Wallace laughed. "Big surprise."

He accepted the pipe from Gormet again. "Hey, any reason why you tried to kill us when we first tried to make contact with you? We didn't threaten you or take any of your shit."

"Wallace," Teagan said.

"What? It's a fair question."

"You killed a voprea," Gormet said.

"Uh, pretty sure I didn't," Wallace replied. "I mean, we were attacked by one when it was protecting its babies, but Duncan didn't kill it. Did you?"

Duncan shook his head. "You know I did not."

"Not you, two others in your camp."

Teagan leaned forward. "Can you describe them?"

"One is dead," Gormet said. "The one you cut open. The other leads your tribe."

"How do you know we cut him open?"

"We watch you."

"Shit," Wallace said, "why the fuck do we even bother keeping watch? Between Vida and these guys, we don't fucking notice shit."

"When did they kill the blow – the voprea?" Teagan asked.

"Only a few days after the orb brought you," Gormet replied.

Teagan turned to Wallace. "Do you remember them killing a blowcat?"

"Fuck, no."

"I don't remember either. If they weren't killing it for food or -"

"They killed it not for food or for its fur but…" Gormet hesitated and Rose cleared her throat.

"For sport?"

"What does sport mean?"

"It means they killed it because it was fun, they didn't have a reason to kill it, they just did it because they could."

"Yes, that is it," Gormet said.

"No," Teagan replied. "Garrett wouldn't do something like that. It must have been attacking them. They must have been defending themselves or -"

"They were not," Gormet replied. "Killing a voprea is an unforgiveable action. It is why we will not allow you to join us in safety behind the wall."

"What if we left Patrick – the one who killed the voprea – behind?" Duncan asked.

"Hey," Teagan said. "Shut your mouth, Duncan."

Duncan ignored him. "Would you allow us to stay with you?"

"We're not leaving Patrick alone to die," Wallace said. "I get that he's a first-class asshole, but if we abandon him, he will fucking die. You want that on your conscious?"

"He is insane, Wallace. You know that."

"I don't give a shit," Wallace said. "We don't leave a man behind. Right, Teag?"

Teagan nodded before turning to Gormet. "We didn't know what the voprea meant to you. If we had, they would never have killed it. We're stronger together. Let us live with you. We'll help you hunt, protect you from the pinkies. We can be an asset to you, Gormet."

Gormet sucked on his pipe. "We do not need your help, big one. We have survived the elidas for nearly a hundred years and will continue to do so long after your bodies return to the dirt and your spirit travels beyond the great gates."

"A hundred years?" Wallace said. "How old are the fucking pinkies?"

"The stories of our old ones tell us the elida were brought by the orb over a century ago. They do not age and, until him," Gormet pointed at Vida, "we believed they could not die. Now we know differently."

"Did your people come from the orb?" Duncan asked.

Gormet shook his head. "No. Although a few of our people have chosen to leave in the orb."

"On purpose?" Wallace asked.

"Yes."

"But, how do you know if it's an orb that sucks you in or spits something out?" Teagan asked.

Gormet pointed to the sky. "When the storm comes from the east, the orb takes. When the storm comes from the west, the orb gives."

Wallace's mouth dropped open. Are you kidding me? Are we seriously that fucking stupid, Teag?"

"Apparently we are," Teagan said. "What happened to the

people who lived in the huts before us? Do you know? Were they people like us?"

Gormet shook his head. "No. Many years ago, a few of our people chose to live beyond the wall. They did not survive long. Much like most of those who come through the orb. You and your people have survived the longest. But, your luck will run out. Your flowers grow for now, but soon they will wilt and die."

They sat in silence for a few minutes. Rose stretched gingerly and Vida pressed a kiss against her forehead. Gormet was sucking contently on his pipe and he studied Teagan when the big man leaned forward again.

"What can we do to change your mind about letting us – all of us - live with you behind the wall?"

"Nothing," Gormet said. "The killing of the voprea cannot be undone."

"But she tried to save a voprea," Teagan pointed to Rose, "doesn't that count for something?"

Gormet nodded. "You are right. The small one and her mate will be allowed to live behind the wall. Now," he gestured behind him where women were carrying platters of meat and fruit toward them, "let us celebrate the death of the elida and the gift of the baby voprea."

IN HER DREAM, SHE WAS BACK IN VIDA'S BED IN THE CAVE. She was naked, and Vida was on top of her, his big body between her thighs and his warm mouth sucking on her nipples. She moaned and arched, rubbing her aching pussy against his dick as he licked and teased and tormented.

"Please," she whispered, "please, I need you, Vida."

"I know, small flower." His low voice sent goosebumps across her skin. "You will have what you need."

The head of his cock pressed against her opening and she spread her legs wide. She felt no fear, only need and want and an aching emptiness only Vida could fill.

"You are mine, Rose," Vida whispered into her ear as he surged forward, filling every inch of her pussy with his hard cock. "Mine."

"Yes," she moaned. "Yours. Please, I want more. I want -"

She woke with a start, scratching absentmindedly at the paste on her shoulder. The moonlight was streaming through the cracks in the hut and she could feel the solid warmth of Vida against her back.

They hadn't spent much time sitting around the fire with the islanders. They seemed nice enough but not speaking the language made things awkward. Not to mention, she was feeling weird about the fact that she and Vida were invited to live with the locals, but the rest of the group was not.

She and Vida were given a hut to themselves. It was on the small side with just a big plush bed of furs. She supposed it would have been the perfect time to try and seduce Vida, especially since he had stripped her naked before taking off his own clothes and climbing into the furs with her, but she was exhausted and embarrassingly weepy.

She didn't want to cry in front of Vida but couldn't seem to help it. Watching both Peter and Brian die in front of her, nearly dying herself, had finally caught up to her, and she had wept hot tears despite her effort not to cry. Vida hadn't seemed to mind. He had held her close, rubbing her lower back and rocking her gently until she'd cried herself to sleep.

She lay quietly, wondering how long she'd been sleeping. She assumed at least five or six hours. She didn't feel as tired and there were no sounds of the locals still gathered around the main fire.

She leaned back against Vida. His big hand was cupping her breast and her eyes widened when she felt his dick pressing against her ass. He was asleep, she could tell by his breathing, but he was also half-hard. Warmth flushed her skin and just like that she was horny.

Crude, Rose.

Maybe, but entirely accurate. She wanted Vida so much, it made her stomach ache. She thought about what Brody had said about middle-of-the-night sex and rubbed her ass against Vida's cock. He hardened some more, his hand tightening on her breast before loosening. He muttered something in his sleep before turning on his back. She studied his face in the dim light, touching his warm chest and the hard muscles of his abdomen before pushing down the furs. He was fully erect now and her pussy tightened and then released an embarrassing amount of wetness.

Fuck, she wanted him, and she was already wet enough to take him.

She straddled him and leaned down to kiss his chest, rubbing her wet pussy back and forth against his cock. The head of him pressed against her clit and she moaned softly before sucking on one flat nipple. Vida groaned, his big hands cupping her hips. He gave her a sleepy look of confusion as she kissed his chest again.

"Little flower? What are you…"

He groaned again when she reached down and stroked his dick. He thrust into her hand, nearly knocking her off of him. She squeezed her knees around his hips as Vida made another low moan, his eyelids drifting shut.

"Does that feel good, Vida?"

"Yes," he muttered. "Do not stop, flower."

She kissed his chest, nipped at his collarbone and sucked on his earlobe. "I want you."

"I want you too." One big hand squeezed her naked ass.

Deciding it was now or never, she crouched over him, holding his cock at the base and pressing the head against her opening. She was soaking wet and Vida groaned, his hips rising when the head of him breached her.

She moaned and pushed down, taking more of his cock. She already felt stretched and full, but she braced her hands on his chest and rose up a little on her knees before pressing down again.

Vida made another low groan as she took a few more inches. His eyes suddenly popped open and she saw a hint of panic in them. "What are you doing?"

"Fucking you," she panted before pushing again. "Oh God, oh that feels…"

"You must stop, small flower," Vida said.

"Are you kidding me? No way." She grinned at him and rocked back and forth a little. "This feels amazing."

"Rose, you must. I do not wish to hurt you."

"You won't." She decided that Vida not actually stopping her himself was a good sign. "Please, Vida. I want this. Besides," she pushed again, and Vida's eyes widened when she took the last of his cock, "you make me so wet, I'm taking your cock like a champ."

She giggled at the look on his face. "See, told you so."

He didn't reply, and she gave him a look of concern. "Vida? Are you all right?"

"So tight," he muttered. "So wet and tight."

"Do you like it?" She braced her hands on his chest again and rode him with slow, smooth strokes.

"Very much, little flower. Move faster."

She did what he asked, rocking her small body against his

larger one. When he cupped her waist and helped her move even faster, she didn't object. She clung to his shoulders for balance, watching his face as he pumped in and out of her. He cupped her breasts, kneading them and caressing them before teasing her nipples.

"Touch yourself."

She did what he asked, reaching down to rub her clit as he thrust back and forth. One big hand held her around the waist as the other touched her breasts and she gasped when warmth rocketed through her body.

"Oh, oh God, that's so good." She rubbed her clit harder, staring at Vida as he watched her fingers rub at her swollen nub.

"Come for me, sweet flower," he suddenly demanded.

She threw back her head and rubbed her clit with short and furious strokes. Her orgasm washed over her in a sweet rush of pleasure and she squeezed Vida's waist with her knees as she came all over his cock.

He cried out at the increased pressure, his hips rising and falling as he pumped himself into her over and over. She leaned over and clung to him, burying her face in his thick throat as he gripped her ass and thrust three more times before emptying his seed deep inside of her. He twitched and rocked in and out of her for a few more minutes before collapsing on the furs. She kissed his neck and he rubbed her back.

"Are you all right, Rose?"

"Yes," she said sleepily. "It was so good."

"For me as well."

She rolled off of him, smiling up at him when he gathered her into his embrace and pushed her sweaty hair back from her face. "I told you I could take all of you."

"You did." A small grin crossed his face. "My sweet flower surprised me."

"Now we can have sex all the time," she said with a sleepy sigh.

She closed her eyes and slipped into sleep, missing the troubled look that crossed Vida's face.

CHAPTER 13

"You should come back with us, Rose. The two of you are safer with us than on your own." Teagan said. "I know this cave feels safe, but it isn't. Not even with the flowers in front of the entrance. You need numbers to survive."

"They're safest behind the wall with the locals. Why did you leave with us this morning? They urged you to stay." Duncan traced the back of the couch.

"I'm not staying there without the rest of you," Rose said. "How do you think I'd feel knowing that I was safe behind that stupid wall while the rest of you aren't?"

"So instead you're going to go off and play house with a blue alien in a giant cave?" Teagan said.

"To be fair," Wallace was sitting at the island and leafing through a magazine from the bookshelf, "this place is nicer than what we've got. They got an actual bed."

"Fuck the bed. You can't survive on your own. I don't care if you have a cave with flowers in front of it and all the fucking goddamn comforts of home," Teagan said. "Sooner or later, the pinkies or something else on this godforsaken island will kill you."

"I won't leave Vida and he won't stay at your camp."

Teagan made a grunt of frustration and Vida said, "Your leader is mad. It is not safe to stay with him."

"We can handle Patrick," Teagan said. "Look, what Gormet said is true. We can't get the goddamn flowers to grow, and we need to figure out a way to convince him to let us stay behind the wall. It'll be impossible without you and Vida."

Rose glanced up at Vida. "When you try and convince him, let us know. Keep Patrick away from us and we'll go with you. But we're not going back to the camp. You know as well as I do that if Vida goes anywhere near Patrick, he'll try and force him to help him take over the locals' home. Vida won't do that and who knows what Patrick will do to him. He is crazy, Teagan. He has some kind of mental illness and -"

"He's not crazy!" Teagan shouted.

Vida pulled Rose behind him. "It is time for you to leave."

Teagan rubbed at his forehead. "And if I don't? Are you going to make me?"

"Teag." Wallace shook his head and Teagan muttered a curse.

"I'll fucking wait for you outside."

He left the cave and Wallace sighed. "Teag's a good man."

"I know he is," Rose said.

"It's just... you know how Brian saved my life in Mosul? Well, Patrick saved Teagan's. It was bad, he almost died trying to save Teag. Teagan thinks he owes him now and they're friends. At least they used to be before Garrett died and Patrick really went fucking nutso. Teagan doesn't want to think the worst about Patrick because he owes him his life."

"His loyalty to Patrick is going to get him killed," Rose said.

"Patrick might be crazy, but he won't hurt one of his own. We take care of each other, Rose," Wallace said.

Rose didn't reply, and Wallace shut the magazine before sliding off the stool. "I guess this is goodbye. See you crazy kids around the island."

"Be careful, Wallace. You too, Duncan."

"We always are, ain't that right, Duncan?"

Duncan nodded, and Wallace rubbed at his forehead. "If you change your mind, you know where to find us."

"Okay. Don't tell Patrick about this place, all right?"

"We won't."

"Will Teagan?"

Wallace shook his head. "No. He doesn't want to admit it, but he knows what you're saying about Vida is right."

He and Duncan left the cave and Rose made a shuddering sigh before leaning against Vida. He squeezed her hip. "Are you all right?"

She nodded. "Yeah, I think so. Just worried about the others."

"Your former mate?"

She wondered if that was jealousy in his voice. "No. I don't care about Solomon. He and Marissa can have each other. I'm worried about Brody and Randy and the SEALs. They won't survive much longer if we don't figure out a way to convince the locals to let them behind the wall."

She smiled up at him. "At least I have you. I don't know what I'd do without you on this island, Vida." A look that she didn't understand crossed his face. "What? What did I say?"

"Nothing. Come, small flower, we will have a bath and then something to eat."

She followed him to the bathing chamber and they both stripped off their clothes and eased into the hot water. Vida washed away the paste from her shoulder. "The wounds look good."

"Not infected?"

He shook his head and she picked up a chunk of soap and scrubbed her hair and body clean as Vida did the same. She smiled at him when they were finished and leaned against the side of the pool, shifting a little when the dull point of a rock pressed against a puncture wound.

"This is nice." She let her legs drift out in front of her as Vida moved to sit beside her. "Don't you think?"

"Yes." He was acting quiet and strange and she touched his arm. "What's wrong?"

"Nothing." He leaned down and pressed a kiss against her mouth. She returned his kiss, parting her lips and sucking on his tongue when he pushed it into her mouth. After a moment, she pulled away and smiled at him. "We don't have to kiss, Vida. I know it's not your thing."

"I want to kiss you," he said. "It is extremely pleasant for me."

"Are you sure?"

He nodded and kissed her again, one big hand cupping her breast as he explored her mouth with long, slow strokes of his tongue. She squeezed her legs together and ran her hands over his broad chest and shoulders before trying to straddle him.

"Wait," he said.

She blushed. "I'm sorry."

"Do not be. I just wish to taste my flower's pussy before I fuck it."

She licked her lips. "I am all for that. C'mon."

She started to climb out of the pool and he pulled her back in. "Where are you going?"

"To the bed?" She gave him a confused look.

He grinned at her. "There is no need." He submerged himself in the water and Rose's eyes widened when she felt his tongue trace along her flat stomach and lick around her belly button.

"Oh God." She spread her legs wide as Vida pushed his large body between them. He slid his hands under her ass, holding her tight as he lifted her. It was too dark in the cave for her to see him under the water, and she cried out when his mouth pressed against her pussy. His tongue licked her clit and she reached under water and clutched his head, rubbing her pussy against his mouth as he licked and sucked. He took his time, his strong hands kneading her ass as he licked her from her opening to her clit. He straightened his tongue and pushed it inside of her before licking his way to her clit again. He sucked on it and when his fangs scraped across the sensitive bundle of nerves, her cries grew more frantic and she stiffened all over before coming with a soft shriek. The sound echoed in the chamber and she rocked back and forth against Vida's face before collapsing against the rock.

He rose out of the water, water dripping down his chiseled body. His cock was huge, and a shiver of lust went through her despite her recent orgasm. He bent and picked her up before stepping out of the pool and walking back to the main chamber.

"Oh my God," she said. "There are definite benefits to you being able to breathe under water."

He laughed, and she nuzzled his neck affectionately. Their bodies steamed in the cool air of the cave and he dried them both with a towel before pulling back the covers on the bed.

She climbed in and spread her legs, smiling up at him as he pushed his large body between her thighs.

"Would you prefer to be on top, little flower?"

"No."

"Are you certain? You can be in control and -"

"No," she repeated. "I want you on top, Vida. I'm not worried."

"I will not hurt you."

"I know."

He kissed her again, long slow ones that made her feel almost drugged with desire. When she was with Vida, it was so easy to forget that she was on a new world and that every day there was the real possibility of dying. He made her feel safe, made her believe that everything would be all right as long as they were together.

Vida bent his head and trailed a path of kisses along her upper chest before kissing the tip of her right nipple. "You are beautiful, flower."

"Thank you," she whispered.

He kissed around her nipple and she moaned when he nipped at the fullness of her breast with his fangs. He tasted her soft skin before finally sucking on her nipple. She buried her hands in his hair and arched her back. He switched from nipple to nipple, licking and sucking until her pussy was aching and it was like she'd never had an orgasm.

She rubbed her pussy against his hard thigh and made a pleading moan. He licked her nipple and smiled up at her. "Does my small flower wish to be fucked again?"

"Yes," she whispered.

He reached down and rubbed her thigh before cupping it and spreading her legs wide. She braced her feet on the bed as he propped himself above her and guided his cock to her warmth. He paused and gave her a grave look

"I will not hurt you. If you need me to stop, just say so."

"I know." There was frustration in her voice. "We've had sex before, Vida, it's fine."

He leaned down and gave her a surprisingly sweet kiss before pushing the head of his cock into her. He took his time, pushing and retreating while he watched her face. She smiled encouragingly at him and raised her hips to meet each of his gentle thrusts until he was fully sheathed.

She touched his face and he turned his head and kissed the palm of her hand. "All right?"

"Yes, it feels good."

"You feel good, flower," he groaned. "Your little pussy is so tight around my cock."

He dipped his head and kissed her again. For a race who didn't enjoy kissing, he sure kissed her a lot. That pleased her more than it probably should have.

He continued to stare at her as he pushed in and out in a slow and steady rhythm. She had a feeling he was holding back, going slower and being gentler than he normally would. But when she tried to urge him to move faster with soft moans and thrusts of her hips, he ignored her. He kept himself propped up with one hand above her and reached down to cup her ass. He lifted her, shifted her slightly and made a slow thrust that brought on an unexpected flash of pleasure.

She gasped, her nails digging into his biceps as he smiled at her. "Did you like that?"

"Yeah," she moaned. "Do it again."

He gripped her ass and thrust and retreated, each stroke driving her need for him higher. Tension and pleasure coiled in her belly and she met each of his thrusts with a hard pump of her hips. She wanted – no, needed – more.

"Please, Vida," she moaned. "I need…"

"What do you need?"

"I don't know," she cried out. "Please!"

He moved a bit faster, sliding in nice and deep and making her moan with relief. "Good, that's so good."

She clung to him, burying her face into his broad chest as he pushed her closer and closer to her climax. When he dipped his head and nipped her throat with his sharp fangs, she cried his name and her slender body stiffened beneath his large one. He lifted his head and watched her intently, thrusting in a steady rhythm in and out of her soft body, as she climaxed around his cock.

He found his own release as the last of her climax pulsed through her. He threw his head back, the cords in his neck standing out as he thrust deep and stayed there. Wetness flooded her pussy. She kissed his chest and squeezed her legs around his hips as he pumped back and forth before pulling out of her and collapsing on his back next to her.

She turned and flung her leg over one muscular thigh. He put his arm around her and stroked her hair as she rested her head on his chest. "That was really good."

"Yes," Vida replied. "I enjoy having sex with you. It is surprising to me that your pussy can take all of my cock, but it is a very pleasant surprise."

She stifled her giggle. She was still getting used to Vida's blunt way of talking. "I enjoyed it too, Vida."

They lay silently for a while before she sat up. "I'm going to get a drink of water. Would you like one?"

He nodded. She climbed out of bed and crossed naked to the kitchen area. She knew Vida was watching her, but she didn't feel self-conscious. Of course, she wasn't sure if that was because the candlelight made everything look better, or because he made her feel beautiful. Maybe it was a little of both.

She returned to the bed with the water and handed him his glass before sliding in beside him. They propped their backs against the headboard and drank their water.

"Are you hungry? It's probably getting close to lunch."

He shook his head. He seemed off to her again, a little moody and closed-off, and she chewed her bottom lip. She hadn't even asked Vida if he wanted to stay with the locals. Maybe he was pissed that she just assumed he'd want to return to the cave.

"Hey, Vida?"

"Yes?"

"Did you want to stay with the locals? I just realized it was rude of me to assume that you would be fine coming back here to the cave."

"I do not wish to stay with them." He set his empty glass on the nightstand next to the bed.

"Okay." She slid a little closer, secretly thrilled when he put his arm around her. "I'm glad. I know there is safety in numbers on this world, but I feel safest when I'm with you."

Another strange look crossed Vida's face and she rubbed his flat stomach. "What's wrong?"

"I am not staying on this world, small flower."

She sat up and drew the sheet up around her naked body. "What do you mean?"

"When there is another orb that takes, I will leave this world in search of my own." Vida studied his hands in the flickering candlelight.

Dismay flooded through her body and she grabbed his hand, squeezing it tightly. "Vida, the odds of it taking you back to your world are astronomically small. Do you understand? There are many worlds and -"

"I know, but I must try."

"But," she squeezed his hand again until he looked at her, "what if you're taken to another world that was like mine? One where they capture you and study you like a bug under a glass. Or what if you land on a desert world? You'll die, Vida."

He didn't reply and feeling an odd sort of panic, she said, "This world is similar to yours, right? You have all the water you need to survive, and people don't care that you're blue or can breathe under water. If you land on another world, they may kill you just for looking different from them. Why risk death to find your own world when the chances of finding it are almost zero percent?"

"I wish to see my world again, flower. To walk the shoreline along my home, to swim in our vast oceans, and to see the sun rise over the Bluff of Vencona."

She swallowed down her rising panic. "Do you have family who are still alive?"

He shook his head. "Both my parents would be dead by now, and I had no siblings. But I had friends and even after all of these years, my desire to return home has not dimmed."

"I understand," she said in a low voice, "believe me I do. I haven't been through what you've been, but I understand being homesick. But, you won't find your world again, Vida."

"You do not know that for certain, little human."

She sighed. "No, I suppose I don't. But the thought of you leaving, of you being alone on a new world where they might-might hurt you or kill you…"

"You could come with me."

Her mouth dropped, and she stared up at him. "What?"

"You could leave this place with me. You would like my world, I promise."

"We won't make it to your world, Vida."

"We might."

She tamped down her frustration at his stubbornness. She was feeling sick to her stomach over the thought of Vida leaving her and the panic in her stomach was steadily chewing its way up her esophagus. "We're safe here."

He gave her a wry look and she sighed. "I know that sounds ridiculous considering I've almost died a few times, but we know the dangers of this world now and how to avoid them. The idea of hopping from world to world, of never knowing what kind of danger we could be in – it doesn't appeal to me, Vida. I'm not adventurous or a risk taker, and I know in my heart that trying to find your world again is a fool's mission."

"You will not go with me then?"

"I'm sorry. I can't, and I wish you wouldn't go either. Please, Vida, I want you to stay here where I know you're safe."

"I cannot, flower."

Stupidly, she could feel tears threatening and she blinked them back rapidly as Vida studied her. It was dumb to cry over Vida leaving. Having sex a couple of times didn't mean they were in a relationship, and just because she was already unnaturally attached to the big blue guy, didn't mean he felt the same about her. Really, she was kind of an idiot for even thinking he felt something more for her than lust.

No, you're not. He acts like you're his mate. You know he does.

She studied the quilt on the bed as Vida continued to study her. He did, but maybe that was just what his kind did when they were sleeping together. She really didn't know that much about him, if she was being honest.

"Rose?" Vida put one finger under her chin and tipped her head up before studying her face. "I am sorry, but I cannot stay. Not even for my sweet flower."

Now the stupid tears did come, and she wiped them away quickly before smiling at him. "Yeah, I know. I'm sorry, I don't mean to make you feel bad."

"Will you take some time and think about coming with me?"

She smiled a little. "I was just going to ask you to think about staying with me. I guess we're at an impasse, huh?"

"When I leave, promise me you will stay with the locals behind their wall of flowers instead of with your friend and the others. You will be safest there."

She didn't want to stay with the locals, she didn't want to stay with Brody and the SEALs. She wanted to be with Vida. But, that wasn't what he wanted, and she wouldn't force him to stay. Not after he spent twenty-five years being held prisoner on a strange world.

His hand cupped her chin. "Promise me."

"If I can convince them to let Brody and the others stay there too, I'll stay with them," she said.

He scowled at her but before he could argue, she said, "I won't live safe behind that wall, while the others fight for survival. Don't ask me to do that."

"You will not survive without me here to protect you," he said. "You are too little and weak."

She shrugged. "I'll get you to teach me some survival skills. Hopefully another orb won't come before I know how to protect myself."

Secretly, she hoped an orb would never come, and then berated herself for her selfishness. Vida wanted to go home and as much as she hated the idea, she wouldn't try and stop him or change his mind. She wasn't his girlfriend or his mate, and she had no right to ask him to give up his world for her.

"Human, you need to stay with the locals. You can't -"

"Stop, Vida. You've made your choice and I've made

mine. I'll be fine. I'm tougher than I look." She flexed her biceps and wiggled her eyebrows at him, but he didn't smile. "Will you teach me some survival skills?"

He nodded but there was still a troubled look on his face. "Yes, little flower, I will."

CHAPTER 14

"Teagan, man, we need to do something. He's getting worse."

"Be quiet, Davis." Teagan checked over his shoulder. They weren't close to Patrick's hut, but sound had a way of carrying in the jungle.

"Davis is right." Wallace sat next to Teagan. "It's been a week since we got back and he's getting worse by the day. Fuck, by the hour."

"What do you suggest we do?" Tegan said. "Patrick is in charge and -"

"We're in the middle of the goddamn jungle. Is the chain of command in our unit something we really need to uphold? Especially when our leader has lost his fucking mind?" Davis asked. "I think it's time we faced the truth and did something. You should be in charge and we all know it. We'll back you if -"

"You're talking about mutiny," Teagan said.

Davis glanced at Wallace and Teagan shook his head. "Seriously, Wallace? You want to start a fucking mutiny?"

"I don't *want* to, but I don't think we have much choice.

You know as well as I do that Patrick isn't fit to lead. Yesterday, he asked me again to tell me what happened with the locals and to tell him where Vida and Rose were staying. I refused, and he threatened to cut off my fucking ears."

Teagan stared at him and Wallace nodded. "Duncan was sitting across from us when he said it. Ask him if you don't believe me."

"I believe you." Teagan scrubbed a hand through his dark hair. "Did you tell him?"

"Of course I didn't. He tried to play it off as a joke, but it wasn't a fucking joke. He's desperate to get us behind that wall and listen, man, he ain't wrong about us needing to be there, but the way he wants to do it is gonna get us all killed. Without Vida and Rose, we don't stand a chance at -"

"Shut up," Davis said.

Wallace shut his mouth with a snap as Patrick, followed by Talla, strolled out of his hut. He studied the three of them before whispering something in Talla's ear. She nodded and moved across the clearing to the table where fruit was piled. As she picked out fruit, Patrick joined them.

"What are you talking about?" He asked.

"The brinos," Teagan replied. "They came close to the camp last night."

"Too fucking close," Wallace said. "I could hear them breathing outside my goddamn hut. I think we need to do something about them. Teagan, Davis and I could dig a pit, lure one toward the pit with some meat. Once it's in there, we use our spears to -"

"Or, we could simply move behind the wall." Patrick studied Teagan for a moment. "Both Wallace and Duncan have refused to share intel on your mission last week. What about you, Teag? You care to share?"

"It wasn't a mission," Teagan said. "It was a hunt gone wrong. Brian died, remember?"

"I remember. Just proves my point that we should be living behind that wall. But you fuckers refuse to do your part."

"Patrick, it isn't -"

"Tell me what happened."

Teagan sighed. "We've told you numerous times, Patrick."

"Tell me again. Wait – let's get everyone out here to hear the story this time. What do you think? Talla, get the others."

Teagan watched as Talla went to each hut. It took only a few minutes for Solomon and Marissa, Doc and Brody, and Daryl and Randy to join them. He glanced up at the tree where Duncan was on watch. The man was watching him solemnly – he knew that Duncan could hear everything that was being said – and he nodded before glancing out into the jungle again.

"Looks like that's everyone." Patrick's voice was deceptively cheerful. "Other than that fat fairy fuck. Where is he anyway? Anyone seen him lately?"

He glanced around at the others. Doc shook his head. "I saw him yesterday at breakfast. Haven't seen him since."

Patrick rolled his eyes. "I'd assume he was dead, but that asshole has a fucking horseshoe up his ass. Teagan, you're up. Tell the others what you told me."

Teagan cleared his throat. "We made contact with the locals, the day that Brian and Peter died. After we saved Rose and the blowcat from the vines, the islanders surrounded us and took us behind the wall to their village. They think of the blowcat as some sort of god, so the fact that we saved one, made them a little more…open toward us."

"You're fucking kidding me." Brody leaned forward. "Why didn't you tell us this before?"

"Because they still won't let us live with them."

"Why not?" Randy asked.

Teagan glanced at Patrick. Fuck it. Patrick wanted them to know, he'd fucking tell them the truth. "Because when we first got to the island, Patrick and Garrett killed a blowcat for sport and the locals saw them do it."

The others glanced at Patrick who shrugged. "How were we to know they worshipped the striped fuckers? Tell them the other part."

Teagan stayed silent for a moment. Fuck, why had he told Patrick about the locals inviting Rose and Vida to stay with them. Wallace and Duncan had told him not to, but he'd wanted to prove something to them. Wanted to make them realize that Patrick was still a good guy.

He'd fucked up.

"Go on, Teag." Patrick's tone was mocking.

"Because Rose tried to save the blowcat and Vida killed the pinkie, the locals invited them to live behind the wall."

Brody released his breath in a harsh rush. "So, Rose is safe."

"She refused to stay without the rest of us."

"Jesus, Rose," Brody groaned. "But she's safe with Vida, right?"

"Who cares?" Marissa said. "That bitch got us all stuck on this island, who cares if she -"

"That bitch is the key to our survival." Patrick stroked Talla's long hair. "We need her and that blue idiot, to get behind the wall. Isn't that right, Teagan?"

"No," Teagan said. "It isn't right. Rose already tried to convince the locals to let all of us stay there. They refused."

"Maybe she needs to try again."

"They won't change their minds," Wallace said.

"Shut up, Wallace." Patrick didn't look at him. "Where in the jungle are Vida and Rose tucked away. Teagan?"

"I told you," Teagan stared steadily at Patrick, "we don't know. Vida wouldn't tell us or show us."

"Is that right?"

"Yes. Why would he? He's not stupid, Patrick. He knows what you want to use him for."

Patrick ran his hand over Talla's hair again. "That blue asshole don't know shit. But we need him to help us take the village."

"What do you mean, 'take the village'?" Solomon said.

"You know what I mean, mister science man. If we want to survive, if we want to," Patrick touched Talla's thigh, "bring new life to this godforsaken rock, we need to take their village. Our only chance against the pinkies and the other dickstick creatures, is the protection of that fucking wall. Our mission is to take it."

"It doesn't belong to us," Solomon said. "We can't just take it from them."

"Since when did you give a shit about anyone but yourself?" Randy asked.

"Shut up, Randy," Solomon said.

"Fuck you. You aren't my boss anymore," Randy replied.

"I've had just about enough of your fucking attitude. You think just because -"

"I don't need to listen to any of your shit anymore, Solomon. Keep your damn opinions to yourself about -"

"Like I fucking care. You were nothing but a shit lab tech and you're still -"

"Both of you shut the fuck up," Patrick snarled.

His hand rested on the butt of the Glock 19 tucked into

his waistband and Teagan frowned. Patrick didn't have any bullets, just like the rest of them.

Solomon turned on him, his usual pale face bright red with fury. "You know what, Patrick? I'm a little fucking tired of you telling me what to do. We're not your damn SEALs and if you think you can just -"

"I said, shut the fuck up." Patrick pulled out his gun and pointed it at Solomon before pulling the trigger.

The sound of the gunfire sent birds squawking from the trees and into the air in a colourful flight of blues and greens. Teagan, his ears ringing, stared blankly at Patrick.

"What the fuck?" Wallace said.

Solomon touched the black hole in the middle of his forehead before blinking slowly.

"Solomon? Baby?" Marissa whispered.

Blood poured from the hole in his forehead and he sank to his knees before collapsing on his face.

"Solomon?" Marissa whispered again.

Doc shook free of Brody's grip and ran toward Solomon. He flipped him over and pressed his fingers against Solomon's throat before staring at Teagan. "He's dead."

"He's what?" Marissa said. "He-he's what?"

"He's dead," Doc repeated. "I'm sorry."

"No," Marissa fell to her knees next to Solomon, "no, he can't be dead. Solomon, wake up, baby. Wake up right now."

She shook him roughly, his head lolled on his neck and already there was a large pool of blood on the ground beneath his head. Marissa began to cry, loud sobs that echoed throughout the jungle.

"Patrick," shock unfurled in Teagan's belly, "what did you just fucking do?"

Patrick shrugged and grabbed Talla's wrist when she started to back away. "Where you goin', sweetheart?"

She froze, giving him an uncertain look as Teagan stepped toward them. "Patrick, you just fucking killed an unarmed civilian."

"One less mouth to feed," Patrick said. "Now, let's talk about how we're gonna convince the blue alien to -"

"Where the fuck did you get the bullets?" Davis asked as Marissa's wails grew louder. "We ran out a week after we fucking got here."

"No, you ran out," Patrick had to raise his voice to be heard over Marissa's sobbing. "I was smart enough to tuck a mag aside just in case."

"Just in case?" Teagan said. "Just in fucking case? You got what, a full mag? That's fifteen fucking bullets we could have used to kill the pinkies. We could have set a trap for them, we could have lured them in and ended all of this in a matter of fucking minutes. We've spent two fucking years being hunted by those pink bastards when you had a full fucking mag we could have used against them. Instead you're using it to kill innocent civilians. What the fuck, Patrick? You've lost your fucking mind."

Before Patrick could reply, Marissa staggered to her feet and ran toward him. "You asshole! I'll kill you! I'll fucking -"

There was another sharp retort of gunfire and Marissa made a startled cry and stumbled to a stop. She stared at Patrick before crumpling to the ground, blood blooming on the front of her shirt.

Patrick lowered the gun as the others stared wide-eyed at him. Talla tore free of his grip and joined Brody who put his arm around her. Doc knelt next to Marissa. She was gasping harshly and she clutched at his hand with panicky tightness before dragging in one final breath. He felt for her pulse before shaking his head.

They stared silently at Patrick who shrugged. "What?"

"*What*?" Davis said. "Stop killing people, you fucking psycho."

Patrick pointed the gun at him. "You keep your fucking mouth shut, Davis." He glanced up at the tree where Duncan was watching him. "Get your ass down here, Duncan. Leave your sword up there."

He waited until Duncan had joined them before smiling at Teagan. "Tell me where the blue asshole and that little bitch are, Teag."

"Patrick, put the gun down. You're sick and you need help. We can help you, okay?" Teagan took a step toward him, stopping when Patrick pointed the gun at him.

"Shut up, and just tell me where they are."

"And if I don't?"

Patrick swung the gun toward Davis. "I'll kill him."

Davis curled his lip at him as Teagan shook his head. "No, you won't, Patrick. Killing civilians is one thing, but you won't kill one of your team."

"The mission comes first, then the team," Patrick said. "Tell me, Teagan."

"No. Taking over the locals' home is not the mission. You don't -"

"This is on you, Teag, not me," Patrick sighed before shooting Davis in the head.

His body hit the ground with a soft thump and there was a moment of shocked silence before Wallace, cursing non-stop, ran to Davis' body. He knelt beside him as Duncan and Doc joined him.

"You cocksucking motherfucker!" Wallace snarled as he stood. "I am going to fucking kill you."

He started toward Patrick, howling angrily when Duncan and Doc grabbed him and held him back. "Let me go, you assholes!" He shouted.

Patrick strode across the sand and pointed the gun at Wallace's temple. Wallace stilled, and Patrick grinned at Teagan. "Tell me or Wallace is dead."

"Don't you fucking tell him, Teag," Wallace growled.

"Do you want more blood on your hands, Teagan?" Patrick said. "Tell me or I blow Wallace's brains out."

"Go ahead and pull the trigger, you festering dick drip," Wallace sneered. "I'm fucking tired of sweating my nutsack off on this goddamn rock anyway. Keep your mouth shut, Teag."

"You got until the count of five." Patrick smiled at Teagan. "One...two...three...four...fi -"

"Wait! Just fucking wait a minute," Teagan said. "I'll tell you."

"Don't," Wallace said. "Keep your mouth -"

Teagan winced when Patrick slammed the butt of his gun across Wallace's face. He dropped to the ground, blood flying from his mouth, as Patrick stepped back and aimed the gun at his head. "Start talking, Teag."

"They have a cave, not far from the waterfall."

"Good," Patrick said. "Was that so hard? Now you're gonna tell me *exactly* where this cave is, and the redheaded faggot and I are going to take a little walk while the rest of you stay here. If you're fucking lying to me, Teag, I'll make you watch as I cut out Wallace's tongue. You get it?"

"I'm not lying."

"Good. Talla, get the rope from the supply hut."

Talla shook her head and clung to Brody's arm. Patrick rolled his eyes and pointed the gun at her. "Go, Talla. I don't want to hurt you, so don't make me."

Tears running down her cheeks, she backed toward the hut.

YAWNING HUGELY, ROSE SAT UP IN THE BED AND PUSHED HER hair back from her face. "Vida? You here?"

There was no answer and she collapsed on her back and stared at the ceiling of the cave. Her growling stomach made her think it was close to supper. Before Vida had taken her to bed, his skin was getting noticeably dry. She had drifted off after sex, no doubt he had gone to the waterfall for both a swim and to rehydrate.

For the last week, they'd gone to the waterfall only during times they were certain that the others wouldn't be there. Even at that, Vida would often boost her up into a tree and tell her to wait while he went ahead and checked the waterfall for anything dangerous. It made her sad that she had to consider the SEALs dangerous now, but they didn't have much choice. She stretched gingerly. Her thighs were aching a little and she moved them carefully.

Not just your thighs.

She blushed. No, not just her thighs. Her pussy ached too. She and Vida had had more sex in the last week then she thought was possible. Not that she was complaining. Despite her soreness, she wanted Vida with a deep-seated lust that was almost embarrassing. She'd never had such satisfying sex in her entire life, and she couldn't get enough of the things Vida did to her.

Yeah, well, maybe you should consider calling an end to the non-stop sex and start learning those survival skills you talked about. You think I don't know what you're doing? Do you honestly believe that if you give Vida lots of sex, you'll change his mind about staying here with you? He had loads of sex on that last world and he didn't stay. You're getting better in bed, thanks to him, but you're not going to convince

234

him to stay with sex. He's leaving as soon as the next orb arrives.

She curled on her side and stared at the flickering candle-light. Her inner voice was right, but the temptation to just ignore it and keep pretending that Vida would always be here with her, was incredibly strong. It wasn't just because of the sex either. She had a very bad feeling she was starting to care about Vida for more reasons than just a supernatural ability to make her come repeatedly.

Starting to? Oh, honey, that train left the station days ago. You're in love with the guy.

She slid out of bed, this time definitely ignoring her inner voice. She wasn't in love with Vida. She hadn't known him for long enough to be in love with him. A person didn't just fall in love with someone that quickly and if they did – there was something wrong with them and they needed psychological help.

Then get your ass to the nuthouse ASAP, because you're crazier than a fucking bedbug, sweetheart. You love Vida and the thought of never seeing him again makes you sick to your stomach.

Yeah, it did. She grabbed the robe that was on the end of the bed and threw it on before marching toward the bathing chamber. Vida was leaving. She needed to get that through her thick skull. She could have sex with him eight times a day and it wouldn't be enough.

Vida was leaving.

ROSE RETURNED TO THE MAIN CAVE FROM THE BATHING chamber, towel-drying her hair as she crossed toward the dresser. She and Vida had done laundry yesterday and while

Freida's clothes were a bit big for her, it was better than having nothing but one shirt and one pair of pants to wear for the rest of her –

"Hello, Rose."

Her blood turned cold and she dropped the towel, clutching her robe closed as she stared at Patrick. He was standing next to the couch, holding a gun to Brody's head and smiling at her. "Miss me?"

"How did you find this place?"

He grinned at her. "Your friends betrayed you."

"No, they didn't," Brody said. "They didn't, Rose."

"Shut up, faggot," Patrick said. "Where's the blue dickhead?"

"He's gone," Rose said. "He won't be back until later tonight."

"I don't believe you, but unless he comes back in the next five minutes, it doesn't really matter. Let's go, sweetheart."

"Where?"

"Back to the camp of course."

"I'm not going with you."

He pushed the gun against Brody's temple and Brody made a low moan of fear. "I'll kill him if you don't."

"You don't have any bullets in that gun."

"That's where you're wrong, Rosie-girl."

"I don't believe you," she said.

"Maybe you should ask your douchebag ex-fiance and his whore if there are any bullets in this gun. Oh wait, you can't. Because I fucking shot them and they're dead."

"W-what?" Rose's mouth dropped open. "Brody, they're dead?"

He nodded. "Yeah. He killed Davis as well. He's got bullets, Rosie."

"I sure do," Patrick said with a small grin. "You've got

236

two minutes to get dressed or Doc's new boyfriend's brains will be splattered across your cozy little love nest."

"WHAT EXACTLY IS YOUR PLAN, PATRICK?" ROSE ASKED. SHE held Brody's hand in a tight grip and glanced behind her at the Navy SEAL. "I tried to convince the locals to let all of us live with them. They won't and that's your fault."

Patrick shrugged. "That's where your blue boyfriend comes in. Once he realizes that I'll kill you if he doesn't help me, he'll be more than willing to help me take their village."

"There's too many of them. Even with Vida's help, you won't take their village," Rose said.

"We'll see."

She chewed on her bottom lip. "Vida doesn't care about me the way you think he does. He won't help you even if you use me as a bargaining chip."

Patrick snorted, and she glared at him. "It's true. He's planning on leaving the island the next time an orb shows up. I'm not invited to go with him. The only thing he wants me for is sex."

"You'd better hope not," Patrick said, "or you're useless to me, sweetheart. And I've got a new policy on what I do with useless people. Just ask Solomon and Marissa."

He laughed and the genuine amusement in it chilled her to the bone. She squeezed Brody's hand and he gave her a sick look before squeezing back. "It'll be okay, Rosie."

She nodded. Vida hadn't really been teaching her survival skills yet, but he had begun to teach her how to find her way around the damn jungle. She was pretty certain they were close to the waterfall. If they could somehow get away from Patrick, they could run to the waterfall. Vida would be there.

He's got a gun, Rose. How are you going to get away from him?

She had no idea, but there had to be something. Some way to –

"What the fuck is that?" Brody said.

He was staring to his left and when Patrick took a step closer and peered into the jungle, Brody dropped Rose's hand. She glanced at him, her stomach dropping at the look on his face.

She shook her head frantically, but it was too late. As Patrick made a grunt of annoyance and reached out to cuff Brody on the back of the head, the redhead turned and tackled the larger man.

"Brody!" Rose screamed as he wrestled for the gun. Patrick headbutted him and Brody howled in pain but held grimly to the gun.

Rose grabbed a baseball-sized rock and ran toward the wrestling, cursing men. The gun went off and something whistled by her ear, so close it made her hair move. Her eyes widened, and she turned to see the bullet embedded in the tree behind her. She kept moving forward, but before she could try and brain Patrick with the rock, the gun went off with another loud bang. Brody staggered back.

"Rose?" She could barely hear him over the ringing in her ears. "I – my leg."

She stared down at his leg, the blood pouring from it made her stomach drop, and she grabbed on to him as he fell. He dragged her to the ground and she pressed her hand over the wound in his thigh.

"Hold on, Brody. You'll be fine. We'll get you to Doc and you'll be just fine."

"Yeah," he muttered. "Fine."

"Actually," Patrick took a couple of steps toward them

238

and grinned. "You're already dead, you just don't know it yet."

He pointed the gun at Brody and Rose threw herself in front of him. "Patrick, don't! Please. Just let me put on a tourniquet and get him back to Doc. Please, Patrick. He doesn't have to die. Give me the chance to…"

Patrick's head cocked, and he turned around just as the brino came lumbering out of the jungle behind him.

"Fuck!" He fired the gun twice at the massive beast, hitting it in the chest and abdomen. The beast didn't slow, just roared angrily and slammed into him, knocking him into a tree.

"Brody! Get up!" Rose muttered into the redhead's ear before standing and putting her arms around his waist. "Up. Now."

He groaned but climbed to his feet. She ducked under his arm and threw her arm around his waist as the brino roared again. He wasn't paying attention to them. Instead, his beady black eyes were trained on Patrick who was staggering to his feet and wiping away the blood dripping into his eyes from the cut over his forehead.

As the brino charged toward Patrick, Rose turned and half-dragged Brody toward the waterfalls. Groaning and panting, he hobbled and hopped along beside her as Patrick screamed in pain and the brino made a third roar. There were three more shots, each one ringing across the jungle. Rose dragged Brody to his feet when he stumbled and fell.

They ran, wobbled, weaved their way toward the waterfall. Rose cried out when Brody fell again and shook his head when she tried to heave him to his feet.

"No, can't do it. Go without me, Rosie."

"No fucking way," Rose puffed. She pulled off her shirt, wrapped it around Brody's leg just above the gunshot wound, and tied it in a tight knot. The blood flowing from his leg began to slow and Rose breathed a sigh of relief.

"Go, Rosie," Brody groaned again.

"No. It's bleeding but I don't think it hit your femoral artery which means you're going to be just fine as soon as I get you to Doc. But we need to get to the waterfall. Vida will be there and he'll help us. Okay?"

"Maybe the brino killed Patrick. Think we could be that lucky?"

"Maybe," Rose said. "But either way, we need to get to the waterfall. C'mon, you can do it. I know you -"

The hair on the back of her neck stood when they heard Patrick's laughter.

"Fuck," Brody groaned under his breath. "That asshole's still alive."

"Rooo-sieeee. Come out, come out wherever you are."

The high-pitched madness in Patrick's voice sent fresh adrenaline skittering through her.

"Goddammit, Brody, get the fuck up now!" She said in a harsh whisper.

"I can't," Brody said. "I'm sorry. I can't fucking walk on it. It hurts too much, and I'll just slow you down. Go."

She looked around in desperation before standing and moving behind Brody. She hooked her hands under his armpits and ignoring his groan of pain, dragged him back toward a large bush. Ignoring the mosquitos buzzing in her ears, she pulled and heaved on him until he was half under the bush.

"Wiggle back," she whispered as she moved around him. She pushed on his good leg, helping him to slide under the bush under he was completely hidden.

"Rooooo-sieeeee. Where are you, sweetheart? You know I can follow the trail of blood from your faggot friend, right?"

Fuck, he was close.

"Stay there," she whispered to Brody. "I'm going to draw him away."

"Rosie, no! Don't!"

She ignored Brody and stepped away from the bush. She put her hands around her mouth and hollered. "Fuck you, you chickenshit asshole! You're a disgrace to the fucking SEALs, you know that? Letting a woman get the fucking best of you."

Patrick bellowed in pure fury and she turned and darted away just as he came limping into view and covered in blood. "I'm gonna hurt you so bad for that, you fucking cunt!"

"You'll have to catch me first, asshole!" She shouted before running full speed for the waterfall. She ran for her life, arms pumping at her sides and her head up. Patrick was in good shape, but the blood on him suggested he'd been injured, and she steadily pulled away from him.

She burst out of the jungle and scanned the waterfall frantically. Vida was nowhere in sight and her heart, already thumping like a frightened rabbit, cranked up another notch. Fuck, what did she do now?

She caught a flash of blue in the pool and her eyes widened. "Vida!" If he was underwater, he wouldn't have heard the gunshots or her screaming. She ran into the water, searching it desperately as she waded further in.

"Vida!" She screamed. "Vida, help me!"

She was almost to the spot where she'd seen the blue. The water was chest deep now and she was close to the drop off. She surged forward, already the coldness of the water was turning her lips blue and making her body shake, and reached under the water. "Vida, are you – shit!"

Her hands pulled up some blue coloured weeds and she tossed them aside before screaming in fear and frustration.

"Rose, what's a pretty girl like you doing on an island like this?"

She turned, her lungs freezing up and her pulse pounding, before she dragged in a lungful of oxygen.

Patrick was standing at the edge of the water and smiling at her. "Not a smart move going into the water, sweetheart. You know I'm a SEAL right?"

"Come in and get me then," she spat at him.

He shook his head and blood flew from the cut on his forehead. "Wish I could, Rose, but that brino did a real number on me. Might have even broken some ribs, if I'm being truthful. Lucky for you, huh? You would never have made it this far, if it hadn't."

Rosie didn't reply, and he raised the gun and aimed it at her. "Come out of the water. I don't want to kill you, but I will."

"No, you won't," she said, but backed up anyway. "You need me."

He shrugged. "You're not wrong. But if you don't come out, I will come in, broken ribs and all."

She shuffled back until the water was at her chin and Patrick gave her a sharp look. "Stop moving, Rose. You're close to the drop off and I know you can't swim. The last thing I fucking need is you drowning. Come out of the pool and I promise you won't be hurt."

"F-fuck you."

He laughed. "Such spirit. I can wait here all day, sweetheart, if I have to. How much longer do you think you'll survive in that cold of water. Hmm?"

"V-vida will rescue me."

"Maybe. Or maybe he won't get here in time." Patrick waded into the pool until the water was at his knees. He continued to aim the gun at her as his other hand pressed against his ribs. "Get your ass over here now."

She shook her head and he sighed and walked toward her. "Fine, we'll do this the fucking hard way."

"St-stay away from me!" She glanced behind her, panic clawing at her insides. She could tread water thanks to Vida, but even if she went past the drop off and even if she managed to not panic and keep her head above the water, Patrick would just swim out to her.

"You should know that I'm very displeased with your inability to cooperate." Patrick moved forward relentlessly, despite his injuries. "We'll need to have a very long talk about – Rose! Goddammit!"

He watched in dismay as Rose took another step back, her arms flailed wildly, and she made a strangled cry before she disappeared under the water.

CHAPTER 15

Teagan blinked rapidly as sweat dripped into his eye. It stung like a bitch and he blinked again before studying Wallace on his left. "You okay?"

Wallace nodded. It had been almost an hour since Patrick had left with Brody, and Wallace was looking like shit. His lip was bruised and swollen, and Teagan could see a dark bruise beginning underneath the dark shadow of stubble. "I'll live. He fucking killed Davis, man."

"Yeah, I know. It's my fault."

"It's not your fault." Randy was on his right. Like the rest of them, his hands were bound behind his back. Patrick had bound each of them with rope and then shoved them to the ground in a neat row and tied the five of them together with a second piece of rope. That rope was tied around one of the four wooden supports in the hut. Randy tried to shift positions and winced. "Shit, I think he dislocated my damn shoulder when he tied me up."

"Seriously?" Wallace said.

Randy shook his head. "Nah, I'm just a wimp when it comes to pain."

Wallace turned back to Teagan. "He's right. It isn't your fault."

"It is. I knew Patrick was losing it, but I didn't want to admit it. Didn't want to see the truth."

"None of us knew he was that bad," Wallace said.

"You fucking should have," Daryl said sullenly. "He was your goddamn leader."

"Shut your fucking mouth, slug fucker, or I'll rip your nutsack off and feed it to you," Wallace said.

"He's right. I should have known. I should have done something and I didn't, and now Davis is dead," Teagan said.

"I don't mean to be indelicate about the death of Davis, but we have bigger issues at the moment," Randy said. "Mainly, what Patrick's going to do to us when he gets back. The only people he really thinks he needs is Rose and Vida."

"And Talla," Duncan said.

Talla shook her head. "I mean nothing to him. I'm just a warm body for his bed."

"He won't kill us," Teagan said, "not if we convince him that he needs us to help him take the village. He can't possibly think that Vida alone can do it."

"He might," Wallace pulled at the ropes that bound his wrists together, "batshit crazy, remember?"

"Yeah." Teagan lapsed into silence.

Wallace touched his bruised lip with the tip of his tongue. "Do you think -"

The faint sound of gunfire echoed to them.

"Shit." Wallace gave Doc a nervous look. "I'm sure Brody's fine."

Doc laughed bitterly. "Yeah. I'm sure those two shots were just warning shots."

"Maybe it -"

Doc was sitting on the other side of Wallace and he stared

at Daryl who was tied next to him and closest to the doorway. "Did you hear that?"

"I didn't hear anything," Daryl replied.

Doc cocked his head and made a shushing sound. "I think Patrick's back."

"He can't be," Wallace said. "The gunshots weren't close enough to ... oh fuck me."

The pinkie stepped into the hut and Teagan wanted to gag at the smell. He'd never been this close to one before and he studied its smooth pink skin and long blonde hair, and the mouth that was already beginning to widen.

"Move!" Teagan roared as the pinkie moved toward them.

"To where?" Talla shouted. "There's no place to go."

"Daryl, look out!" Doc screamed.

Daryl screamed as the pinkie dropped to his knees. He grinned and bit into Daryl's face., his teeth sinking into the flesh and bone with a loud cracking noise. Daryl screamed again, the sound muffled in the pinkie's mouth. Blood sprayed out, coating Doc's chest and Wallace's legs.

The pinkie tore Daryl's face off and chewed up the warm flesh. Daryl, blood and gore covering what remained of his face, screamed a final time as the pinkie reached out and popped his left eyeball with one sharp nail. He pulled Daryl's eye from the socket and sucked the eyeball into his mouth as Daryl's head dropped forward and his body went limp. The pinkie swallowed Daryl's eye before turning toward Doc and studying him.

"Fuck," Doc whispered.

He scooted backwards on his ass, Daryl's body dragging along with him, but the pinkie stood up, darted forward and lifted him as easily as a child. Wallace snarled in pain as he was dragged halfway up with Doc, his bound arms bending unnaturally.

"Doc!" Teagan shouted as the pinkie's mouth opened and its jaw elongated again. Its fangs protruded, the smell of blood and rot intensifying, and Doc made a scream that was half fear and half defiance as the pinkie yanked his head back.

"Goddammit, no!" Teagan shouted.

He watched in surprise as the pinkie stiffened. He dropped Doc to the ground – he landed half on Wallace who made a grunt of pain – and stared down at his chest. Something sharp and silver protruded from the middle of it. Blood, shockingly red against the pink skin of the creature, ran in tiny rivulets down the pinkie's chest.

"What the hell is that?" Randy rasped.

"My sword," Duncan replied.

The sword was yanked free and the pinkie stood still for a moment, staring at the gaping hole in its chest before it fell face forward onto the ground of the hut.

"Arden?' Teagan said.

The fairy lowered Duncan's sword. "Hey."

"Holy fuckballs," Wallace said, "the fucking fairy just killed a pinkie."

"I'm not just a fucking pretty face, dickhead," Arden leaned the sword against the wall of the hut and examined a pimple on his belly. He popped it with a quick jab of both thumbs and grunted in satisfaction at the splat of yellow pus that landed on the dead pinkie's back.

"How did you get my sword?" Duncan asked. "It was in the tree."

Arden rolled his eyes. "I got fuckin' wings, don't I? Idiot."

"You can fly with those things? This I gotta fuckin' see," Wallace said.

Arden ignored him. He squatted and, using Duncan's

sword, cut through the rope that connected them before beginning to cut through their individual bonds. "Your dumb shit leader's gone crazy."

"Tell us something we don't know," Wallace said as Arden sliced through the rope that bound his wrists.

"Flowers don't work on the pinkies anymore." Arden freed the rest of them before handing the sword to Duncan.

"What? How do you know that?" Teagan asked.

Arden just shrugged. "Seen it. They killed a dozen of the locals last night who were out hunting. They were covered in flowers and it didn't even stop them. The pink fuckers have been making themselves immune to it, the past few months. I seen 'em rubbing the flowers on themselves, shit like that."

"Great. Just fucking great," Wallace said. "If Patrick doesn't fucking kill us, the pinkies will."

"Yep," Arden said.

"We get the gun from Patrick and we use those goddamn bullets to kill the motherfucking pinkies." Teagan stalked out of the hut and the others followed him. "He's only used five bullets, we take him down and take the gun – plenty left for us to lure the pinkies in and kill them."

"If he had a full mag," Doc said. "He didn't confirm that he -"

They all stiffened as more gunfire rang out. When it ended, Randy said, "How many gunshots is that total? Did anyone count?"

"Seven." Doc, Duncan and Wallace said in unison.

Teagan grabbed the machete that was sitting on the slab of wood that served as their table. "Talla, Doc and Randy, stay here. Wallace and Duncan, let's go."

"I'm not staying here," Doc said.

"Like fucking hell you aren't. We can't risk you getting

RAMONA GRAY

hurt," Teagan said. "We'll find Brody and bring him back to you."

"No," Doc said. "I'm going with the team."

"I'm not staying here with just Randy," Talla said. "If the flowers don't protect us from the pinkies anymore, then we're sitting ducks. He's not going to be any help." She glanced at Randy. "No offense."

"None taken," Randy polished his glasses before picking up a spear that was leaning against the table. "We all go together. Safety in numbers, right?"

He studied Teagan who nodded. "Yeah, let's go."

"Where to?" Wallace said.

"The cave first. If they're not there, we check the waterfall."

"What if they're not at either place?" Doc had ducked into his hut and returned with his med kit on his back.

"We'll cross that bridge when we come to it." Teagan gave them all a grim look. "Move fast and stay fucking quiet."

"Yo, Arden, what the fuck, man?" Wallace said.

The fairy had grabbed some fruit from the table and was sitting down on the log next to the fire. "What?"

"You just gonna sit there and eat fucking fruit while we save our friends?"

"I did my part and saved your asses, didn't I?"

"We could use your help."

Arden bit into the fruit before flipping him the bird.

Wallace shook his head and grabbed a spear. "Fucking fairies."

W HEN THE HAND SNAKED AROUND R OSE'S CALF AND PULLED her under the water, she supposed she was lucky she didn't inhale a lungful of water. Instead, her body, in adrenaline racing survival mode, had gasped in air and snapped shut right before she went under.

She stared wide-eyed at Vida as he turned her to face him and cupped her face. He smiled at her and she wanted to weep with relief. Instead, she clung to him as he pulled her close and then swam away from the edge of the drop-off.

Deeper and deeper they went, and she could feel panic starting to churn in her belly. She tried to hold her breath, but she could see a stream of bubbles rising in front of her face as her air slowly leaked out. Her lungs were beginning to scream for air and she squeezed Vida's shoulder and then pounded on his back.

He stopped immediately and held her around the waist as she gave him a look of pure panic. A silver-coloured fish swam by them, followed by the sleek, black body of an eel. Before she could try and pantomime to Vida what was wrong, he was cupping her face and fitting his mouth over hers. She opened her mouth and moaned with relief when Vida blew a hard breath of air into her lungs. He pulled away, stared at her for a few seconds, then gave her a second lungful of air before he drew her up against him again and resumed swimming.

He stopped twice more to give her air before she realized where he was taking her. The water was getting choppier and even deep underwater, she could hear the roar of the water-falls. Vida swam for the surface, and when their heads broke free of the water, she gasped for air for several minutes, clinging to Vida as he held them both above the water.

She stared up at him, confused and a little surprised by the way he was looking at her, before he cupped her face and kissed her fiercely. She returned his kiss, clinging tightly to him until he pulled his mouth away.

"I am sorry, my flower," Vida had to shout to be heard above the sound of the waterfalls. "I should never have left you alone. Are you hurt?"

She shook her head. "N-no. I'm f-fine." Other than being completely numb. She'd been in the water too long and even Vida's body heat wasn't enough to keep her warm. She stared at the sheet of water falling steadily in front of them. "A-are we b-behind the waterf-falls?"

"Yes."

The cliff behind the falls had been worn away by centuries of falling water, and Vida swam toward it. He boosted her onto a ledge. "Stay here for a moment, sweet flower."

He disappeared under the water before she could stop him. She waited a tense few minutes before he reappeared. He boosted himself out of the water and sat next to her. He cuddled her close, kissing the top of her head and rubbing her cold skin.

"W-where did you go?"

"To see where the mad one is. He still searches the water for you."

"Th-thank you for saving my life," she said.

"What is that metal machine he carries that makes so much noise?" Vida asked.

"It's called a g-gun."

Vida kissed her again. "Stay here, sweet flower. I will kill the mad one and return for you when he is dead."

"No!" She grabbed him when he started to slide off the ledge. "No, Vida, you'll be killed."

"I am stronger than him," Vida said. "Do not worry."

"You don't understand. That gun is very dangerous. He can kill you with it."

"How?"

"Guns are very powerful weapons. They fire metal objects called bullets and those bullets can tear through your flesh, even through bone, and kill you. Do you understand? If he shoots you in the head or a vital organ, you will die."

"My kind heals quickly, little human," Vida said. "The water heals us."

"It won't heal you from this. Trust me."

He hesitated and this time she cupped his face and kissed him. "It won't, Vida. You can't just go after him. He wants you to help him take the village, but he also won't trust you. If you go after him, he will kill you."

"We cannot sit here forever like frightened children," Vida replied. "I can kill him."

"Only if he doesn't see you," Rose said. "If I distract him, keep his attention, you can come up behind him and-and snap his neck like you did the pinkie, right?"

She cringed at how casual she sounded in planning the murder of another human being, but Patrick had already murdered three people. They couldn't let him live.

"It is too dangerous. You will stay here and -"

"No! Vida, you don't get how dangerous the guns are. If Patrick shoots you, you will die. This is our best plan. Please, trust me."

"What if he shoots you with this metal weapon?"

"He won't. He thinks he needs me as his prisoner to convince you to help him."

He studied her before nodding. "All right. You will distract him while I swim behind him. Take a deep breath and hold tight to me, Rose."

"Okay." Her body was shaking from cold and fear.

Vida cupped the back of her head and rested his forehead against hers. "I will keep you safe. I promise."

"I know. Vida, I -"

"You what?"

She shook her head. Now was not the time to tell him she loved him. "Be careful, okay?"

"Do not worry, sweet flower. Take a deep breath."

———

"CAVE IS EMPTY." TEAGAN SAID. HE, WALLACE AND Duncan joined the others by the second smaller cave that Vida obviously used for cooking.

He glanced at Doc. "No blood or signs of struggle."

Doc nodded, his face was strained, and he kept running his hand repeatedly through his hair until his blond hair was sticking up in short, erratic spikes. "Yeah, okay. We go to the waterfall next."

Teagan led them through the jungle. He was dripping with sweat and he could hear the harsh panting of the others, but he didn't slow his pace. As they drew closer to the falls, he could smell the metallic tang of blood in the air.

"Hold up." He held up his left arm and the others stopped as he took a few steps forward. He peered around a clump of shrubs. "Fuck."

"Guess we know what he used the bullets for." Wallace had joined him, and he spat on the ground before arming the sweat from his forehead.

"What is it?" Talla called.

"Dead brino," Wallace kicked at the dead beast as the others joined him and Teagan. "Fuck me, this thing stinks worse than a cow's ball sack."

"Cows don't have ball sacks," Randy joined him and squatted next to the brino, "bulls do."

"Tomato, tomahto." Wallace held his hand over his nose.

"There is a blood trail leading toward the waterfall." Duncan was studying the ground.

"Could be Patrick's blood," Wallace said.

"It could be Brody's blood or Rose's." Doc ran his hand through his hair again.

"C'mon, we need to keep moving," Teagan said.

They continued toward the waterfall until the trail of blood ended in a pool of blood seeping into the ground. Duncan crouched and studied the blood as Wallace studied the jungle around them.

"Maybe it – fuck me!" He screamed shrilly as a hand snaked out of the bush next to him and grabbed his ankle. He pulled away, raising his spear as Doc pushed him back.

"Brody!" Doc was already squirming into the bush and after a few seconds he said, "Teag! Help me!"

Teag pushed past the prickles. Doc was squatting next to Brody who looked pale and exhausted, but kissed Doc enthusiastically when Doc pressed his mouth against his.

"Let's get him out of here," Teag said. He and Doc carefully dragged Brody out of the bushes.

"It's really good to see you," Brody said.

"Fuck, man, you just about gave me a goddamn heart attack. As it is, I think I peed my pants a little." Wallace was leaning over with one hand on his chest.

"Sorry, Wallace," Brody grimaced as he moved his injured leg.

"Babe, what happened to your leg?" Doc touched the tourniquet that was around his leg.

"Patrick fucking shot me. I was bleeding like a stuck pig, but Rose tied a tourniquet. You okay?" He studied Doc's face.

Doc nodded as he shrugged out of his med kit. "I'm fine. Just like you're going to be fine." He gave Brody another quick kiss before resting his forehead against his.

"Where's Rose now?" Teagan asked.

"I don't know for sure. She said she was going to lead Patrick away from me. I'm assuming she went to the waterfall but…"

"We need to keep moving," Teagan said.

"I need to stabilize Brody first," Doc said. "You guys go on. We'll be fine."

"We can give you five minutes to -"

Shrill screaming tore through the air and Brody's eyes widened. "Rose!"

"Randy and Talla, stay with them!" Teagan snarled. "Wallace and Duncan, you're with me."

WHEN ROSE EMERGED, THE WATER WAS ONLY WAIST DEEP AND she wasn't far from the shore. In front of her, she could see Patrick's broad back. He had moved away from the drop off and was scanning the water and the jungle around him.

"Fuck," she heard him mutter, "the stupid bitch drowned herself."

Vida had already swum away. She splashed back in the water, hoping to make some noise to catch Patrick's attention. When he immediately spun around, she tried to look terrified – it didn't require much effort.

"There you are!" He gave her a jolly smile, his gaze dipping to her hardened nipples against the translucent material of her bra.

She crossed her arms over his chest and he laughed. "Don't worry, sweetheart. You're not my type. At all."

He waded toward her. "I thought you'd drowned, Rose. Didn't you say you couldn't swim?"

She held out her shaking hands. "Don't come near me."

He gave her a weary look. "Stop pissing me off. I've had a really long fucking day and I'm tired."

Behind him, Vida rose out of the water. Rose kept her frightened gaze trained on Patrick's face.

Patrick stopped moving and studied her. "Do you know what I hate, Rose?"

"Stay away from me."

He gave her another weary look as Vida reached for him. "What I hate is -"

Rose cried out when Patrick whirled around and aimed the gun at Vida. He fired, and Rose screamed Vida's name as he clasped his hand over his stomach and gave Patrick a puzzled look.

"Well now you've just fucked everything up, you stupid, dumb Smurf," Patrick sighed as Vida stumbled back.

Screaming Vida's name, Rose surged forward in the water. Before she'd even taken a few steps, Vida's eyes closed and he sank below the surface of the water.

"Vida! NO!" Rose screamed.

Patrick turned and waded toward her. He grabbed her by the hair and she shrieked and screamed, beating at him with her fists as he dragged her onto shore. One of her flailing fists caught him in the ribs and he bellowed a curse before punching her in the face.

She fell onto her back, the water lapping at her feet, her ears ringing and her breath coming in harsh pants. Vida was dead. Disbelief and shock flooded through her.

Vida was dead. The man she loved was gone forever.

Hot tears flowed down her cheeks as Patrick, holding his ribs with one hand and the gun with the other, stood over her.

"I'm going to kill you," she moaned.

He laughed and pointed the gun at her. "With Vida dead, you're of no use to me, Rose."

His finger pressed down on the trigger as something large and fast-moving tackled him. The bullet whined past Rose's ear, burying itself in the sand beside her skull. Patrick screamed in pain as Teagan landed on him with a hard thud.

Teagan knocked the gun from his hand and punched Patrick twice in the face. Blood poured from Patrick's nose and Teagan punched him a third time before grabbing the gun. He scrambled off Patrick and pointed the gun at him as Patrick made a low laugh and struggled to sit up.

"Rosie, you okay? Wallace helped her stand and she clutched at him.

"Vida! Vida is dead! He shot him. He shot him and…"

She started to cry, and Wallace pulled her into his embrace as Duncan studied the water.

"I'm so sorry, Rosie. I'm so sorry." Wallace rubbed her lower back as Patrick spit out a mouthful of blood before staggering to his feet.

"Teag, old buddy, what are you going to do? Huh? I saved your life in Mosul and now you're gonna repay me by killing me? Someone on your own goddamn team."

"You killed Davis," Teagan said.

Patrick shrugged. "It was necessary for the mission."

"There is no fucking mission!" Teagan shouted. "You killed Davis and the others because you've lost your goddamn mind, Patrick."

Patrick was slowly backing toward the jungle. "I guess we'll just need to agree to disagree."

"Stop moving," Teagan said as a pinkie stepped out from the jungle.

"If I don't?" Patrick asked. "You don't have the guts to

kill me, Teag. We both know it. You're weak and that's exactly why Garrett put me in charge and not you. He knew you couldn't cut it. He knew you –"

He stopped and raised his head, sniffing the air like a dog, before turning. The pinkie was right behind him and it cocked its head as Patrick stumbled back.

"Teagan, Teag," Patrick gave him a terrified look as he pressed his hand against his ribs. "Shoot it for fuck's sake."

Teagan stared at the gun in his hand. "Why waste two bullets killing you and the pinkie, when I can just use one?"

"Teagan?" Patrick whispered, "Buddy, please."

"Good-bye, Patrick," Teagan said as the pinkie grabbed Patrick by the arms and dragged the screaming, struggling man into his embrace.

"Don't look, Rosie." Wallace tried to turn her face and she pushed his hand away.

"He killed Vida," her voice was low and emotionless. "He deserves to suffer."

She watched unflinchingly as the pinkie, its jaw distended and its teeth protruding, buried its face in Patrick's neck. He screamed piercingly as the pinkie tore the skin off from the base of his throat, up the side of his face and into his scalp.

It chewed Patrick's flesh in an almost thoughtful manner as the blood poured from Patrick's face and he screamed repeatedly. The pinkie dipped his head again and bit off Patrick's nose, crunching it down. Patrick made a gargling sound as the blood poured into his open mouth. The pinkie bit off both his lips and Patrick made one final scream, his teeth bared to the sky, before the pinkie tore out his throat. Blood sprayed and the pinkie lapped at it delicately.

"Teag." Wallace's voice was thick with repulsion. "Kill it, man."

Teagan raised the gun and aimed it at the pinkie before

whistling sharply. The pinkie raised its head, tattered pieces of flesh and meat hanging from its fangs and stared at him. Teagan pulled the trigger and a black hole appeared between the pinkie's eyes. It dropped like a stone, Patrick's dead body falling on top of it.

"Well, fuck," Wallace said. "That was fucking awful. I don't think I'll ever fucking sleep again."

Two more pinkies came out of the trees. They studied the body of the fallen pinkie with disinterest, stepping over both it and Patrick's body without a second glance. The one on the left flicked its forked tongue out and Duncan made a sound of disgust.

"Kill them."

Teagan aimed at the one on the left and fired. The bullet hit it in the mouth and blood and teeth flew as the bullet tore through the pinkie's soft pallet and into its brain. It fell to the ground with a muffled thud. The pinkie on the right stopped and stared at the body before turning toward Teagan.

There was no anger or fear in its gaze. Instead it seemed more confused than anything. It studied the gun in Teagan's hand and took a step back when Teagan aimed the gun at it.

"Shoot it, Teag," Wallace said.

Teagan pulled the trigger and fear swept through Rose when there was only a loud click.

Teagan pulled the trigger again. "Fuck!"

"What's wrong?" Rose could hear the panic in her voice.

"Misfire." Teagan tossed the gun aside.

"Of course it fucking misfired," Wallace said with a groan.

"Now what?" Teagan said.

Wallace glanced at Duncan and tightened his grip on his spear. "We kill this fucking thing the old-fashioned way. You ready, Duncan?"

Duncan nodded, readjusting his grip on the handle of his sword. Teagan pulled the machete from his belt and said, "Move in close and tight. Don't give him a chance to – fuck, Wallace watch out!"

The pinkie had darted forward with its unnatural speed. It wrapped his hand around Wallace's throat and lifted him. Wallace drove his spear into the pinkie's thigh and it made a high-pitch squealing noise before tossing him like a rag doll into the trees. He hit a tree with a harsh thud, slamming his head against the rough bark before falling to the ground. He didn't move, and Teagan roared with anger before attacking the pinkie with the machete.

The pinkie dodged his swing before grabbing Teagan's arm. He sank his nails into Teagan's flesh and, snarling and hissing, twisted Teagan's arm until Rose heard his arm snap. Teagan screamed, and the pinkie dropped him to the ground before turning and ducking. Duncan's sword whistled through the air where the pinkie's head had been only seconds earlier.

The pinkie yanked the spear from his thigh and dropped it on the ground. He reached for Duncan and Duncan danced back, swinging the sword with wide and powerful sweeps. Duncan was fast, but the pinkie seemed to be almost a blur as he avoided Duncan's sword.

He raked his claws across Duncan's chest, shredding his shirt and ripping open the skin. Duncan stumbled back into the water, pressing one hand against his chest as blood poured out of the slashes. The pinkie followed him into the water as Duncan raised his sword.

The pinkie made a squealing sound of triumph that turned to pain. He stared in disbelief at the spear that was buried in its side. Rose, her arms trembling, shoved the spear in a little further. The stench of the pinkie was over-whelming, and she gagged and then screamed when the pinkie wrapped its hand around her throat and lifted her into the air.

Choking and gasping, she tore at the hand as her feet dangled in the air. She kicked at the pinkie, a little surprised when he dropped her into the water and turned away from her. The air she had just dragged into her lungs, escaped in a startled whoosh as she followed the pinkie's gaze.

Vida, his blue skin glistening in the setting sun, emerged from the water like an ancient and powerful god.

"Vida?" Rose whispered.

He walked toward the pinkie and Rose's eyes widened when the pinkie turned and tried to run. It had only taken a few steps when Vida's arm wrapped around its neck. It screamed and hissed, clawing at Vida's arm with its nails as Vida dragged it deeper into the water.

It shrieked again and tried to twist its head to sink its fangs into Vida's powerful arm. Vida's arm tightened around it, and the pinkie made one final scream before Vida dragged it under the water and they both disappeared.

"Rose!" Duncan was staggering toward her and she struggled to her feet. "You okay?"

"Are you?" She studied the blood on his chest and he nodded.

"I think so. The beast scratched me up some."

"Vida's alive," she said.

He smiled at her. "He is."

He hugged her with one arm as she scanned the water anxiously.

"I'm going to check on the others."

She nodded but stayed where she was as Duncan moved toward Teagan. "Are you all right, Teagan?"

"Broke my fucking arm, but I'll live. Check on Wallace."

She heard Wallace's low groan. "I'm fine. What happened to the last one? Where the fuck is it?"

"Vida has it," Duncan said.

"What the fuck is he doing with it?" Wallace's voice was growing stronger.

"Drowning it, I believe," Duncan said. "Give me your hand."

"Fuck, my head hurts. Fucking thing rattled my brains. Probably got a goddamn concussion. Teag, you okay?"

"Broken arm."

"Jesus. That's gonna hurt like a bitch when Doc sets it."

"Yeah, I know."

Rose ignored the men behind her. She was still scanning the water and panic was starting to set in. What if the pinkie had overpowered Vida under the water? What if he was hurt or -"

The water rippled, and she cried out when Vida emerged again. He smiled at her and she stumbled forward, nearly falling into his arms. He lifted her, and she kissed him hard on the mouth.

"Oh, Vida." She began to cry, and he kissed away the tears before carrying her to the shore.

"Shh, small flower. Do not cry."

He set her down and she studied his stomach. There was obvious bruising and when she traced her fingers across his abs, he winced and sucked in his breath but there was no wound from a bullet.

"How?" She whispered.

"I told you, flower, my kind heals quickly in the water."

"I thought it killed you."

"It did not."

She threw her arms around him and stared up at him. "I love you, Vida."

A look of surprise crossed his face before he scooped her up again and started toward the others. "Come, flower, it is time to go home."

"HEY, BIG GUY." WALLACE EASED DOWN ONTO THE FALLEN log next to Vida. "I never did say thanks for saving our lives yesterday."

"You are welcome." Vida stared at the hand Wallace was holding out to him before saying, "How is your head?"

Wallace dropped his hand and grinned at him. "I got a hard head. Doc says I got a mild concussion, but it could have been a lot fucking worse. At least I didn't have to have a bullet dug out of my thigh," his gaze drifted to Brody who was sitting across the fire with Doc, "or a broken arm set, or stitches in my chest without fucking pain meds."

"That is true." Vida wasn't studying Teagan or Duncan. Instead, his gaze was on Rose who was standing at the table with Randy and helping him cut up fruit.

"Everything okay with you two?" Wallace nudged him.

"Why do you ask me that?" Vida replied.

"Because things seem to be a bit off between you since we all nearly got killed by Patrick and the fucking pinkies."

Vida didn't reply. Things were strange between him and his flower. Had been since she told him she loved him. She'd been quiet and withdrawn since they'd gone back to the camp, and although she was eager to make love to him last night, she had fallen asleep almost immediately afterward.

She'd been avoiding him all day and he didn't know if it was because she regretted telling him that she loved him, or if she was angry that he hadn't said it back.

"Well? You okay?" Wallace prompted.

"She told me she loved me."

"Yeah, I was there. You didn't say it back. Is it because you don't love her?"

Vida shook his head. "No, I am bonded with my sweet flower. Have been for many days now."

"Bonded?"

He shrugged. "Bond – love, it means the same thing to my kind."

"Ah. Maybe you should mention that to her before she decides you're a real dickweed and goes after someone with a smart mouth and a rock-hard body." Wallace grinned at him. "That's me, by the way. I'm referring to myself."

"You are not to go near my flower. If you do, I will -"

"Relax, big guy. I'm kidding." Wallace clapped him on the back. "Why didn't you say it back to her then?"

"I do not know," Vida admitted. "It surprised me to hear that she loves me even after I told her I would not stay on this world with her."

"That was a dick move," Wallace said. "Maybe you'd better go tell her you love her. And say love not bond, ya idiot. Women want to hear the L word."

Vida stood and stared into the jungle. "The others are coming."

"Others? Who?" Wallace lapsed into silence as about a dozen locals walked into their camp. They studied them silently before Gormet stepped forward.

"Hello again."

Teagan, his arm splinted with branches and strips of fabric, stood. "Hello, Gormet."

"We have come to extend an invitation to join us in living in our home. We know the elida have killed your mad leader, and we know that you have destroyed all of the elida. The invitation is a taken of our thanks."

"Do you mean token?" Randy asked.

"What does token mean?" Gormet turned to him.

"Uh, like a symbol or reason for your thanks."

"Then yes, a," Gormet paused, stumbling a little over the word, "token."

"Oh sure," Wallace said, "now that we got nothing to be afraid of, you want us to live with you."

"There are still the blowcats and brinos," Randy said.

"Good point."

"Are we all invited?" Teagan asked as he glanced at Vida.

Gormet nodded. "You are. Regardless of your decision, you will join us tomorrow evening for food and in celebration of the death of the elida."

He nodded to all of them before he and the other locals left.

"Jesus," Wallace rolled his eyes, "he's a pushy little guy, isn't he?"

"Are we going to live with them?" Brody glanced at Teagan.

Teagan shrugged. "We can take a vote on it."

Vida stood and walked to Rose and Randy. "Small flower, I must speak with you in private."

She gave him a wan smile. "We're just about to eat dinner."

"It will not take long. Come." He took her hand and led her to her hut. He had wanted to go back to the cave last night, but Rose had insisted on going with the others back to the camp.

He pulled the fur across the doorway of the hut and studied Rose in the dim light. "Are you all right, flower?"

"I am." She smiled again at him but took a step back and folded her arms across her torso when he reached for her.

He frowned. "Do you no longer love me?"

Her face turned bright red. "I, uh, what?"

"Yesterday you said you loved me, but today you will not allow me to touch you."

She licked her lips. "I do still love you."

Relief flooded through him. "After dinner we will return to the cave."

She gave him an oddly nervous look. "I, um, I did want to talk to you about that."

"What is it?" He was aching to touch her, to pull her into his embrace and soothe away the anxiety he could practically smell on her.

"Whatever the group decides – living with the locals or staying here at the camp – I'm going to stay with them."

"I do not wish to stay with them, flower. I want to stay in the cave."

"I know," she said, "and you will. I just – I won't be with you."

"You will not stay with me in the cave where you are safest?"

"It's safer now without the pinkies around and I think it's best if we, uh, put some distance between us."

"Why?"

He could see the frustration building on her face. "It's just best for both of us to not keep doing what we're doing."

"Why?"

"Oh my gosh!" She scowled at him. "Are you going to make me say it? Fine. I am in love with you and you are not in love with me. As soon as another orb comes, you're going to leave me. Maybe that'll only be a few months or maybe it'll be a few years. Either way, I can't – I mean, I love you and knowing that you're eventually going to leave... it's breaking my heart. It's just better if we end things now. Do you understand?"

"No," he said, "I am not leaving you, small flower."

Her jaw dropped. "You – what?"

He couldn't stand to not be touching her anymore, and he pulled her into his embrace before pressing a kiss against her mouth. "I love you, small flower and I will stay on this world with you for the rest of my life."

"You love me," she whispered.

"Yes."

"Since when?" She gave him such a look of confusion that he smiled.

"I have been bonded to you since the first time we mated. I just did not want to admit it to myself. But you are my bondmate, and I will never leave you."

"But what about your world?" She said. "You're giving up your chance, no matter how small it is, to find your world again."

"I do not care." He bent and kissed her again. "I love you, small flower, and all that matters to me now is you and the children you will someday carry in your belly."

He rubbed her flat stomach and nuzzled her neck. "Will you accept me as your mate and bond with me for life, Rose?"

She cupped his face and gave him a sweet smile. "Yes, Vida. I will."

EPILOGUE

Two years later

"Well, for being blue and having teeny horns and gills, he's a pretty good looking kid." Wallace studied the baby he held in his arms. "What's his name again?"

"Vitali," Rose said. "It was Vida's father's name."

She smiled at Vida who took the baby from Wallace. He kissed the baby's cheek before raising him to his shoulder and patting his back gently.

"How did the ritual go last night?" Duncan asked.

"Good, I think." Rose glanced at Vida. "I mean, I didn't exactly know what was happening, but Vida assured me that his and Vitali's takenas have bonded."

"That's good." Duncan smiled at her and she squeezed his arm as a loud clap of thunder made the cave shake a little.

"Before I forget," Teagan was sitting on the couch next to Wallace, "Doc said to tell you that he and Brody and Amina would be by tomorrow morning as long as the weather has cleared by then. They want to do another check on the baby."

Amina was the islanders' medical woman and despite the language barrier, she and Doc worked well together.

"All right. Thanks, Teagan," Rose said.

Wallace suddenly grinned at Rose. "Did you hear the news about Talla?"

Rose shook her head. "No, what news?"

"She's knocked up."

"Really? She and Randy are having a baby?"

"Yep. She'll be popping out a little baby science nerd in six months."

"That's awesome. Good for them." She moved to the couch and sat down on a stool in front of it. She stared at the three men solemnly. "You can still change your mind."

Teagan smiled at her. "We need to go, Rose."

She pressed her lips together and glanced at Vida. "You won't find your world again. You know that."

"We know."

"Then why are you leaving? Things are good here. Safe and -"

"We cannot stay," Duncan said gently.

"We should get going." Wallace stood up. "Gormet thinks the orb is going to appear in less than two hours."

"Nothing I can say will change your mind, will it?" Rose said.

"No," Teagan said.

She sighed and stood as Duncan and Teagan did as well. "I'm going to miss all of you so much."

"We'll miss you too, Rosie-girl." Wallace hugged her hard before grinning at Vida. "Keep her safe, big guy."

"Why would I not? She is my mate and the mother of my son."

Wallace laughed as Rose hugged Duncan and then Teagan.

"Be careful," she whispered into Teagan's ear. "I hope you find what you're looking for."

Teagan smiled at her and kissed her cheek. "Thank you, Rosie-girl. Take care of your boy and your man."

"I will."

***

"YOU SURE YOU WANNA GO THROUGH WITH THIS, TEAG?" Wallace had to yell to be heard over the continuous thunder. Lightning flashed across the sky, lighting up the grim lines in Teagan's face as he nodded.

"I am. You?"

"Fuck, yes," Wallace shouted. "Duncan, you gonna pussy out on us?"

Duncan shook his head and adjusted the sword around his waist. His hair was plastered to his head from the driving rain. He stared at the cliff as the wind began to pick up and a small round light appeared. "Here we go."

As the wind howled and thunder and lighting shook the island, the orb grew larger until the glowing ball of energy was as tall as they were. The wind was sucking them toward it now and the three men glanced at each other before walking toward the light. The light grew stronger and it pulsed in a bright flash as the men entered the orb and disappeared.

***

Keep reading for an excerpt from Book Seven of the Other World Series "Elena Unbound".

ELENA UNBOUND EXCERPT

(OTHER WORLD SERIES BOOK SEVEN)

The screams that echoed through the forest made his horse neigh nervously and the hair on the back of his neck stand up. The screams were full of rage and fear and he automatically rode toward them. He'd been travelling for many days and he was weary and ready to be in a bed again, but he couldn't ignore her screams.

As he grew closer, the woman screamed for a third time and there were louder grunts and growls of men. He dismounted, tied his horse to a tree ard crept closer on foot. He peered around a large oak tree, and anger swept through him.

Two men with stained and ripped clothing were pinning a woman to the ground. She was thrashing and kicking furiously at them. Like most of the women from this area, she was tall with full breasts and wide hips. A small grin crossed his face when she suddenly bent her knees and kicked the man leaning over her, directly in the stomach.

Coughing and retching, he fell back as the man pinning

her arms down roared with anger. The man she had kicked stood up and retched once more, spit flying from his mouth. With an angry snarl he fell on her, pulling at her heavy skirt.

She shrieked, the sound thin and birdlike in the cold air, and reared up, her back arching off the ground. He stepped out from behind the tree as the man on top of her balled his hand into a fist and punched her in the face. She slumped back against the ground, moaning dazedly and the two men grinned at each other.

"She's a feisty one."

"Aye. I love 'em that way too," the second man said. He reached for her full breasts. Before he could squeeze them, a sword appeared and tapped him lightly on his outstretched arm.

He looked up, his mouth dropping open to reveal black and rotting teeth. Before he could speak, a large fist smashed him directly in the mouth and he sagged to the ground, teeth and blood flying from his mouth.

The other man jumped to his feet, reaching for his own sword.

"I would advise against that." He held his sword loosely in one large fist.

The man hesitated and then grabbed the handle of his sword. He gave a small gasp of surprise and looked down to see the stranger's sword buried in his belly.

"What?" He whispered.

Traven yanked the sword out and watched disinterestedly as the smaller man fell to the ground, blood pouring from his stomach. He died quietly, his mouth gaping like a fish.

He put his sword away and turned to the woman. She was still lying on the ground moaning softly. He bent over her and she pushed weakly at him. "Do not touch…"

Her eyes rolled up and her head sagged to the side as he picked her up with a loud grunt. He carried her to through the trees to his horse and steadied her on it before swinging into the saddle behind her. He pulled a short piece of rope from a saddle bag and lashed her wrists to the saddle horn before pushing her back against his wide chest. Her head lolled on his shoulder until with a soft snort, her face fell into the curve of his thick neck. He dug his heels into the sides of his horse and continued on his way.

Elena buried her face against the warm skin before pressing a soft kiss against it. Her cheek was hurting as was the back of her head and she frowned in thought. Why did it hurt? Had she fallen? She kissed his warm, hard flesh again, sighing happily when his arm slid around her waist and pulled her closer. God, she'd missed a man's touch. His hand was stroking her ribs just below her breasts and she arched her back encouragingly. How long had it been since she felt a man's hand cupping her breast? Too long.

A part of her knew this was a dream, knew that she was alone in her cold bed, but she suddenly desperately wanted it to be real. It felt real – the man's breath washing over her cheek and neck was bringing goosebumps to her skin and his hand was heavy and delightfully warm against her side. The swaying of the bed was a bit strange, but she ignored that part. She wanted to be touched, to be reminded that she was a woman with needs and desires that had been ignored for far too long.

"Please," she whispered before nipping at his neck.

The man inhaled sharply before squeezing her side. "Wake up, girl."

She frowned and shook her head before kissing his neck again.

"Girl, open your eyes."

His rough voice demanded obedience and she reluctantly dragged her eyelids up. She squinted at the light trickling through the trees before she straightened. She could see her breath and the breath of the horse that she was riding on.

Her eyes widened as she remembered where she was and what had happened. She'd been captured by the horrible men in the forest. Her hands were bound to the saddle horn and, panic rushing through her, she turned her head to bite the throat of her captor.

He was quick, she'd give him that. His hand wrapped in her hair and held tight, preventing her from sinking her teeth into his throat.

"Enough, little minx. While I enjoyed your sweet love bites, I don't believe that's your intention now, is it?"

She flushed bright red, her grey eyes darkening to slate as he tugged her head up so he could study her face. It wasn't one of the men who had captured her in the forest but that didn't mean she wasn't in trouble.

"Where are the other men?" She asked.

He shrugged. "One is dead, the other will live if he wakes before the animals of the forest dine on him."

She yanked at the rope that bound her wrists. His horse neighed nervously, and he put his heavily-muscled arm around her waist and pulled her back against him. "Be still, you're spooking my horse. Relax, I won't harm you."

She looked around and then tugged at her restraint again. "Why am I tied up?"

"I was worried you would think I was one of the men in the woods and would struggle. I didn't want you tumbling from the horse and breaking your neck."

"I'm not going to struggle. You can untie me."

"Aye, I could."

He made no move to untie the rope and she sighed with frustration. "Please?"

"What's your name?"

"Elena."

"Why were you in the woods alone, Elena?"

"I wasn't alone. I was travelling with two companions. Those men attacked us and killed them." She cleared her throat. "I ran, but they caught me."

"These companions – were they your lovers?"

She twisted around to glare at him. "What? No, they were not my lovers."

"Then why were you with them?"

"We were travelling for supplies for my employer."

"Whose home do you belong to?"

"The Lord Enderson's."

He inhaled sharply, and she glanced at him. "Do you know him?"

"Aye, in a manner of speaking." He shrugged his cloak from one arm. She stared at the armband that announced his allegiance to the Lord Enderson. The blue and gold was a startling contrast against the drab brown of his shirt.

"You're one of his men. Are you returning from the war?"

"Aye."

"So it is true, the war is over." She glanced at him again. "What of the Lord Enderson? Does he still live?"

"Why do you ask that?"

"Because the rumour is that he died in the last days of the war. Did he?"

"No. He will be home shortly."

She mulled that over for a moment. "Lord Barten will be thrilled."

He frowned at the obvious sarcasm in her voice. "What do you mean by that, girl?"

"Nothing." She stared up at him again. He was one of the largest men she'd ever seen, which was saying a lot considering how big the men were in this area. His face was nearly hidden behind a long, bushy beard and his hair was past his shoulders. It was wild and thick, the sides held back with a small piece of leather, and she could see small bits of leaves stuck in it. She could barely see his mouth beneath the overgrown beard, but she had no problem seeing the scar that started at his hairline and coursed down his face, disappearing beneath the thick coating of hair that covered his jaw. It had just missed his left eye and she flushed a little when she realized he was staring at her mouth, his light green eyes darkening with an emotion she easily recognized.

Quickly, she turned around, her heart beating frantically in her chest, as he bent his head into her throat and inhaled.

"You smell good, girl." His voice had deepened into a thick purr. Whether it was his voice or the way his hard hand was rubbing her belly slowly and gently, an ache, one that she had thought was gone forever, started up in her lower belly.

"Thank you, my lord. Would you please untie me now?"

"It has been a long time since I have been this close to a woman." He placed a gentle kiss on her throat.

She shivered, ignoring the surprising pleasure she felt at the touch of his mouth against her skin. "Do you always grope women you have just met, my lord?"

"Not always."

She bit back the laughter at his reply. She was shocked by her sudden need for the man who had saved her life. Was it because she had come so close to being raped and murdered by the men in the woods? Was her relief at being unharmed, thanks to the man behind her, bringing out her need? Or simply the fact that she'd been alone for so long? She had no idea, but it would not do to let him even have a hint that she was finding his touch pleasing.

He slid his hand up her ribcage and very carefully cupped her breast with one large hand, rubbing his thumb over the nipple.

"You should stop, my lord. You saw what happened to the last men who touched me by force." She hated how breathless and needy she sounded. She didn't want to be attracted to him.

He grunted. "Aye, I did. You are lucky I showed up when I did."

"I would have been fine." She blushed a little at her obvious and foolish lie.

He laughed, a rich, warm sound that made her whole body tingle. "Aye, perhaps. You did seem rather adept at kicking.

"Although," he said as her traitorous nipple hardened under his touch, "it does not feel like I will need to use force."

He kissed her neck again before kissing his way to her ear and sucking lightly on her earlobe. His beard tickled, and a little moan escaped her mouth.

When he pulled on the string that laced her shirt closed, she told herself to object, to demand he not touch her. Instead, she arched her back as he unlaced it and pulled her shirt open, exposing her bare breasts to both his gaze and the cool air. He inhaled sharply at the sight of her large firm breasts. Her pink nipples hardened as he put his heavy thighs over hers, pinning her legs down against the sides of his horse.

His horse neighed and sidestepped a bit and he patted it on the side of its large neck. It calmed and continued to pick its way through the trees as he cupped her left breast. He kneaded it gently before pulling on her nipple, smiling with satisfaction at her soft moan.

He switched to the right breast, cupping and rubbing and lightly pinching her nipple until her back was arching. She turned her face toward him, pressing her lips against his. He immediately angled his mouth over hers and kissed her hard. She opened her mouth wide so that he could explore it with his tongue. He flicked his tongue against hers and when she timidly slipped her tongue into his mouth, he sucked hard on it, making her moan.

He dropped the reins and used both hands to cup her breasts. He squeezed and rubbed them, pulling with rough fingers on both her nipples, and rubbing his crotch against her ass as she sighed and moaned. He licked her neck before sucking hard on it. The pressure of his mouth left a large red mark and he made a soft noise of satisfaction deep in his throat.

"You seem to be enjoying my touch, sweet Elena," he murmured into her ear.

The sound of his deep voice broke the haze of desire that had enveloped her, and she squirmed against him, blushing furiously. What was she doing? She didn't even know his name.

Humiliated by her reaction to the stranger and her inability to resist his touch, she lied to him. "My lord, I belong to another. If he finds out that you -"

"Where is your collar?"

"I do not wear a collar. My – my man is secure enough that he does not require me to -"

He laughed. "No man lets his woman go without a collar. If she shares his bed, she wears the collar that tells other men she belongs to him."

"He does not believe in such barbaric practices. He understands that women are not property to be -"

She gasped when he slipped his hand under the waistband of her skirt and cupped her pussy. He gave a grunt of surprise at the feel of the soft hair between her legs.

"Why do you have hair here?" He asked, his fingers stroking the soft curls.

"Because I am a woman and not a little girl," she snapped. She tried to move her legs out from under his, but it was impossible. He actually used his legs to push her legs back, spreading them further apart and giving him better access to her warmth.

He rubbed a bit of her hair between his fingers. "Why do you not do what the other women do and remove your hair?"

"Why should I? Because you would prefer it? It's my body and I refuse to remove all the hair just to please a man."

Traven grinned to himself. Elena had spirit and he loved how she reacted to his touch. He stroked the hair that covered her pussy again. After years of being with women who were shaved, or plucked, or waxed completely bare, the feel of her soft curls was an exciting change. His cock was so hard it was nearly painful, and he pressed it against her ass again. Her ass pressed back against him before she made a soft huff and glared at him.

He placed a kiss on the tip of her nose before looking around. It was growing darker and he would have to find shelter for them soon. He was close enough to home to recognize the area and he frowned briefly, trying to remember the layout of the land. If he was correct, there were a series of small caves not far from here. One of them would provide enough shelter for the evening.

He was still cupping her warm core, his fingers gently stroking the curls as she trembled against him. He made a sudden decision. If he gave her pleasure now, made her come, she would be more open to the idea of letting him fuck her later. He was going to fuck her tonight, he knew that as well as he knew his own name, but he needed her warm and willing. Showing her how easily he could make her come would be the fastest way to make that happen.

He slid his index finger between her pussy lips and found her clit. He rubbed it with firm pressure and she stiffened against him before trying to back away from his hand. It pushed her ass into his cock and he groaned into her ear. Her clit was hardening and swelling under his touch and he pinched it lightly, grunting with satisfaction when she moaned, and her juices began to flow over his fingers.

"I hate you," she muttered.

"Aye, I can feel how much you hate me." He slid his finger easily inside of her.

"Ohhh," she sighed. Her pelvis thrust upward, and her bound hands squeezed the saddle horn. He slid his finger out and then added a second, pushing both of them inside her velvety core. Her pussy was very wet now, it sucked eagerly at his fingers, and he curled them inside of her and rubbed the front of her pussy wall with the tips of his fingers.

"Oh my God!" She cried. Her wet walls clamped down around his fingers, trapping them inside of her and he groaned with delight at the thought of her doing that to his cock later. He pressed again, and her entire body trembled against him.

"Does that feel good, Elena?" He whispered into her ear.

"No!"

He nipped her neck. "Do not lie to me. Do you like having my fingers in your pussy?" He licked her neck, soothing his earlier nip.

"Yes," she moaned, and he rewarded her honesty by rubbing her clit roughly with his thumb.

She moaned again, letting her head fall back on his shoulder as he circled and rubbed her clit. She was growing close, he could see it in the way she was turning her head back and forth on his shoulder, in the way she was rubbing her lower body frantically against his hand, and he stopped touching her.

She cried out in frustration. "My lord, please."

"Do you belong to another?"

She didn't answer, and he brushed her clit with the tip of his thumb while he pushed his fingers deeper inside of her. She gasped and jerked against him.

"You said you have a man. Do you?"

"Please touch me," she whispered, and it took all of his willpower not to immediately do as she asked.

"Tell me the truth. Is there another who touches you the way I am touching you now?" He rubbed her wet and swollen lips without touching the small pink nub nestled between them.

"No," she gasped, "there is no other – only you."

"Good." He licked her mouth and she opened it immediately, sliding her tongue between his lips and exploring his warm mouth with frenzied abandonment.

He moved his fingers in and out of her as he stroked her hard clit. He kept his mouth firmly planted on hers and swallowed her loud cry of pleasure when she suddenly stiffened and arched her back. She collapsed against him as wetness flooded his fingers.

Spooked by her squirming, his horse tried to gallop

forward. He tore his mouth away from hers and tugged on the reins with his free hand, returning the horse to a slow walk. He pulled his hand out from under her skirt and slipped his index finger into her mouth.

"Suck."

She closed her mouth obediently around his finger, her small tongue licking and sucking it clean. He shuddered against her, his cock throbbing in his pants. He pulled his finger free of her mouth and sucked on his second finger. He tasted her on his tongue, groaning at her good, clean taste as she attempted to sit up.

He pulled her back and cupped one bare breast, her nipple a hard little pearl against his palm, before he clicked his tongue to his horse and dug his heels into its sides. It quickened its pace and he kept his hand firmly around her breast as he searched the growing darkness.

ABOUT THE AUTHOR

Ramona Gray is a Canadian romance author. She currently lives in Alberta with her awesome husband and her super cute dog. She's addicted to home improvement shows, good coffee, and reading and writing about the steamier moments in life.

For more information about Ramona, check out her website at

www.ramonagray.ca

facebook.com/RamonaGrayBooks

twitter.com/RamonaGrayBooks

instagram.com/ramonagrayauthor

amazon.com/Ramona-Gray/e/B00OD26SAM

bookbub.com/profile/ramona-gray

ALSO BY RAMONA GRAY

Individual Books

The Escort

Saving Jax

The Assistant

One Night

Sharing Del

Filthy Appeal

Forbidden Bliss

Shadow Security Series

Dead of Night

Edge of Night

Dark of Night

Undeniable Series

Undeniably His

Undeniably Hers

Undeniably Theirs

Undeniable Series Boxset

Working Men Series

The Mechanic

The Carpenter

The Bartender

The Welder

The Electrician

The Landscaper

The Firefighter

The Cop

The Paramedic

Working Men Series Bundles

Working Men Series Books One to Three

Working Men Series Books Four to Six

Working Men Series Books Seven to Nine

Other World Series

The Vampire's Kiss (Book One)

The Vampire's Love (Book Two)

The Shifter's Mate (Book Three)

Rescued By The Wolf (Book Four)

Claiming Quinn (Book Five)

Choosing Rose (Book Six)

Elena Unbound (Book Seven)

Other World Series Box Sets

Other World Series Books One to Three

Other World Series Books Four to Six